JANE KNIGHT

Her Fae Lovers

First edition

This book was professionally typeset on Reedsy.
Find out more at reedsy.com

This book is dedicated to you the readers,
Thank you for all of the kind words and feedback that you guys
have given me over the course of my writing journey. Without you
guys I would have never taken this adventure or created these
characters and the worlds they live in.

XOXO,
Jane

Contents

Prologue

"The Seelie and Unseelie court's sentence you four to confinement for your crimes until the blood has forgotten the atrocities you have committed against them." The woman spoke, her voice ringing loudly through the clearing as her autumn-brown eyes passed over the four beings.

"No, it's not fair." The red-haired man shouted, his copper-colored curls bouncing around him. His words slurring as his cheeks flushed, glassy jade eyes scanning the Queen and King as he fell to his knees ready to plead with them.

"Shut up, Lu, before she chooses a different punishment. Do you want to be trapped within the trees?" The unearthly beautiful sea-green eyed man said through clenched teeth. He fisted his hands at his sides as he shook with barely concealed anger. He looked over at the woman swollen with child. No, not a woman. She was far too beautiful to be just a mere mortal. He pushed his white-blonde hair out of his eyes and turned to glare at the red-eyed man that stood at his side.

"They will forget with time," He stated, pushing his hair over his shoulder with an uncaring shrug before crossing his arms over his chest.

"I think it might be longer than you expect." The Seelie Queen spoke once more. She looked at the four creatures in front of her. Turning her head, loose blonde curls swaying in the evening breeze. She cast her eyes on the tallest of them, "Have you nothing to say, Puca?"

"It would make no difference. You have already decided our fate." The auburn-haired being shook his head. His gold glowing eyes met the Queen's angry glare before turning to look at his King. He looked back down, his shoulders dropping.

"So it shall be," The Unseelie King said, holding his hand out to his counterpart, his midnight eyes meeting her ever-changing ones. Their hands met, and a circle formed around the four creatures. Bright white sparkles seemed to dance along their skin as Lu let out a pain-filled wail. Mushrooms and flowers sprouted in the soft earth around them as a magical wind-whipped painfully against their skin.

Suddenly the wind stopped and in the center of the circle where the creatures once stood, an oak puzzle box covered in runes sat.

Chapter One

ᴥᴥᴥ

ola walked around the antique shop. It was filled with all kinds of hidden treasures that she couldn't wait to discover. She picked up a broach that was made from human hair, a piece of mourning jewelry.

Sitting it down, she couldn't help but think that the light brown and copper strands must have a sad backstory. She loved little shops like this. Each item seemed to tell her a story as she studied a figurine of two lovers strolling side by side their hands clasped, before moving on. She glanced up at the tinkling sound of bells and looked towards the door, her eyebrows scrunched together.

That was strange no one had come in. Shrugging her shoulders, she turned back to all the pretties. Maybe it had been the wind?

She loved everything about this particular antique shop, the cozy feeling the shop had come from it being set up inside an older Victorian style home. The soft scent of jasmine tea filled the air from the small kitchen at the rear of the house.

She paused, her emerald eyes taking in the new necklaces, the glittering glass beads sparkling in the sunshine from the windows. They caught her interest.

While those pretty baubles were eye catching she had a gut feeling that she was here for something else. Lola moved about the room, fingers trailing across dusty surfaces as she walked. It felt like something was calling to her and it wasn't something she had ever experienced before, almost like an invisible pulling sensation.

Lola moved deeper into the house. She tucked a strand of her purple hair behind her ear and followed the pull into a darkened room. She didn't know if this room was off-limits, but she had the strangest feeling like she wasn't supposed to be there. She moved to an old mahogany writing desk that sat in the corner of the room.

There it sat.

A small oak box, barely bigger than a bible. She touched the box. The warmth that met her fingertips made her frown. How was it warm to the touch? Bending down, she examined the strange intricate carvings that littered the scarred surface were symbols she was unfamiliar with. She had a gut feeling that this box was more than it seemed. Lola picked up her newly found treasure and headed to the register, with a smile on her full lips.

"Hi Erik," Lola said as she approached the tall blond man. He turned to look at her from behind the register as he pushed up his wire-rimmed glasses.

"Lola, it's good to see you again," Erik said with a toothpaste commercial-worthy smile.

Lola felt her cheeks heat up in pinpricks of warmth as he smiled at her. She looked down at the box in her hands. She wasn't used to men as handsome as him smiling at her. His dimples flashed at her as he ran a hand through his wavy hair.

"It's nice to see you as well, it looks like you got in a lot of interesting finds," Lola said, sitting the box down on the glass counter. She crouched down to look at the trinkets inside the case. A leather-bound journal catching her attention. A rust-colored stain covered the spine. She wondered what stories it held within its bound pages.

"That is a journal from an English girl in the late 1800s. Her vernacular was surprisingly modern. I think she may have been insane, or maybe she had a touch of foresight after reading the journal. Would you like it as well?" Erik asked as he wrapped up her purchase in the brown paper before placing it into a lavender paper shopping bag.

"I don't think so, it kinda gives me the heebee-jeebees," Lola said, standing up and glancing at Erik. She smoothed out her skirt and pushed her hair out of her eyes.

"I know what you mean, I felt the same way when I opened the crate it came in," Erik replied with a wink of his gray eyes. Lola looked away, her blush deepening as she bit her lower lip nervously. Erik told her the price, and she paid, happily accepting the bag from him. Before she turned, heading towards the door, his hand on her arm stopped her in her tracks.

"I was, I'm sorry," Erik said, pulling his hand back as she looked up at him in surprise. "I was wondering if you'd like to stay and have some tea with me, or maybe another time if you're busy today."

"I can stay," She smiled shyly up at him.

"That's good, um. I mean, I'd like that." Erik said as he let out a sigh of relief.

Lola had the feeling that he, much like she tended to do, had over-thought the interaction. Erik turned and headed to the small kitchen, Lola followed him at an easy pace. She sat her bags on the counter and leaned close to study the antique tea set that Erik had sitting on the counter.

"The details on the teacups are exquisite," Lola said as she picked up the delicate china cup to study the mauve and yellow hand-painted roses.

"It's a 1950s Roslyn Fine Bone China set, very hard to come by nowadays. They weren't open for very long," Erik said as he poured the fragrant tea into the delicate teapot and topped it with the lid. He pulled out a tin of shortbread cookies and placed them onto a matching plate.

"I bet this china has some stories it could tell us," Lola said as she gently placed the teacup back onto the saucer.

"That's what I like about you Lola, you realize that everything has a story. I appreciate that quality. Too often people are drawn in by modern and sterile things. You see the history, the magic of an item as I do." Erik said as he picked up the tray that the tea set was on.

Lola blushed as she grabbed her bags and followed him into the sitting room. It was filled with figurines and a grandfather clock that could be heard throughout the entire house when it chimed. He sat the tray onto a regency era drum table. The rosewood gleaming in the afternoon sunlight.

Lola sat in one of the high back overstuffed chairs. They were beautiful to look at. They were not comfortable though, and she shifted about trying to find a comfortable position as Erik handed her the teacup and saucer.

"Thank you, the tea smells delicious." She inhaled the floral steam as he gently placed the shortbread on the table between them before picking up his own teacup and taking a sip as he sat down.

"I thought the jasmine would be a good choice for such a nice day." He said with a smile as he pushed his hair back out of his eyes and sat the teacup down onto the saucer.

"It is," Lola agreed, not sure what else to say as she eyed the lemon curd shortbread. They were a favorite of hers.

"I need your help," He said, cool gray eyes peeking at her over the rim of his glasses.

"I don't know how much help I would be," Lola said as she picked up one of the cookies and took a bite.

"I just need someone to run errands for me occasionally, when I can't get away from the shop. I've always felt that I could I trust you." Erik said with a hopeful smile.

Lola thought over his offer as she nibbled on the cookie. It would help her to get to know Erik better and see if she and the handsome shopkeeper had anything other than a love of antiques in common. It would also get her a little extra income, which sadly these days she needed the money. Lola worked at the local plant nursery and the cold months always meant she wasn't needed at the business and her paychecks were starting to reflect that.

"When would I start?" She asked as she sat the cookie on the edge of the saucer, picking up the teacup to take a sip of the lightly sweetened tea.

"Tomorrow, if it doesn't interfere with your other job." Erik sat his teacup and saucer down with a smile. He pulled out a cream-colored envelope from his vest pocket and handed it to her. Their fingers brushed as she accepted the vellum envelope. She felt a spark of something she couldn't name flare to life in her chest, it felt almost magical.

Erik looked at their touching fingertips, he pulled his hand back flexing his fingers. "The information about the item you're picking up and the payment is enclosed."

"As long as it's not dangerous, I can help," Lola said as she tucked the envelope into her bag that rested by her feet. She finished her tea and shortbread, sitting the teacup and saucer on the table as she stood.

"I would never put you in any danger, thank you for having tea with me today." He said as he stood. The bells on the door made a tinkling sound as another potential customer entered the shop.

"I guess I'll see you tomorrow evening," Lola said as she picked up her bags and headed towards the front of the shop.

"I look forward to it," Erik said as he walked her to the door, Lola watched as he turned away to greet the shopper that had come in earlier.

Stepping outside and back into the real world was a shock to her system. The almost magical feeling she felt inside the antique shop always left her excited for a time when she could return. The crisp cool air swirled around her, making her purple hair dance in the wind and she smiled, feeling a connection to something else. Something more powerful than herself.

Lola closed her eyes, absorbing the feeling, before the honking from a random car passing made her jump. She let out a deep sigh. Time to get back to reality. She walked down the sidewalk heading home, a hop in her step as she thought about the job and the box that she carried. She knew exactly where she wanted to put it.

Humming quietly, she all but skipped down the sidewalk. Sometimes she felt like she was born in the wrong time with how much she enjoyed antiques and just being in nature. The connection that she felt to a higher power when she sank her fingers into the soft earth, was something she had yet to find a way to put into words.

* * *

Lola unlocked the door to her apartment, it wasn't a large apartment. It did have a nice kitchen and she enjoyed that feature. She sat down on the couch, her purchase clutched to her chest as a small smile played on her lips. It was almost like she could feel something special about the box. Something otherworldly that called to her. She carefully pulled out the paper-wrapped item and sat it on her knees. She felt like a kid on Christmas morning.

She carefully peeled back the paper until her prize was revealed to her. Smiling as she picked it up, letting the paper fall to the floor as she brought it up for closer inspection. The symbols looked vaguely familiar to her, and she brought her index finger up to trace the lines. Lola dropped the box and jumped off on the couch, sure that she had felt sparks of electricity.

Had she finally gone crazy?

Throughout her childhood, they had teased her for being different. The whispers still bouncing through her head, haunting her.

She must finally be cracking. This was the way her brain was manifesting her insanity. Lola picked up the box again and traced the next symbol.

The same thing happened. She closed her eyes, letting out a deep breath. This had to be a very vivid hallucination.

Lola opened her eyes, her heart pounding as she repeated the tracing pattern. Sometimes skipping around to a different symbol in a seemingly random pattern. The wood felt warm in her hands. She sat it down on her small lavender colored coffee table. Watching the box, waiting for it to explode. She wondered if maybe Erik had spiked her tea with some kind of drug or if she really was finally going insane.

She shakily brought her hand up, holding her breath as she traced the last symbol. Small sparkles seemed to shimmer in the air. It would have been pretty if Lola wasn't so terrified. The lights moved towards her, playing across her skin in a flurry of multicolored shimmers.

Backing up, she worried her lower lip as they followed her. Then they flew back towards the box in a flurry of movement. She let out the breath that she had been holding, stepping closer to see what it would do next. A feeling of weightlessness flowed through her as her feet left the ground and she went flying backwards. Tossed by an unseen force.

Lola's world started to go dim but around her. The small living room erupted into an explosion of colorful lights that made the previous one seem like a sparkler compared to a roman candle.

Chapter Two

"Is she dead?" The deep, rolling brogue was unfamiliar to her. Lola was afraid that someone had broken into her apartment and after possibly going insane, she was about to be murdered.

"No, I think she's coming to." A lighter, but still very masculine voice said from somewhere near her right side.

"Go halainn," another voice said from further in the room.

"She is, but you shall not lay with her." A grumbling voice said from somewhere near the couch.

"I do as I please, and if she wants to, I wouldn't be opposed. It's been a long time, she's pretty enough even if her hair is a strange color." The voice that had said the strange words said, his voice coming nearer as he moved closer.

Lola opened her eyes slowly. She was lying on the floor with two men standing above her. No, that wasn't right. They may look like men, but something about them screamed other to her. She closed her eyes, willing them to be gone when she opened them.

They were not. She let out a shriek and tried to crab walk away from them, slamming her tender head against the wall again. She fell back to the floor and brought her hand up to probe the knot on the back of her head.

"If you're planning to rob me, then go for it. I don't have much, but there's money hidden in my sock drawer. Please, don't hurt me" Lola said with a wince. Her head was throbbing and her stomach felt queasy. Did she have a concussion? Was that what this odd feeling was?

The man with curly red hair stood up, a smile on his face as he patted the coin purse that hung at his waist. He stood, heading towards her bedroom.

"Lu, you're not stealing her money." A hand shot out to grab his arm. Stopping him in his tracks.

"She told us where it is, I would only hold it for safekeeping," Lu said with a frown. It had been so long since he had any money that wasn't his own in his hands.

"Lu," the dark-haired man warned.

"Fine," He huffed as he moved to sit on the couch with a pout.

"If you aren't planning to rob me, why are you in my apartment?" Lola asked as she looked between the three men crouched around her. The throbbing got worse as she spoke, and she rubbed her eyes.

"You have set us free from our prison," The man with white blonde hair spoke.

"I think you have me mistaken," Lola said as she moved to sit up in a more comfortable position.

"No, you have the box that they trapped us in." The man spoke again. He brushed his hair out of his face.

Lola was pretty sure she saw gills along his high cheekbones.

"I think I may have bumped my head harder than I realized. That box couldn't fit you guys. This must be some elaborate prank. Yeah, that's got to be it. Why would four hot guys who look like they're going to a comic con or a renaissance festival be in my apartment dressed this way? It's just a prank or I'm hallucinating. That's right, I've started to finally crack and I'm imagining you guys." Lola said in a rush as she pointed at the men.

The dark-haired man with red eyes reached over and ran his hand up her calf with a dark smirk as his hand crept higher until he reached her thigh.

"Hey, oh no you don't. Owww!" Lola yelped as he pinched her inner thigh.

"Oh, we're real acushla," The dark-haired man who had pinched her said with a smirk. He rubbed her thigh where he had just pinched her, soothing away the pain.

"Hands, keep them to yourself," Lola said, pushing his hand away as he let out a chuckle that made something inside of her body clench tightly.

"Don't worry, the next time I touch you. You'll beg for it." He said as stroked her skin one last time with a smirk.

"Great, my subconscious likes pain," Lola said as she buried her head in her hands. A masculine chuckle made her head snap up, and she winced at the movement.

"I must remember that for later, but no. We are real, ignore Bodach. He's only teasing," He said as he took her head in his hands, "Looks like you've knocked your head good. Close your eyes, for a moment."

"Why?" Lola asked as she looked up at the man with dark auburn hair.

"So I can heal you." He said smiling down at her, Lola felt

her breath catch in her throat at his closeness. She closed her eyes, feeling his breath fan across her face. She could see sparks behind her eyelids as she felt his warm fingers probe her scalp, making the pain fade away.

"Thank you," Lola said, opening her eyes to look up at him. His golden luminescent eyes were studying her face with an intensity she wasn't used to.

"If you're done Puca, maybe we should introduce ourselves so we can thank our lovely host?" The man with gills said.

Lola stood up and looked around the living room. It looked like a tornado had torn up the room. Books were scattered on the floor, her lamp was knocked over, the blub smashed, and torn pages were scattered about. The box sat on her coffee table, opened. She looked at the man they had called Lu as he sat glaring at the box.

Had they really come from inside that box, or was she really losing her mind? They felt real enough, she'd give them that.

The man with white-blonde hair and gills stepped up to her, "Go halainn, I'm Merrow." He said taking her hand in his and kissing the back of her hand. His lips lingered on her skin as he looked up and winked at her with his sea-green eyes twinkling with mischief.

"What does that mean?" Lola asked as she pulled her hand from his.

"You're beautiful, and he's not wrong. I'm Bodach." Said the red-eyed man with dark hair who had pinched her earlier.

"Thanks?" Lola said, confusion coloring her voice as Bodach caressed her wrist with long thin fingers. The man with dark auburn hair pulled her hand away and gave her a sheepish smile.

"Sorry, we haven't seen a woman in a really long time.

14

Forgive our behavior, I'm Puca and the one pouting is Lu." He said with an almost shy smile.

"I'm Lola and I've got so many questions right now," Lola said, looking between the four men and the box that sat on her coffee table still.

"Ask away." Puca said as he tucked his hands into his trouser pockets.

"You said someone trapped you in that box?" Lola asked as she pointed towards the small oak box that was obviously too small to hold four very well-built men inside of it.

Men, who were currently standing in her living room, okay so she was using the term men loosely, very loosely.

These men were obviously not human like she was. She could feel the other-world difference floating about them, could almost see it swirling around their auras. Lola couldn't put her finger on it as she looked at them, but she had the feeling like she should know who they were.

"We were imprisoned inside of it. Yes." Puca answered her as he bit his lower lip, looking at her. His golden eyes studying her closely. He could feel the pull of magic faintly coming from her.

"Why?" She asked with a frown.

"That's a long story-" Bodach started to say as he looked down sheepishly.

"He stole a fairy's child and switched it with a Changeling." Merrow blurted out with a glare towards Bodach.

"Maybe not that long, and to be honest the child didn't feel like fae neither did her mother. How was I to know?" He asked, shrugging his shoulders as he raised an eyebrow.

"You could have not involved us," Lu said with a glare from the couch.

15

"Where's the fun in that? The family we gave the child to had several pretty daughters. I knew you guys wouldn't want to miss a chance with their type." He glanced over at Lola with a smirk, "Succubus."

Her eyes widened and she looked away, a blush coloring her cheeks.

"Afterwards, we couldn't find them again when we realized our mistake." Merrow mumbled, his eyes downcast and his shoulders slumped.

Lola looked over at him. She worried her lower lip with her teeth, not understanding why seeing him upset bothered her.

"How about I make us some tea?" Lola said, her voice sounding high and nervous to her own ears, making her cringe.

"Tea, do you have anything to warm it up?" Lu asked, making Lola frown.

"A tea kettle?" She shrugged her shoulders as she moved towards her tiny kitchen.

"He means spirits?" Bodach said with a chuckle at her innocent response.

"Oh, you mean like alcohol?" Lola asked. She had some wine in the fridge from this weekend.

"Aye, I'd love some whiskey. If you have it," Lu said perking up.

"I've got some white wine in the fridge." She offered hopefully.

"Settled then," Lu said, pushing up from the couch a happy hop in his step. His copper-colored curls bouncing as he walked towards the kitchen behind Lola. His eyes lingering on the swell of her hips.

Lola pulled the wine from the fridge and set it on the cabinet.

Planning to get him a wineglass when he snatched the bottle up and took a long pull from it. Lu swallowed hard and then grimaced.

"This isn't wine, it's barely a step above water." He said with a frown.

"Well, it's yours now, thanks for ruining it for everyone else." Lola crossed her arms under her breasts. His eyes flickered to her chest before he looked away. She let out a sigh of frustration. She'd been hoping to have a glass after this crazy night.

"It'll have to do for now," Lu said, taking another pull from the bottle as he sauntered back towards the living room. Bottle sloshing in hand as he plopped heavily down on her denim couch.

Lola frowned as she filled the kettle at the tap and then placed it on the stove. She turned on the burner as she tried to collect her thoughts. Maybe this was all a very vivid hallucination, even though her guests claimed it wasn't. She pulled out two boxes of tea and bit her bottom lip, looking between both small boxes.

Peppermint tea or Earl Grey, which would they prefer? She wished she had some chamomile. She could do with a little bit of relaxation.

Merrow came and leaned his hip against the counter, pushing his white-blonde hair over his shoulder as he watched Lola looking between the two boxes. He pushed away from the counter to look over her shoulder, and Lola was acutely aware of his body against hers. He smelled like the fresh waves of the ocean.

"I don't think we want to drink something made of man, I'd go with the peppermint one," Merrow whispered in her ear as he rested his hands on her hips. Smirking as she shivered.

"Hands, buddy," Lola growled in warning as she slammed the boxes down on the counter and turned to look up at him, he took a half step back. Still much too close for her tastes. "You guys need to learn to keep your hands to yourself."

"Tis been a long time since any of us has laid with a woman. Especially one who is such a beauty as you," Merrow said, his voice husky as his pupils dilated. His sea-green eyes searched her deep emerald ones.

"Well, it'll be a bit longer still, I've got no plans to sleep with any of you." Lola's cheeks heated up as she looked up at him. She hadn't missed the compliment on her looks, and it made her stomach feel like it was full of butterflies.

"You sure about that, Ghra?" Merrow said as he smirked down at Lola. His eyes twinkling with mischief and promises of something she didn't have a name for.

"Stop hogging her all to yourself, Merrow," Bodach said as he came into the small kitchen and Lola felt the room heating up. She didn't know if it was the stove or the two beautiful men that stood before her.

Merrow stepped back with a glare towards Bodach. Maybe it was the tension between these two? Judging by their clothing, they had been trapped in that box for a long time. Who was she to judge?

Lola turned back towards the counter and busied herself pulling out her mismatched tea set. One day she would have one like Erik's til then she would make do with the small cups painted with cheerful daisies and morning glories.

Filling the teapot up with boiling water, she tossed in a few tea bags, sitting it onto the tray. She planned to take it into the living room. Lola didn't look at the two men shooting daggers back and forth as she lifted the heavy tray in her arms and grimaced at the pain in her shoulder.

Frowning, she realized she must have hit the wall harder than she first thought.

Lola winced at the pain stabbing through her shoulder as she picked up the wooden tray. She sat it back down quickly. Rolling her shoulders before lifting it again.

"You're still hurt?" Bodach asked as he caught the grimace marring her pretty features. He glared over at Merrow before stepping closer to her.

"It's fine, I'll ice it later." She said turning to take the tray into the living room and to get away from the tension she felt between the two men.

"Let me," Bodach said, stepping forward to take the tray from her hands. Lola released it as he pulled the tray closer to his broad chest.

"Thank you," Lola said, looking up at him. She had never seen a person with crimson eyes before and she bit her lip, studying him. His eyes were larger than a normal person's, his features almost delicate with a slightly squared jawline.

"It's my pleasure," he said, his lips tilting in a smirk as he caught her admiring glance. Something tightened low in her stomach, a blush rising in her cheeks at the way he said pleasure.

What type of spell were these creatures weaving?

Lola turned to look at Merrow, and he raised an eyebrow at her as he crossed his muscular arms across his chest. She moved away, all but running into the living room as Bodach sat the tray onto the coffee table in front of Lu.

"Merrow suggested mint tea," Lola said, the words coming out faster than she meant them too.

"Aye," he said, sitting beside Lu on her small couch, "Better than a tea of Earl Grey."

"You drink tea made of flesh?" Puca said, his lip curling in disgust.

"It's just named after him, not made from him. We're not cannibals." Lola said as she handed Puca one of the delicate teacups. "Well, I mean, some humans are. None around here that I know of, maybe the guy in 3B."

Lu gave her a look and she held up her hands. "I'm just kidding. I doubt Sam would let in any tenants like that."

"'Tis good to know, go halainn." Puca said, breathing in the steam from his tea. A soft sigh of pleasure escaping his lips, making Lola's eyes widen. She didn't understand why her body was responding to them the way it was. Was it because they were fae? Was this some super secret power they possessed?

Lola grabbed a plush floor cushion and sat down, looking at the men that filled her small living room. She had the strange feeling of other-worldliness again as she took in their clothing. It was so out of place in her modern apartment. They stood out from her colorful aesthetic in their leather trousers that looked soft to the touch. Shirts that didn't look soft though, she knew they were. Lola's eyebrows scrunched together. How was she supposed to get them out of her apartment?

Where would they go?

They looked like they were headed to some LARP convention or something. She bit the inside of her cheek as she thought about the errand she was going to run for Erik tomorrow. What would she do with her new guests while she was busy?

Shaking her head as she looked about the room, she'd worry

about that tomorrow. Maybe she could claim they were cousins or- who was she kidding, no one would believe that?

They looked like models off of the covers of the cheesy romance novels she liked to read. While she with her wild purple hair, piercings, and curvy figure would never be considered a traditional beauty. Mostly, she was fine with that. Something about the looks they cast her way had made her wish she had put more effort into her clothing choice and makeup today.

She sipped her tea, trying not to think about the way Bodach's eyes were trailing up her body as he sat close to her. Her face flushed and she didn't want to understand why.

"What are you?" He asked, his voice a low grumble as his eyes met hers.

"I, I don't understand what you're asking." She said, tucking a strand of hair behind her ear.

"You are not a mere mortal, I can smell it on you," Puca said from where he sat on the couch.

"Pretty sure I've been human my entire life," Lola said with a frown. She didn't have any family she could ask. Her parents had passed away when she was younger. Her grandmother had raised her until she too had passed away last summer. Lola felt a pang of loneliness. She was the last one left of her bloodline. Even if she had wanted to ask her Nana about this, she wouldn't be able to.

"Aye, I smell it as well," Merrow said, his elbows on his thighs as he leaned forward to study her.

"Must be the hair," Lu said before taking another pull from the wine bottle.

"Oh, that's just dye." Lola said, "I don't like my natural color and I think this suits me better."

"What is your natural color?" Puca asked, his lips tilting in a half-smile as he watched her with his golden eyes.

"Um, it's strawberry blonde. So not really red, not really blonde." She answered, running her fingers through her hair nervously. She wasn't used to having so many eyes on her.

"I bet it looks like spun gold in the sunlight," Puca mumbled as he thought about how she would look with her natural hair color spread on the ground. The sun shining through the trees, painting her pale flesh brighter as he watched her Merrow worshiping her. His head buried in between her thighs as she panted his name. He felt his cock twitch in response and he looked over at the other man with a knowing glance.

He knew he had said they wouldn't lay with her, but something about Lola called to something in him. He had felt it the moment he had healed her, felt it when his magic had touched her. Dancing under his fingers, tasting him as his magic had tasted her. He knew he wanted to taste her as well. To see if she tasted as sweet as her magic, like honeysuckle flowers that perfumed the summer evenings in his childhood.

Chapter Three

"So let me get this straight, you're a merman," Lola said, looking at Merrow as he turned his head to the side, brushing his hair away from his high cheekbones. Letting her see scattering of scales across the top of his cheeks, framing his eyes. She sat her teacup onto the coffee table and leaned forward to study them intently.

"Aye," he answered.

"And you're a leprechaun? I thought you guys were a lot smaller." Lola asked, turning to face Lu as he finished his wine.

"I can shrink if ye'd like," he said with a slight slur as he sent a wink Lola's way. She blushed, looking down before glancing over towards Bodach.

"And you're, well, a child thief?" Lola frowned, she didn't really like that.

"I like to think of it as a child rescuer. I rescue children from homes where they are not loved and take them to homes where they will be cherished." Bodach said as he watched her with his red eyes, studying her in a way she'd never been looked at before. She looked at her hands before glancing back up again.

"Looks like you're not very good at your job," Lola said, motioning to his former prison.

"Accidents happen," he said, shrugging his shoulders as she turned to face Puca.

"And you, you're a-"

"Bringer of good and bad fortune, yes," Puca said, smiling down at her from his spot in the oversized red chair that sat in the corner. He steepled his fingers under his chin, resting his elbows on his crossed legs as he watched her interacting with his brethren.

"Okay, well now that that's cleared up. I'm going to go take care of our cups." Lola said, standing up from her spot on the floor. She looked around at the men in her apartment and covered her mouth as she fought back a yawn. This day had been long. The adrenaline was finally wearing off. She placed her teacup on the tray and started picking up the empty ones from the coffee table. She picked up the tray. Her shoulders stiff and painful still, she turned ready to take the dishes to her kitchen.

"I'll take that for you," Merrow stood up from his spot on the couch and stepped forward. His fingertips grazing her hand as he took the wooden tray from her.

"Thank you," Lola said, looking up at him with wide eyes. She was used to doing things herself. It was strange to have two men offer to help her in one evening. Merrow turned towards the kitchen and Lola followed him. He gently set the tray down as she moved to the sink.

Lola turned the water on and put the stopper in. She added dish soap and watched the bubbles foam up. She let out a soft sigh, picking up the first cup to carefully wash it.

Merrow leaned against the counter, his arms crossed as he watched her. She could feel his gaze on her and feel the burning in her cheeks. She wasn't used to so many men paying her so much attention, watching her like they were dying of thirst and she was a glass of water.

"You can go back and sit with your friends if you'd like," Lola said, looking over her shoulder at the blonde-haired merman.

"The view is better in here," he chuckled. She reached for one of the bright orange dish towels folded neatly under the sink. Turning, she tossed it towards him.

"You can help me then," Lola said with a smile as he caught the brightly colored towel. Merrow stepped closer and she could feel the heat of his body radiating against her skin. His smell enveloping her, making her feel almost drunk.

Peeking at him through her dark lashes, she must be more tired than she realized. She studied his sharp features, high angular cheekbones with hooded eyes that were now watching her as well.

She handed a teacup and gave him a nervous smile as they made short work of the dishes. Merrow stacked them on the counter, unsure of what to do with the cups and teapot.

Lola let the water out of the sink before drying off her hands. She reached over, watching as Merrow sucked in a breath at her nearness. "Here, let me." She said, taking one of the cups and opening the cabinet above the sink. Placing it on the shelf.

After she was done, they made their way back into the living room. Lu was lying on the couch, his arm tossed over his eyes as he snored softly.

Bodach and Puca were talking softly in the corner.

Covering her mouth as she yawned again, Lola made her

way to the hallway to get some blankets for her guests. They would have to make do with her living room floor, although they were pretty she wasn't up for sharing her bed. Trying to hold in a giggle at the thought. She grabbed several quilts and sat them on the chair in the corner before heading back towards the closet to grab them some pillows.

Grabbing one of the handmade quilts and shaking it out, she covered Lu's sleeping form up. Turning to look at her other guests, a slight frown marring her delicate features.

"I'm sorry I don't have anywhere else for you guys to sleep. I can help you guys make a pallet." She said nervously, not feeling like a very good host.

"We could always join you," Bodach said as he prowled closer. There was a twinkle in his eyes as he spoke. Lola felt her heart beat faster at the promise in his eyes.

"A world of no," Lola said, thinking about the three men in front of her. They were all handsome, and she had no problems imagining herself with them. What their hands would feel like trailing softly over her pale skin as they undressed her, lips teasing, tasting as they went.

"Are you sure?" Merrow said, moving closer. Lola backed up a step and bumped into the couch, tripping and falling onto Lu. She let out a small yelp.

Strong arms wrapped around her, pulling her closer to his chest as he felt her soft curves pressing against his body. He mumbled in his sleep, tightening his grip as she tried to pull herself away.

"Lu," Puca said roughly, rousing the other man from his sleep. "Let her go."

"Soft and warm, she is." He said sleepily as he brought his hand to her hair, caressing the silky strands.

"Aye, but she wants up."

"You ruin all me fun, Puca." He said with a loud yawn, untangling his arms from around Lola and letting her stand up as he rolled over.

"Thank you," Lola said, as she straightened her shirt.

"You should go to bed, Go halainn." Puca said softly, his voice barely above a whisper.

Lola looked up at Puca. Her cheeks flaming red, her wild purple hair a mess. He was right. She was tired even through the embarrassment she felt at falling on Lu and the way he had held her. She bit her lip as she turned away from the men and trudged down the hallway to her bedroom.

"Let me know if you need anything," she said over her shoulder.

Lu's body had been surprisingly muscular underneath her. She shook away the thought and opened the door to her bedroom. Reaching into the darkness, feeling the smooth white wall for the switch. Finally finding it, she flipped the switch on. Letting out a sigh of relief.

Lola knew it was a silly fear for an adult to have. Being afraid of the dark, but that didn't make it any less real for her. She closed the door behind her as she stepped into the softly lit room and fell face first onto her bed.

Burying her face into the handmade quilt, her body sinking into the soft surface as she thought about the quilt beneath her.

The one she and her grandmother had made together the winter before she had passed away. Sitting by the fireplace with their sewing machines set up. Humming away quietly while they chatted. It was a good memory, one that she would treasure forever.

It filled her with happy thoughts just looking at the purple and yellow squares, wrapping herself in it felt almost like a hug from her grandmother and she savored the feeling.

What she wouldn't give to hear her grandmother's voice one more time. The melodic southern tones always make her feel at ease. She felt a pang of loneliness as the ache in her chest deepened.

She kicked off her shoes and burrowed deeper into the bed, twisting her body so she could pull the covers over herself. Not bothering with getting cleaned up. She could shower in the morning, maybe they would be some elaborate hallucination and she would be alone again.

* * *

"She's like us," Puca spoke. His deep voice filling the quiet room, his golden gaze lingering on the closed bedroom door.

"Aye, she is," Merrow said from beside him, his arms crossed as he looked at the door and then back to his friend and oftentimes lover.

"She even looks fae," Puca said, moving to the quilts that sat on the chair.

"That she does," Merrow agreed as he stared at the closed door. Thinking about the girl on the other side, even if her hair had been its natural color. He would still be able to tell she was fae.

"We shall find out, leannan." Puca said as he nudged Merrow's shoulder. He handed the merman a blanket and motioned for him to lie down on the pallet as he stripped his shirt off.

Bodach was making a pallet for himself as he listened

to the two men talk about Lola. He had to agree that she was something else. Something about her stirred to life the darkness that lay in him.

He couldn't help but wonder what type of fae she could be?

He lay down on the soft quilt and felt his head sink into the down pillow he let out a sigh of pleasure. He closed his eyes.

Inside of their prison, they hadn't had bedding this soft, they hadn't had bedding at all and this felt like heaven. It would be even better if Lola were curled up beside him. Her warmth seeping into his skin. He bit his lip softly as he thought of the swell of her breasts pressed against him. He could trail his hand from her silky hair down across her shoulder, over the curve of her hip. His hand caressing the soft curve of her bottom before the sharp smack of his hand made her moan with a sharp gasp.

He opened his eyes, shaking his head. What was Lola that she made him feel like this?

Bodach had never felt this way about anyone before, human or not. He rolled over onto his side, trying not to imagine how she would look after a good tumble. Her purple locks loose about her shoulders. Her lips swollen from his kiss as she curled up next to him. Wearing nothing but a satisfied smile.

He bit his lower lip harder with a growl. It was going to be a very long and uncomfortable night for him.

On the couch Lu lay, his arm tossed over his eyes as he feigned sleep, listening to Merrow and Puca. He couldn't help but smirk at the growl he heard coming from Bodach, he knew that sound well.

It was the sound of frustration, and a small part of the leprechaun took great pleasure in that sound. Just as he had for much of their time in that cursed box. He himself was feeling just as frustrated as he thought about how Lola had felt against him. Her chest pressed to his own as she had struggled against him. Waking something in him that he hadn't felt in ages, longing.

A longing desire for the touch of a lover. He wanted more, though. Something about how she had spoken to him earlier as he drank her wine had piqued his interest. Lu couldn't wait to see how far he could push her. To see how she looked with her eyes sparkling in anger. Would her skin flush, or would she be covered in that blush that made her glow earlier?

Chapter Four

❧

*L*ola rolled over onto her back as she scrubbed the sleep out of her eyes. She'd been having the strangest dream. In it, she had been trapped in a dark room. No way to get out, just endless darkness. The only sound was her ragged breathing and the frantic pounding of her heart as she desperately dragged her hands across the smooth walls. Trying to find any way out.

She bit her lip as she looked around the bright sun-filled room and let out a deep breath. It was quiet and still. She wondered for a moment if she had imagined everything that had happened yesterday.

A loud bang came from the kitchen and she sat up, eyes wide. Either someone was breaking in or there really were fae creatures in her apartment. She untangled herself from the warm bedding and her feet hit the floor. She grabbed the baseball bat from under her bed before opening the door.

The polished wood and leather laces feeling comfortable in her hands as she brought the bat up. Ready to swing hard and

31

fast at any intruder. Her heart was beating fast in her chest as she tightened her grip on the bat. Sneaking down the hallway. Holding her breath as she walked into the living room. She scanned the room, taking in the tossed around blankets on the couch.

"What-"

Lola swung the bat as hard as she could, her eyes widening as Bodach caught it with his hand. Trapping the wood in his fist and then using it to pull her forward before she could let go. He wrapped his other arm around her waist and pulled her closer.

He smirked down at her, his red eyes twinkling in amusement as he took in her tangled locks and her surprised expression.

"Did you think we were just a dream?" He asked, letting go of the bat and as his eyes searched hers.

"Yes," Lola whispered as she looked up at Bodach. The bright sunlight streaming through his hair reminding her of a raven's feathers almost blue and black when the sun hits it just right. She shook her head, clearing her throat before she spoke, "Well, a hallucination."

"I'd be offended, acushla. If you weren't so lovely upon waking." His lips twitched as he tried to fight back a smile. He brought his hand up to brush her hair behind her ears.

Merrow propped his arms on the pillow, his eyes narrowing as he watched Bodach run his fingers through Lola's hair. He didn't like the way his friend looked at her, he knew that look well. Full of hunger and longing, glancing over at Puca, his long dark auburn hair fanning out over the pillow, his face relaxed in sleep. It seemed like they would have competition in trying to woo Lola.

"Falbh a ghabhail do ghnuis airson cac!" The shout rang out from the kitchen, filling the apartment, making Lola jump away from Bodach. The sound of a pot clanging against the counter made Lola hurry to her kitchen.

"What are you doing?" She asked Lu as he stood glaring at her stove.

"I can't figure out this bastair," he growled, dragging a hand through his copper colored curls.

"If you were trying to destroy my kitchen, good job," Lola told him. Her full lips pressing into a thin line as she stepped into the small room and started putting things back in order.

"I was trying to fix you breakfast," Lu said, a blush coloring his cheeks as he sulked.

"Oh, well, thank you for the thought," Lola said, smiling over her shoulder.

"I didn't mean to wake you yet, but how do you turn this on?" He asked, motioning to her stove.

Lola pulled out a box of matches and struck one before turning the knob and lighting the burner. She looked back over at Lu with a soft smile. Wondering what stoves must have been like before. Or did they even have stoves? That was a question she decided to save for another day. He already looked embarrassed.

"Why don't you get the eggs out of the fridge," she suggested. Pointing to the cream colored antique fridge that sat in the corner of her kitchen, "and I'll get breakfast started."

Lu nodded at her as he pushed himself away from the counter and did as she asked.

Lola busied herself fixing coffee as Lu brought the eggs to her. She sat them on the counter as she finished measuring out the grinds for all of her unexpected house guests. Next, she grabbed a mixing bowl from underneath the counter and sat it down. She opened the egg crate.

"Would you mind grabbing some chives from my window?" She asked before handing him her kitchen scissors.

Lu grabbed the scissors from her hand. His fingertips grazing her palm, making sparks fly as their skin met.

"That's odd," Lola said with a frown.

"It's just your magic responding to my own," he said, a smile playing across his face as he turned to do as she had asked.

Lola shook her head, trying not to think about what had just happened as she went about cracking the eggs into the bowl. Grabbing her whisk from the mason jar that sat beside her sink. She pulled out the cutting board and a knife, so Lu could chop the herbs. Beating the eggs with the whisk, Lola bit her lower lip. Last night had been much different from her normal Wednesday evenings.

Normally she'd read a book or watch some cheesy television show, maybe have a glass of wine before bed. Not accidentally open a puzzle box that was a prison. Releasing four super hot guys into her small apartment.

Guys who seemed very interested in her.

Lola placed a pan over the open flame with a bit of butter stepping over to the toaster she added bread to it. Moving back to the pan to give it a swirl. The steady thwack, thwack of Lu chopping the chives at the counter was soothing as she moved about the kitchen.

The toast popped up and Lola grabbed it from the toaster, moving it between her hands as she grabbed a plate.

"What magic is that?"

"The toaster?" Lola asked.

"Toaster." Lu repeated, watching as Lola added more slices

to the slim silver device and pressing the little lever.

He did the next round, picking up the toasted bread and studying it closely. He grabbed two slices and added them to it, moving closer to watch as it went down and the coils inside of the device turning orange.

Lola smiled to herself as she added the eggs to the pan before dumping the chives in. She stirred the eggs until they were fluffy. The smell making her mouth water, she glanced over at Lu, "Would you mind grabbing the plates with the toast for me?"

With a nod, he picked up the plate with the neatly stacked toast and moved over to her.

Lola nodded her head in thanks as she turned off the burner and started plating out their breakfast. She stacked plates in Lu's arms before moving to the coffee and getting it setup into a carafe. She took it to the living room, before scurrying back to the kitchen to grab the plates that Lu missed.

"Breakfast is served," Lola said as she and Lu walked into the living room. She handed a plate with scrambled eggs and toast to Merrow, as Lu did the same to Bodach. The carafe of coffee sat in the middle of the coffee table as they all sat down to eat.

"Smells mouth watering, acushla" Bodach said as he leaned over his plate, his eyes not on the food but on Lola, making her shiver at the tone of his voice.

"Thanks, Lu and I worked great together." Lola said, glancing at the man beside her.

"Aye, we do make a good team." His green eyes sparkled in the morning light as he handed her a cup of coffee. Lola's fingers brushed against Lu's and the familiar sparks washed over her, making her suck in a breath.

Lola picked up her fork and took a bit of her eggs, glancing over at Puca who was still asleep. The morning light bringing out the red tones in his long hair. "Should we wake him?" She asked, looking at the men that sat around her small coffee table.

"Only if you want to fight or rut?" Bodach said with a dark smile. He wasn't keen on sharing her just yet, but he could only imagine how she would look pinned beneath Puca's body. Her eyes sparkling with shock, maybe even lust as the other man's hardness pressed against her.

Would she roll her hips into him, or shy away from his touch?

Bodach shifted uncomfortably as his cock hardened. He bit his lower lip, trying to fight back a moan as she looked up at him.

"What do you mean?" Her innocent question made him groan.

"Puca wakes up ready to take anyone to his bed." Bodach said, his lip twitching as he slowly blinked.

"Oh? Oh. I guess we should let him rest then." Lola said, the tops of her cheeks heating with a blush as she looked down at her coffee.

Glancing down at the black liquid, Lola didn't see the wide grin that spread across Bodach's face as he sat back. Merrow did, and he realized that he and Puca would have to act fast if they wanted a chance to be with the enchanting young woman.

Lu looked at Lola, he wondered if she knew that her innocence drew them in like moths to a flame?

That mixed with the fire that he could see lurking in the depths of her eyes made him hunger for her. He knew the others felt the same, just by the quiet conversation he had overheard last night between Puca and Merrow. It was obvious to him that Bodach was taken with the girl.

How his gaze lingered on her and the uncomfortable way he shifted in his seat.

"So I have some errands to run today." Lola said, trying to change the subject away from beds and taking.

"You do?"

"I do, I don't just stay home all day. I have work, well sort of." Lola said, taking a bit of her eggs.

"Do you not have a man that provides for you?" Lu asked. He had seen no evidence of a man in her home, but that didn't mean that there wasn't one away.

"Ummm, no. It's just me. So the errand I'm running is part of my job." Lola said. Taking a sip of the dark coffee, grimacing at the bitter liquid. She was supposed to have gone to the grocery store this morning.

Other things had interrupted those plans.

Four other things, three of which were watching her as they ate their breakfast and one was snoozing on her living room floor.

"I can go with you," Lu and Merrow said at the same time, then turned to glare at each other.

"I offered first, it should be me." Merrow said, tilting his head to the side with a glare.

"I've made breakfast, you should stay and clean as thanks." Lu countered.

"Bodach. I choose Bodach." Lola blurted out, to stop the two men from fighting further.

"Why him?" Lu asked as he pressed his lips together. His tight curls bouncing as he swung his head around to glare at the other man.

37

"He's not fighting while I'm drinking my coffee." Lola said with a shrug as she finished off her coffee. Standing up, she took her plate into the kitchen before they could argue further.

"You heard her, she chose me." Bodach smirked, his red eyes glimmering as they met Merrow's gaze and then flickered over to Lu's.

"Just because she hasn't figured out you're a jackeen." Merrow said as he finished off his breakfast and moved to follow Lola.

Lola stood at the sink rinsing her plate off, Merrow moved to stand behind her. He studied the long line of her neck. Her hair was pulled up into a high ponytail, soft strands escaping to lay against her skin. Merrow couldn't help but wonder how she would respond if he ran his lips across the smooth skin.

Pinning her body against the counter so he could take his time teasing and exploring her body.

"You just going to stand there or are you going to help?" Lola asked as she looked over her shoulder.

"You should tread carefully when dealing with Bodach." Merrow said as he stepped closer and Lola turned the water off, turning to face him.

"You seem to always corner me in the kitchen." Lola said looking up at him, and Merrow fought the urge to brush her hair from her eyes. "Why should I be careful around him and not you?" She asked biting her lower lip as he stepped even closer and Lola could feel the heat of his body through her clothing. Smell the soft scent of his skin, he smelled of the beach and burning driftwood.

Merrow's fingers moved to brush a loose strand of hair away from her face, his fingers tracing over her high cheekbone. Lingering and savoring the warmth of her soft skin. "You should be around me as well." He said leaning closer to her. His lips hovered over hers and Lola's eyes widened as his lips started to inch closer to her.

Chapter Five

$\mathcal{L}$ola walked down the sidewalk, looking down as she touched her cheeks. Thinking about the kiss that had almost happened with Merrow. She didn't know if she had wanted him to kiss her or not when Lu had interrupted them. His bright eyes studying them intently before he raised a thick eyebrow at the merman.

"Cleaning, aye?" He asked as he stepped into the kitchen, shaking his head. Breaking up the moment, Lola looked back up at Merrow as he studied her lips before stepping back. His sea-green eyes moving to hers as she let out a breath she hadn't realized she had been holding.

She couldn't help but wonder what he would have done if they hadn't been interrupted?

"Aye, we are." Merrow frowned as he looked over at Lu with a scowl.

"I guess I'll be heading out then," Lola said, stepping away from the handsome man, "If you get bored, you guys can watch some television. I've got Netflix." She said missing their confused looks as she headed into the living room.

"Are you ready?" Bodach asked as he moved to stand.

"Almost, I need to get changed and we can head out." Lola said, pausing as she walked past Puca. She looked around the messy living room. Debating on if she should ask her guests to pick it up when I hand snaked its way up her ankle. With a shriek, she jumped away.

"What are you doing?"

"Waking up from a pleasant dream, into an even lovelier realm." Puca said, his voice gravelly with sleep as he propped himself up onto his elbow. Admiring the way the light filtered through the thin cotton of Lola's shirt. She stepped back, almost as if she could escape the heat of his gaze only to back up into Bodach. Her back hitting his chest as he wrapped his arms around her waist.

Lola let out a gasp as his arms around her tightened. She looked from Puca to Bodach. Felt sparks dance across her skin as she felt him bury his face in her hair and breathe her in. Heat moved through her body at his soft groan.

Puca moved to stand. His chest was bare, and she marveled at the way his muscles moved and bunched under his skin as he moved closer to her. Her gaze moved to the fine line of downy hairs below his belly button and she felt her blush spread further. She looked up quickly into Puca's penetrating golden gaze with a gulp.

She understood why it was called a happy trail as she bit her lower lip. Her hands moved to Bodach's arms and she'd meant to pry herself for his grasp. Instead she gripped his muscular arms. It was hard to think as Puca sauntered closer to her, his eyes hungrily devouring her in, like he was a starving man and she was a tasty treat.

"No having." Lola squeaked out, "You said no laying with me."

"Aye," he said with a smirk as he stepped closer, "It's been a long time and the mornings are always harder."

Lola felt Bodach run his nose along her neck and she shivered. His breath made goosebumps form on her skin and her nipples hardened. "It's always a struggle in the morning." His voice tickled across the shell of her ear as his lips grazed the outer shell. Making her jump away from the loose circle of his arms. Putting some distance between herself and the two men.

"Look, I'm not that type of girl." Lola exclaimed, looking between the two men.

"What type is that?" Puca asked her as he dragged his hands through his hair, as his tongue darted out and he licked his lower lip.

"You know the type that all the guys want." Lola said looking away, trying to ignore the way her face flushed with embarrassment. Boys hadn't liked her growing up, yes she had dated. Nothing more serious than a few one night stands, and the attention from these four men had her feeling things she had never felt before. Sure, she had the lustful thoughts just like any normal woman did. Mostly about Erik, but they paled in comparison to how she was feeling right now.

"We are no mere men." Puca said. His hand moved from his chest to his abdomen and Lola had a moment where she desperately wanted that hand to be hers. She longed to run her hand over the hard plans of his abs, feel his muscles contract under her touch as her fingers traveled lower.

"No," Lola squeaked out, as she felt desire coil low in the pit of her stomach. Pulsing through her body like a wave.

"No?" Puca asked as he bit his lower lip, his eyes promising pleasure that Lola couldn't even begin to imagine.

"No." Lola said, stepping towards the hallway. She knew if she stayed any longer her no would be changing to a yes.

Shaking her head, Lola tried not to think about what happened this morning.

She glanced over at Bodach. His red eyes were covered with a pair of her dark sunglasses with big lenses that made him look almost comical. The sun glinted off of his black hair, catching the deep blues and greens of it. Bodach caught her stare and his lip twitched up into a grin as he tilted the dark glasses down to catch her eye.

Lola looked away, her cheeks heating up. "We're almost there." She said, looking down at the address on her phone. She looked around at the buildings that surrounded them. They were in a residential neighborhood, the homes looked older, Americana with their deep porches and wicker furniture. It was beautiful. She couldn't help but think about all of the history these homes must have seen.

'In one hundred feet your destination will be on the left.' Lola's phone rang out in the quiet afternoon and Bodach frowned.

"'Tis strange for a map to talk." Bodach said and Lola couldn't help but smile.

"I told you already, it's a cell phone. It's not only a way to get in touch with people over substantial distances. But it has maps and directions which makes things so much easier." Lola said smiling up at him.

"Still seems like a spell to me, the future is quite strange."

Lola couldn't help but agree with him, she could only imagine how he and the others must feel. How much they had missed out during their confinement. Everything must seem so different for them.

'You have arrived at your destination.' The voice chimed out again, making Lola laugh as Bodach pressed his lips together, sliding the glasses back into place.

"Would you like to come in with me?" Lola asked as she tucked her cellphone into her bag.

"Nay," he said, shaking his head as he looked at the chimes beside the door. The thick iron bells clanging in the slight breeze.

"I'll be quick then."

"Take your time, I'll be waiting for you." Bodach said as he leaned against the porch railing. Looking out over the yard, he let out a sigh as the door closed behind him.

* * *

Lola stepped outside, the brown paper package clutched close to her chest. The redwood jewelry box wrapped up nice and safe. She glanced around the porch for Bodach. He had chosen to stay outside, Lola could understand that. If she had been trapped for as long as he had in that box she wouldn't want to be indoors more than she had to either.

Debating with herself about planning a picnic for the men, she wondered if they would like that? Maybe they could go for a hike on one of her favorite walking trails.

Looking out onto the well-manicured lawn, she frowned. Bodach wasn't there. Lola walked down the steps, looking around she wanted to kick herself. Where could he have gone?

Things were so different from the time he had come from. She bit the inside of her cheek as she walked down the sidewalk. He couldn't have gotten very far, could he? Maybe he had gotten bored and decided to head back to her apartment?

Shifting the package in her arms, she reached into her bag to grab her cellphone, then stopped herself. Of course, he didn't have one of those, so calling him would be useless.

Shifting the package again, Lola moved down the sidewalk. Her eyes scanning across the yards of the surrounding houses. The further she got, the more worried she became when she remembered the park they had passed, Bodach was a child thief.

Well, rescuer.

Same difference. She picked up her pace, worrying her lower lip as she went. Hopefully, he would be there and she could get him back to her apartment and out of trouble in no time at all.

* * *

Lola felt the anxiety ease up the closer that she got to the park. There off to the side, under a grouping of trees, was Bodach. A soft smile playing on his lips as he watched the children running around. Even with the glasses blocking half of his face, Lola could see the way he was relaxed with his arms held at his side. His back against the tree, the normal dark, seductive smirk gone.

"You had me worried." Lola huffed out as she moved to stand beside him, her eyes moving to the children playing tag.

"Worried for me, that touches my heart. That you would worry for someone like I."

"Well, worried for what might happen." Lola shifted from

foot to foot.

"These children are loved, they are safe." His words were soft and Lola glanced over at him.

"Well, of course, everyone loves their children."

"Nay, not everyone. There are those who need my help to place them with the fae that will help them flourish." He said glancing away from the children, his eyes meeting Lola's gaze.

"That's what you do? Take them so they have a better chance?" Lola asked, looking away from him, feeling her cheeks heat up.

"Aye, it's what I do."

She couldn't help but think about her own childhood. It had been sad. At the same time filled with happiness, her grandmother had made it memorable teaching her to garden.

The blistering sun beating down on her freckled shoulders as she and the older woman had their hands in the dirt. Enjoying the feel of the rich soil as they had planted flowers in her garden. It had been hard, but she was thankful that she had her to lean on.

"How about I take you back home and then I'll go drop this off?" Lola asked, shifting the box in her hands. Bodach stepped forward, taking the box from her, his fingers grazing hers with that smirk back on his lips.

"Ready to end our time together so soon?"

"It's not that," Lola said with a pause as she thought about how to word her next sentence. "I just worry about you guys, the world has changed a lot."

* * *

Back at Lola's apartment, things were not as they should be.

The kitchen was cleaned, the dishes put away.

"Are the two of you planning to seduce her?" Lu asked as he flopped onto the couch, putting his feet onto the coffee table.

Puca looked over at him as he sipped his coffee. The lines around his eyes let Lu know that he was smirking behind his coffee cup.

"If we are?" Merrow asked, brushing back his white blonde hair as he studied the book in his hands. Flipping back to the cover, he looked at the models with a sigh of boredom. "It says it's about mer-folk, but he does not look like one of ours."

"I think it's supposed to be the girl." Puca said, his grin deepening. "She has a tail."

"That's not what we look like either," Merrow said with a frown.

"I know, leannan. I've seen."

Merrow looked up, peeking over the book at Puca, "Yer teasing me."

"Aye."

Lu frowned as he watched the two men banter.

How was he supposed to have a chance if they were already planning their courtship of their pretty host? He looked over to the strange dark mirror that sat across from him on a stand. Nodding to himself as he started to come up with a plan.

Standing up, he decided he would try to do something helpful. He picked up his blankets from the night before and began folding them when a log rectangle box fell from the couch. Leaning down, Lu picked up the item. Pressing on the small soft buttons and what he had believed to be a badly kept burnt mirror blared to life. The strange sounds of people talking filled the room.

"What magic is this?" Merrow asked, sitting his book down

as he leaned forward to study the images on the screen of one man punching another.

Lu pressed another button. The screen changed, this time to a sobbing woman. The three watched as a man took her into his arms.

"Is this a scrying mirror?" Lu asked, captivated by the couple on the screen as the woman looked up at the man.

'I'm sorry, my love.'

'Sarah, I love you. We will find a way.'

Lu pressed the button. Something about that felt like he was intruding on a moment he shouldn't have been.

"Lu is controlling it." Puca said, watching the two as he sat down his coffee cup, "I don't feel any spirits coming from it."

"I'm not doing it." Lu said, tossing the remote towards Puca.

Puca easily caught the hard black rectangle. Pressing another button, the fight from before appearing again and the men sat sucked into the action packed-drama.

Chapter Six

Opening the door to her apartment, the cool air hit Lola in the face and she let out a soft sigh of pleasure as she walked in. Slipping off her shoes. Bodach stepped behind her, his body responding to the sound she made as his eyes moved along the exposed skin of her shoulders. He found himself wanting to hear that sound again.

"Where shall I put this?" He asked, shifting the box in his hands. Bodach had a strange feeling about it, but didn't want to say anything to alarm Lola until he was sure.

"Oh, um. On the coffee table is fine." Lola said over her shoulder as she walked to the kitchen. She passed Lu, Puca, and Merrow smirking to herself as she caught sight or what they were watching with a roll of her eyes. "Really guys?"

"Your scrying mirror seems to be broken." Merrow glanced over to Lola as he spoke, his face flushing at being caught in this act of voyeurism.

"The television?" Lola raised an eyebrow, "Seems to be working just fine to me."

"But these men, they're all in love with this one woman." Lu said pointing to the television. "Puca senses no magic from it, and they seem mortal. Most mortals, they don't mate like the fae do."

Lola moved into the kitchen, speaking loudly as she went to the cabinet and grabbed a glass, "It's trash tv, it's all staged. It's fake you guys."

"But this Springer man, he says they are in love." Lu said louder, unable to look away.

"They only say that so more people will watch." Lola yelled back as she turned on the tap filling up her water glass. "It's all pretend. Fae take more than one lover?" Lola called out. She felt her cheeks darken at the thought of that. She'd the feeling from Bodach and Puca earlier that they didn't mind sharing. From the way that Merrow and Puca interacted that they had been intimate as well. Who was she to judge?

"Aye, some of us do. Trash tv?" Lola heard Puca mumble as she turned the water and took a sip of her water. She turned, heading back towards the living room, to see Bodach had joined the others as they all sat leaning forward.

"Yes, a television show for the sake of drama. It's all pretend, chances are these people will go back home to their boring lives and never talk again." Lola said as she moved to sit down. Enjoy the fight that was happening on the screen as she finished her drink.

She looked over at the three, as Lu winced in sympathy at the punch that was thrown on the screen. Puca leaned forward, his hands on his knees as he studied the people closely. Lola couldn't help but think about their interaction earlier, the way he had sauntered over to her.

How his hand had traveled over his muscled torso as

Bodach's arms had tightened around her waist. Her face flushed, she looked back towards the television. Trying not to think about the men that sat in her living room. How Merrow's eyes had filled with heat as he had warned her away.

She shivered as she took another sip of her water, and Lu glanced over at her.

"Are you cold?" He asked as he reached his arm around her shoulder.

"Oh, no you don't." Lola said scooting away. "This isn't a Netflix and chill kind of moment."

Lu's chest pressed against her arm and the muscles she felt under his shirt surprised her. Yes, sure. She had felt them last night as she lay sprawled above him. Now she felt them moving against her. He wrapped the quilt that he had folded earlier around her shoulders and gave her a smirk.

"What is this net flicks and chill you speak of."

"It's uh, it's. Nevermind." Lola muttered. Looking away from his curious gaze as she took a gulp of her water, finishing it off. "I need to take the jewelry box to Erik, and then I'll come home. You guys enjoy the television."

Merrow looked away from the drama unfolding on the television as one of the men threw a punch at one of his lovers. "Do you not need help to carry the box? Or someone to walk with you?"

"No, Erik's shop is close by. I'll be back before you guys know it." Lola stood, stretching her arms above her head before taking her glass to the kitchen. She walked past the men sitting on her couch with a bounce in her step and a slight smile. The tops of her cheeks still covered in faint traces of a blush.

Merrow thought as he watched her walk, his hand on his

chin. Was this Erik person someone she was close to? A suitor, perhaps? He tapped his foot against Puca's tilting his head in the direction she had gone. Puca looked away from the screen. "It is interesting."

"More interesting than Lola having another male admirer," He lifted an eyebrow as he pressed his lips together before speaking. "Other than us?

Puca turned to look at him with a frown. He wasn't bothered by the others being interested in her. Well, he was, but he could understand the attraction. The thought of another, besides the four of them he didn't like.

When Lola returned, Merrow couldn't help but notice the swipe of color on her full lips. Lips that were quirked up with a smile as she hurried past them, slipping on her shoes. The faintest traces of vanilla lingering in the air. Puca watched as well, his keen gaze taking in the fact that her hair had been brushed. It seemed that he and his brethren would have some competition.

Lola moved in front of them, picking up the box from the coffee table, "I'll be back soon." She said before moving to the door, not waiting for a reply.

Puca and Merrow turned to one another, before both men moved to stand.

"Where are you going?" Lu asked, looking away from the screen in confusion, his thick brows knit together.

"Didn't you see how she looked? She is interested in this Erik." Puca said as he moved to stand in front of the television.

"What are we going to do about it?" Bodach asked as he leaned back onto the couch, his eyes meeting Puca's.

"Follow Lola." Merrow said as he turned towards the front door, the others following him out.

* * *

Walking down the sidewalk, Lola was lost in thought. Unaware of the four men that followed her. She turned down the street, stopping to wait at the crosswalk as she waited for the light to change.

Shifting the box to her side as she clutched it with one arm. Smoothing her ponytail. Before all but skipping towards the antique shop as the light changed. An older gentleman with red hair and deep chocolate eyes held the door open for her. His toothy grin sent shivers down her spine.

"Thank you," she whispered as she hurried past him, unable to shake the eerie feeling he gave her.

The bells twinkled above the door as Lola walked into Erik's antique shop. It was quiet except for the whistling of the kettle. "Erik?" Lola called out as she stepped up to the cash register. Sitting the box down gently on the counter, she brushed her hands over her top, smoothing the material down. She couldn't wait for Erik to see it.

Walking out of the back room with his nose buried in a book. He moved towards the front and Lola couldn't help but grin as she watched him adjust his glasses on the bridge of his nose. "Sorry, lost myself for a bit."

"Good afternoon Erik, what are you reading?" Lola asked, dragged her finger under the tape pulling the paper open.

"Oh, just some research." Erik answered as he closed the book and sat it behind the counter. He stepped closer to Lola, and she jumped at his nearness. The fae men that she'd been around lately had her on edge, and she was overly aware of Erik. How his body heat seemed to seep through her clothing, the soft scent of his cologne.

She was always aware of his nearness.

Today it was more so than normal. Dragging her finger across the brown paper, Lola jumped and pulled her hand away.

"Oww," Lola lifted her hand, the blood dripping from the paper cut.

"You're hurt," Erik said as he grabbed her wrist. "I've got a first aid kit in the kitchen." He murmured as he let go of her wrist and turned towards the kitchen, Lola following behind him.

"I don't know where my head is." Lola said as she moved into the kitchen. She turned the kettle off while Erik searched under the sink for the first aid box. "Why do you keep your first aid box in the kitchen?"

"A friend once told me that the most bleeding happens in here."

"Odd thing to say." Lola said as she leaned her hip against the counter, watching Erik.

"He was an odd fellow, brilliant fun at parties." Erik said with a smirk as he turned around holding the red and white box.

"I have a hard time picturing you at a party." Lola said, biting her lower lip. Fighting down a smile as he sat the box down on the cabinet and opened the lid.

"I used to go to quite a few, nowadays I live a simpler life." Erik smiled as he meticulously lined up the antiseptic and bandages. He picked up a cotton ball and held his hand out to Lola. She held her injured hand out, and his smile deepened as their hands touched. "This might sting a bit, I do apologize."

"It's just a paper cut. I can take care of it."

"Lola, let me take care of you." Erik said in a soft voice as he dabbed the cut clean.

Lola felt her heart beat faster at his softly spoken words.

"Erik-" Lola whispered.

"I feel things for you." He said as he dabbed the antiseptic onto her cut. "Things that I haven't felt for a-" he paused as if he were thinking of the right words to say. "Things that I haven't felt in a very long time."

"Erik, I'm not sure what to say." Lola said. Watching as he placed the bandage on her fingers. She had longed to hear those words and now that he had spoken them, she didn't know how to react.

"You don't have to say anything, I just wanted you to know that I like you. I'd like to pursue you, I mean to say I'd like to pursue a relationship with you."

Even though he had bandaged her fingers up, he still held her hand in his. Lola felt her breath catch in her throat as she looked down at their joined hands. She wondered if he felt the same sparks that she was feeling now.

"Erik, I-"

"Lola, you don't have to say anything right now. The reason that I asked for your help was not just because I do need help. But it gives me an excuse to spend time with you." His fingers squeezed hers gently as he turned away, moving to clean up the bandages and cotton balls he had sat on the counter.

"I'd, um." Lola said pausing for a moment to collect her thoughts, "I'd like to spend time with you too."

Erik turned to look at her, his gray eyes locking with her eyes. As she looked up at him through lowered lashes.

"You have no idea how long I've waited to hear you say that." He said biting his lower lip as he stepped closer to Lola.

Lola looked up at him, her eyes widening as she sucked in a

deep breath. "Erik-"

The bells over the door chimed and Erik looked at Lola one last time before turning away. He stepped out of the room, greeting the customers as Lola raised her hands to her cheeks. Feeling the heat under her palms as she tried to calm herself down. She didn't know if it was her longtime crush on the shop owner or the fae men at her home that had sent her libido into overdrive.

"Lola, I, I think you have a visitor." Erik called out, pulling Lola from her thoughts.

Stepping out of the kitchen, Lola walked towards the front with a frown.

Why would she have a visitor at Erik's shop? Then she saw him, his golden eyes blazing as he looked at her and her mouth went dry.

Puca stood stiffly by the front door, his jaw clenched as he looked from her to Erik. She knew that he found her attractive, that he may have said that they wouldn't sleep with her. The look in his eyes said something else, that he wanted to throw her over his shoulder and drag her back to the apartment.

Pushing her hair out of her eyes, she tried to quash down the thrill that thought sent through her. She knew she shouldn't feel this way for someone she'd just met.

"Erik, this is my friend Puca." Lola said introducing the two before she turned back to look at Puca, "Puca, this is my boss Erik. What are you doing here?" She said barely holding her smile in check as she spoke through her teeth.

"I came to offer to escort you back home." Puca stood taller. Smoothing the front of his shirt as he looked from Lola to Erik, he didn't like the way the other man's eyes kept traveling back to Lola. Didn't like the way that his eyes met his with a silent challenge.

"It's good to meet you, Puca." Erik said, extending his hand out for the other man, his lip quirking in a half smile. Lola held her breath as she watched Puca's eyes slowly move from Erik's hand to his eyes.

"Aye, you as well." Puca said, finally taking the hand extended towards him. Puca's jaw clenched and Lola knew if she hadn't been watching him, she would have missed it. Looking back down at Puca's hand, she noticed the burn marks on his skin as he released Erik's hand and tucked his own back at his side.

"Erik and I were just wrapping up here, then we can head home. What happened to your hand?" Lola asked, watching the two men stare each other down.

She moved to lean over the counter, looking at the box she had brought in earlier as she grabbed Erik's notebook and a pen. Opening it up, she frowned at the strange symbols she saw scratched onto the crisp white paper. Shaking her head, this was not her business. She flipped to a blank page, writing her number down. She left it open for him, her cheeks heating up with a blush. "I wrote my number down so you can call me later."

She moved away from the counter, unaware of the eyes that had been watching how her dress had lifted up, giving both men a brief flash of her bare legs.

Unaware that Puca was fighting with himself, with the ache he had felt since he woke up. The urge to push her over the counter and press himself against her soft curves was one he was fighting with. He wanted to taste the soft flesh of her exposed shoulders, to tease her until she begged for his touch. Or for him to taste her. He felt his body respond to the thought of tasting Lola.

"I'd like that. Maybe we can have dinner later." Erik said, pulling Puca from his fantasy. The bells above the door chimed and a tall, lithe woman came into the store. She pushed her blonde locks out of her eyes as she looked at the three.

"Good afternoon," Erik said in greeting. Turning to look at Lola one last time before he moved to talk with his latest customer.

Lola bit her lower lip as she watched him walking away before she turned to look up at Puca, "I said I'd be home after I came here. Why did you follow me? And what happened to your hand?" She asked as she pressed her lips together.

"Because go halainn, I'm very taken with you."

"What?" Lola asked in shock as he stepped closer to her.

"I plan to court you." Puca said as he reached up, pushing a lock of her hair behind her ear.

"You don't even know me."

"I want to, though," Puca said as he reached down to grab her hand and lace their fingers together. He pulled her towards the door and Lola looked down at their joined hands. She couldn't help but think about the way her heart beat faster at his words. Butterflies flared to life in the pit of her stomach as he pulled her from the store, the door closing behind them as they left.

Erik came back to the front of the store with a frown. Looking towards the bells above the door, his frown deepening before he moved to the counter. His fingers tracing over her hastily scribbled number as he pulled out his phone, he saved her number and sent her a text.

Meanwhile, outside, Merrow watched from a shaded stoop as Puca pulled Lola down the sidewalk, "Do you think she knows?"

"I don't think she does. Good thing Puca was with us. Or she'd still be in there." Lu said, wishing for a drink. He looked at the buildings around them, wondering which one contained a tavern. He could use a strong ale after the morning they'd had.

"Iron bells."

"And the door knob from the way Puca flinched." Merrow said, hoping they were okay. He too was glad Puca was with them. Out of the group, he was the oldest and strongest and could handle things that they could not. Bodach pushed away from the shade where they stood.

"Where are you going?" Lu asked as he watched Bodach's retreating form.

"After them. Our darling has a temper that could easily match Puca's." He said with a smirk as he shoved his hands in his pockets, ready to watch the sparks fly.

Chapter Seven

*L*ola stopped, pulling her hand from Puca's grasp. As she came to a stop and looked up at him, "I said I was coming back home soon, what are you doing?"

"Getting you out of danger." Puca turned to look at Lola. Her cheeks were flushed and her eyes shone in the sunlight.

"I wasn't in any danger." Lola said as she glared up at him, "Erik is my friend."

Puca held up his hands showing her the healing scorched skin, "There is something in there that isn't safe."

Lola stepped closer, taking his burnt hand in her own so she could study his palm, "Don't be ridiculous, why are you hurt? And why do you think there is something in the store that's dangerous?"

"Iron, it was on all of the doors. The windows too, even the bells." Puca said, watching the wisp of purple hair that escaped her ponytail and caressed her shoulder.

"I don't understand."

"Iron hurts my kind. The runes traced into the box you

found us in were sealed in it. I don't know why it didn't hurt you." He brought his hand up, pushing that strand of soft hair behind her ear as she looked up.

"I found the box at Erik's."

"How well do you trust your friend?" Puca whispered, as he watched her teeth worrying her lower lip. Frowning at the color flaring to life on her cheeks, knowing that it wasn't for him, but for the other man.

"I trust him a lot." Lola glanced away, even as she spoke the words she didn't know if they were true. She wanted them to be. From a young age she had learned to trust her intuition, as her grandmother and mother had taught her to do. Now was one of those times where if she thought about it. That yes she had always been attracted to Erik, did she trust him though?

"Puca just doesn't want you to trust him because he fancies you." Bodach said as he got closer. He pushed the glasses down the bridge of his nose as Puca's gaze met his. "Isn't that right, my friend?"

"If she trusts him, that's all that matters. Even if I do not."

"You don't even know him." Lola said, pressing her lips together as Bodach stepped closer to her. She could feel the heat of their bodies, and this time she couldn't blame it on the cramped space of her kitchen as Puca moved closer to her. Trapping her in between their muscular bodies.

Merrow slowly ambled closer, his eyes taking in the sight of the three of them. He smirked to himself as he watched Lola's eyes travel from Puca to Bodach.

"Looks like they're either going to fight over her or take her together." Lu said as he caught up with Merrow.

"Aye, I know which I prefer." Merrow chuckled as he glanced over at his friend.

"I'm sure you do, your type are not very picky."

"What are you implying, Lu?" Merrow said as he turned to look at the leprechaun.

"Just that I know your kind, anything to scratch the itch." Lu said glancing back towards Puca and Bodach, "It's hard to hide it in the box, you were never good about hiding it before."

"No, I wasn't. She's different. If I get her I don't think I'd be able to let her go."

"If the others get to her first?" Lu asked, knowing that he wanted her as well. He didn't mind sharing with the other men. It was hard to think of a time when it hadn't been the four of them.

Even before their entrapment. He didn't think he'd even know what to do without them after so long together. Lu didn't like the way his chest clenched painfully at the thought of them all not being together after they escaped the box for good.

"I don't think I would want it any other way." Merrow said softly, and Lu let out a deep sigh.

"You both stop it. I can't think when you do that." Lola huffed out, pulling Lu's attention back to the trio.

"Do what go halainn," Puca asked as he stepped forward, his lips tilting up with a smirk as his body pressed against hers. His chest pressing against her breasts, feeling her nipple harden through the thin material of her dress.

"That sexy thing that you're doing right now that makes me feel all trapped, but in a good way." Lola slapped a hand over her mouth, her blush deepening as Bodach ran his fingertips over her arms and up her shoulders.

"Trapped, but in a good way. I like it." Bodach said as he felt goosebumps rise under his touch along her smooth freckled skin.

"I didn't, I didn't mean to say that last part." Lola stammered out as Bodach stepped closer, pinning her body between the two of them.

"What if we want you too?" Puca asked as he brough his hand up to cup her cheek. Forcing her to meet his gaze.

Lola looked up into his eyes, desire. Hunger for her shown clear as day. She looked over her shoulder at Bodach, seeing the emotions reflected across his stoic features. "Food, we need food."

"Not the answer I was hoping she would go with." Lu said with a laugh.

"Me either," Merrow said as he and Lu moved closer.

"Groceries, we need more, since you guys are staying with me." Lola said, moving from between the two men. She didn't know why she felt so hot and bothered. Why she wanted to give into them and what they seemed to offer. Smoothing her hair down, she brought her hands to her cheeks, feeling the warm heat of her blush under her palms.

What was it about the fae men that made her feel this way? That made her want to give into them and the promises that their eyes held.

* * *

Grabbing a basket as she walked into the store, Lola frowned as she looked at it. Realizing that she was going to need a cart instead. She put the basket down and moved to get one of the carts, the fae already heading into the store. Lola couldn't help but smile as she took in their wide eyes and amazed expressions as they passed displays promoting various items.

"So you come here for all your food?" Lu asked as he slowed down from the others to walk beside her.

"Most people do nowadays, I mean there are people who have gardens and do the whole hunting thing." Lola said with a shrug as she walked along, pushing the cart. "Did you umm, did you do a lot of hunting before?"

"Aye, well, mostly foraging. We bartered a lot, my mum kept a garden."

"Interesting, we don't really barter and I don't have enough space in my apartment to do a proper garden. Maybe one day I can have a house with a small garden." Lola let out a wistful sigh, and Lu couldn't help but envision a future with her. One where her belly was swollen with child as they both worked in their garden. A toddler with copper curls playing in the yard with another sibling. He smiled to himself as he looked over at Lola.

"I think that's a fine thing to have." Lu said as he watched Lola step away from the buggy and grab a bag full of apples.

"I think so too. Is there anything in particular you guys like?"

"You," Lu smiled at her, watching the blush flare to life as it covered her cheeks.

"I mean to eat." His eyes met hers and she felt her blush spreading into her hairline, "Food, I mean food."

"We are not picky, anything will be fine." Lu smirked as she looked away from him, moving to grab a carton of strawberries.

"That's good." Lola said as Lu moved to take the cart from her hands.

"Let me," his hands brushed against hers and Lola bit her lip as she watched the tops of his cheeks turn red. She dipped her head in thanks as she moved to the vegetables. Grabbing some carrots and potatoes with an idea to do a stew for dinner. She grabbed a few more things before walking over to look at the fresh-cut flowers.

"In your garden, do you want flowers?"

"Yes, I think roses would be lovely." Lola said as she brought her hand up to touch the pale white petals of a rose. "Or maybe daisies." She added before stepping away from the bouquets. She walked away, grabbing more of the groceries she knew they would need, placing them into the cart before moving to head down an aisle.

Lu followed behind her, his eyes tracing her curves. Even in the harsh lighting, she glowed with a beauty that took his breath away.

Lola looked over her shoulder, "Is there anything you missed when you were trapped?"

Lu bit his lower lip as he looked at Lola. There were a lot of things he missed. A woman's touch, a barrel aged whiskey, his mother's baked bread. "There were mostly little things. I missed dancing with a woman."

"I'm not sure I'd be a suitable partner, but we could dance." Lola said as she moved closer to the cart, dropping in a box of tea bags.

"I think you would be an excellent dance partner," Lu said as he stepped around the cart and held his hand out to her. His eyebrow raised as he bowed, waiting for her to take his hand.

Lola bit her lower lip as she looked down the aisle. With a giggle, she placed her hand in his as he pulled her close. His hand coming to rest on her waist as he held her close, spinning them around to the soft jazz that poured through the store's speakers.

She looked up at Lu as he smiled down at her, twirling them about. He was humming a tune under his breath as he moved. Her body was pressed against his, her palm resting on his shoulder. He wrapped his arm tighter around her waist. She felt his muscles flex and her eyes widened.

"Lu," Lola shrieked with a giggle as he lifted her up so her feet were off of the ground. Her cheeks flushed as she realized how close together they were. How she could feel the racing of his heart under her fingertips as he sat her back down.

"See an excellent dance partner." Lu said, resting his forehead against hers.

Lola brought her hands to his waist, feeling the soft cotton of his shirt under her fingertips as she breathed in his unique scent. Warm whiskey with hints of herbs that made her mouth water. Her heart fluttered in her chest as his warm breath fanned across her lips, Lola closed her eyes. Tilting her head up, waiting for him to press his lips against hers.

Lu studied her face, her closed eyelids. The way her lips were softly parted waiting for his kiss, he drank in the sight of her. Fireflies flaring to life in his stomach as he closed his eyes.

"Found you." Merrow chuckled, making Lola and Lu jump apart. He held out a sausage on a toothpick, a smirk on his face as his eyes met Lola's, "I brought you a sample." He held out his offering to her as he bit into the one in his other hand.

"Thank you," Lola said, looking away from his smile as a blush covered her cheeks. Lola peeked over at Lu as she tried to take the toothpick from Merrow. He held it up, a teasing glint in his eyes.

"Don't I get anything for bringing you something?"

"I can get my own free sample." Lola said, not meeting his

gaze as she turned back towards the buggy.

"I'll take it." Lu snatched the bite away, biting into the delicious morsel as he scowled at the merman.

"I didn't interrupt anything, did I?" Merrow asked, his lips twitching up into a half smile as he met Lu's glare.

"Nothing that won't happen sooner or later." Lu said after he finished his bite of the meat.

Chapter Eight

*A*fter the grocery store, Lola and the fae headed towards her apartment. They got everything unloaded and a quick lunch was made and enjoyed while Lola introduced the men to cartoons. Their laughter filled the room until Lola's phone chimed, pulling her attention away.

Lola looked down at her phone, unlocking the screen to see a message waiting for her.

Erik: Just check to see if you made it home safely.

Lola brought her fingers to her lips, smiling while looking down at the screen as she typed back a message.

Lola: I did. What are you doing?

Erik: Thinking about you ;)

Lola blushed as she tucked her legs up on the couch. She was absorbed into the device and didn't notice the golden eyes that studied her. Moving along her long, pale toned legs down to her pale pink polished toes. Puca bit his lip, fighting back a groan as he watched her from across the room.

Jealousy flared to life as he watched her staring at the

rectangle in her hand. The way that it made her smile. He liked that smile. He just wished it was turned to one of them.

"Lola." Bodach said and Puca realized he hadn't been alone in his study of their hostess. She worried her lips, looking over at the other man, and Puca smirked to himself. He knew that look well. The other man was thinking about taking her over his knee.

Puca wondered how she would respond to being spanked? He couldn't help but wonder if her cheeks would flush as her eyes flashed with anger? Or would she lift her hips up to meet his hand? Her teeth biting her lower lip as she fought back a moan as he rained down blow after blow.

Puca shifted uncomfortably in his seat as his trousers got tighter at the idea of spanking Lola. He dragged a hand through his hair.

"Yes, Bodach?" She asked as she looked up, tucking her phone beneath her leg. Lola felt guilty over texting Erik, she didn't know why.

"Would you like to come to the kitchen with me?"

"I um, I guess so." She said watching as he unfolded his long legs and stood up. She sighed as she moved to follow him, and Puca smirked to himself.

He had a feeling he knew what was about to happen. It would either end up with tempers flaring or a very interesting turn of events.

* * *

Bodach leaned against the counter, his arms crossed across his chest. Lola walked into the kitchen and looked at the dark-haired man. Curious as to what he could need.

"Bodach-"

Lola looked up at him as he stepped forward. The hunger in his eyes taking away any thought she had to say anything. As she stopped in her tracks, for a moment she had the urge to run from him. To flee back to the safety of the living room with the others.

"Lola," he said as he stepped forward, his hands coming up to gently cup her face. She gazed up at him with wide eyes as he caressed his thumb over her cheek. His finger trailing along her neck, making her shiver. The way that her name fell from his lips was spoken like a caress or a kiss.

"Y, y, yes?"

"What makes you smile like that?" Bodach said softly as he bit his lower lip. His gaze moving to her lips as her tongue darted out, moistening her full lower lip.

"Like what?" Lola asked as she watched his pupils dilate. His red eyes darkening with something she didn't have a name for.

"As if someone made you feel like you are the only girl in the room." He said, moving his fingers to her chin to keep her from looking away.

"Oh, um. Erik sent me a message on my phone." Lola said as his thumb moved along her jaw.

"What would you say if I were to make you feel like the only woman in the world?" Bodach leaned closer and Lola took a deep breath as her eyes traveled to his lips.

"I don't know."

Bodach trailed his hand down her side, his other one tangling in her ponytail. "Do you want to find out?"

Lola looked at him through lowered lashes. She did want to find out. Her heart beat in her chest as she nodded and his lips pressed against hers. Softly at first, as he moved them so she was pressed against the counter.

His body pressed against hers as his tongue moved along the closed seam of her lips with feather light, teasing touches. Bodach let out a low groan as her lips parted under his questing tongue. She tasted just as sweet as he thought she would. Her hands fisted into the back of his shirt as her eyelids fluttered closed.

Bodach felt his cock stirring to life at the hesitant way her tongue moved against his. He wanted to lift her up onto the counter. To press himself against her sensitive core, to trail his fingers up her thigh. He'd never wanted anyone as much as he wanted her right now from just a simple kiss. He gently tugged at the strands of hair around his fingers and smirked at the way she gasped.

Lola pressed her body closer to his as he pulled back, letting her catch her breath.

"Well?" Bodach said as he trailed his fingers over her collarbone.

"What? Why? I don't understand." Lola said as she struggled to get her breathing under control. Her head swam from his kiss. Or maybe it was the lack of oxygen.

"Do you feel like the only woman in the world?" Bodach asked as he trailed his nails over her shoulder, making her shiver as she felt the coil of arousal snaking through her body.

Lola looked at Bodach. She brought her fingertips up to swollen lips.

"Do you?" He asked again, "Does my kiss wipe everyone from your mind?"

Pressing her lips together, Lola met his hungry gaze. She thought about his question, in a way it did.

In another way, it didn't. It made her wonder what it would be like to be with him and the other fae men.

Would Merrow's kiss steal her breath away like Bodach's had?

Would her toes curl if Puca pulled her hair, making her gasp in pleasure and pain?

Would her heart flutter as Lu's lips pressed against hers?

"Does it?" Bodach asked as he leaned closer to her, and she could feel his hard length pressed against her abdomen. "Does it make you wonder what it would be like, to be with us?"

"Yes," Lola breathed out. She watched Bodach's lips twitch with a half smile. He leaned in, pressing his lips to hers once more, she moaned at the feel of his hands moving along the sides of her breasts. Teasing, feather light touches that had her shaking, craving more of his touch. She brought her hands to his waist to slide them up his shirt, splaying her hands over his tight abs.

The shrill ringing startled Bodach, and he pulled back. Looking towards the sharp sound. Shivering at the feel of her fingers tracing over his muscles. "What's that sound?"

"That's my cellphone." Lola muttered as she pulled her hands away from him, Bodach backed up watching her leave the room. He wanted to pull her back to him, to see where her wandering hands would take themselves while he was tasting her.

Placing his hands on the cabinet, he took a deep breath. Trying to will the ache in his cock away.

* * *

Lola scurried into the living room, grabbing the phone off of the couch and retreating to her room. Looking at the screen she worried her lower lip, Erik's name flashed across the screen. She swiped her thumb across the screen, bringing it to her ear as she moved to sit on her bed.

"Hello?"

"Hi Lola, it's me Erik." He said with a long pause, "Of course, you know it's me. We've been texting. You have my number."

Lola smiled to herself. His nervousness was cute. "I do."

"I was wondering if you were busy tomorrow morning?"

"No big plans," Lola picked at the seam of the quilt underneath her.

"Would, would you like to come over for tea or maybe coffee?" Erik asked.

She could hear the nervousness in his voice. It made her heart beat quicker in her and her cheeks flood with warmth. It wasn't the same as she felt with Bodach, when he had kissed her. Or even how she felt when she and Lu had danced in the store. She couldn't help but wonder if this was a date or strictly business. Maybe he had another pick up envelope for her.

"Sure, sounds like fun." She said, covering her cheek with her hand.

"Good, I'll see you in the morning." Erik said before ending the call.

Lola lay back on the bed as she sat her phone on the bed, the kiss still fresh on her mind as her lips tingled from Bodach's kiss. She wondered what would have happened if they hadn't been interrupted.

She didn't see the sea-colored eyes that watched her from the hallway as Merrow stood in the darkness. Hidden in the shadows.

73

The way that Bodach had looked at him when he had come back into the room. Told him all he needed to know about what had happened between the two in the kitchen. His smug smirk had been all the conformation that he needed after the way she had all but fled the living room after grabbing the small black rectangle.

Her skin was flushed, eyes glassy with lust, and her lips swollen. Her beauty called to him, he longed for her to look at him like that.

Merrow wished he had been witness to what had happened in the kitchen, sure he wished it was him. He wanted her, there was no doubt in his mind after seeing her pressed between Puca and Bodach earlier. Even as he had watched her dance with Lu. A smile on her face as the leprechaun had spun her around, her girlish giggle music to his ears.

He wanted to step into the room, crawl up her body. To see if her lips still tasted of Bodach, to breathe in her sweet scent. To settle himself between her thighs, to feel the soft curves of her body as she moaned beneath him. Or maybe she would be silent in her pleasure. Either way, he couldn't wait to find out.

Watching as she covered her face, he fought down the desire. There would be plenty of time for him to have a moment with her later.

* * *

Erik hung up the phone and looked around his shop with a sigh. He wanted to leave this place as much as he loved it here. It was beginning to feel like a prison. He let out a chuckle at the thought.

Glancing at the woman who sat across from him, he let a

smile spread across his lips.

Soon, he could get out of here.

"Do you think it will work?" The woman asked him as she pushed her blonde hair out of her eyes. "That she will want to be with someone like you?"

"We shall see." Erik sighed as he poured more tea into her cup.

"The one before her didn't choose you." She smirked, her brown eyes twinkling with mirth.

"Lola is different. I know she's the one." Erik said as he sat the teapot down and picked up his own teacup taking a sip, he hoped his words were true. He didn't know how much longer he could stay here and keep his sanity intact.

Chapter Nine

ola's lips parted with a gasp at the feel of his hands on her breasts. Those fingers moved, plucking at her nipples. Making her bit her lower lip, arching her back as she tried to hold back a moan. His lips pressed against her throat, and she rolled her hips, needing more from him.

Wanting more.

His teeth scraped across her collarbone before his tongue soothed her skin, gently sucking into his mouth. Leaving love bits that would mark up her skin long after their lovemaking. Lola gasped at the nails that scrapped over her hip bone. Fingers moving lower to gently tug at the curls between her thighs, making her whimper. She felt lips press against her ribs in feather light kisses that had her panting as the lips that had been on her collarbone moved lower. Biting at the top of her breasts. Those lips trailed lower and the fingers that were plucking at her nipples moved. Allowing the other man to engulf one tight peak as the other set of lips kissed their way to her other breast.

Lola pulled at the restraints that bound her wrists. She wanted to touch them. Opening her eyes, she peered down her chest at the golden eyes as he gently sucked at her nipple. Alternating that gentleness with sharp nips of his teeth that made her toes curl. Her gaze moved to the other man. His emerald eyes sparkling as his tentative licks to her nipple got bolder, and he sucked the hard bud into his mouth, making her body clench up in anticipation.

The fingers that had been tugging at her curls moved to tease through her wetness. Dragging it closer to her clitoris. Lola threw her head back against the pillow as he circled the throbbing bundle of nerves. Merrow let out a laugh as he pressed his lips against her shaking thigh.

He watched Puca and Lu tease her nipples. His finger moved in a slow circle, making her bite out his name.

She looked over to the man that lay beside her. His fingers stroking through her hair as he whispered her name. Bodach's words would have made her blush if she wasn't so lost in the passion they were stirring to life within her.

Merrow's tongue replaced his thumb and Lola bucked her hips up, trying to guide him where she needed him most. As he sucked his clit into her mouth.

The shrill ringing of the alarm clock made Lola growl in frustration as it pulled her from the dream she had been having. The dream that she desperately wanted to finish. She was so turned on, could feel the wetness on her panties.

Slapping her hand to stop the loud sound. She tossed her arm over her eyes and let out a sigh as she pressed her thighs together, trying to get some relief from the need that she felt.

Lola had never been with more than one lover at a time, but the idea of picking just one of them didn't sit well with her.

Bodach's question had stirred to life a curiosity in her that she couldn't seem to get rid of.

She did wonder what it would be like to be with them, and the dream made that desire so much worse.

Through dinner her eyes had kept drifting over to Bodach's, before glancing away again. Lola couldn't understand why she was feeling this way about not just one of them, but all of them.

Did it have something to do with the fact that they were fae?

Lu had said her magic responded to his, and that's why it felt almost magical when they touched. Flares of desire coursed through her as she thought about touching him. Would her touch make his heart beat faster?

She couldn't help but wonder how each of them would respond as she tried to get her hormones under control.

It wouldn't do to go out there like this, her skin practically crawling with need for them. Her phone chimed, and she puffed out her cheeks, reaching out to grab the annoying device. Swiping the screen open, she checked the text message.

Erik: Looking forward to seeing you soon :)

Lola bit her lip. It seemed like it was a date then. Her fingers flew across the screen as she tapped out a reply. Dropping the phone to the bed, she sat up and moved off the bed with a yawn, stretching her arms over her head. Linking her fingers. She stood and walked to the closet, scrubbing her face as she walked.

* * *

Puca stretched with a smile on his face as he glanced around the room. Looking at the sleeping men as they shifted uncomfortably. His own body thrummed with need, and beyond her door he could hear Lola moving about her room.

He couldn't help but wonder how she felt about the seeds he had planted in her dreams. If she would act on it, or would he be forced to pursue her further? He didn't mind the thought of that either. There was something thrilling about luring a pretty woman like Lola in.

Once he got a taste of her, he planned to hold her close. There would be no slipping away or her. He wondered if they could convince her to come with them when everything was over and they were free to return home.

Just the thought of showing Lola his world sent a thrill through him. He wondered if she would enjoy the beauty of their realm as much as he was enjoying her beauty. Her door creaked open, her soft footsteps padding down the hallway. He shifted, rolling over to look up at her. His body pressing against Merrow.

A moan slipped from his lover's lips and he watched her step into view. Cheeks flushing at the sound as her eyes met his, she pushed a lock of hair behind her ear as her eyes widened.

"Did you sleep well, go halainn?" Puca asked, his voice gravelly with sleep. Lips twitching up into a smirk as his hand moved over Merrow's firm chest, tracing the muscles before plucking at his nipple.

"I, I did." Lola answered. Her eyes were drawn to the fingers that Puca ran over Merrow's chest and the way the other moan bit his lip. He was still asleep, but she couldn't help but notice the way the sheets tented with his arousal. "Wait, is, is, is Merrow naked?"

"Why don't you come closer and find out?" Puca said, his hand trailing lower, tracing well-defined abs.

Merrow huskily whimpered her name with a soft moan. Moving his hand beneath the sheet. Puca watched her, the way her gaze hooded as her eyes gleamed in the morning sunlight. Glued to the way his hand stroked Merrow, the sheet blocking her view. He bucked his hips up to grind his erection into the hand that squeezed him.

Lola worried her lower lip as she watched Puca's smirk deepen into a grin as his hand gripped the other man. Fisting his cock, working his lovers member faster. Making a moan slip from Merrow's lips.

"I think I'd be safer over here." Lola said with a gulp as she backed up, trying to put more distance in between herself and them.

"I don't know about that," Bodach's voice was husky as he stretched from his spot on the floor. His eyes taking in her pale legs. Legs that he had been having a very vivid dream about, thrown over his shoulders as he lapped at her. The last traces of the dream still on his mind and he could almost taste her against his lips.

"Coffee, I'm making coffee." Lola sputtered out as she all but ran from the room, Bodach's wicked chuckle filling her ears.

"I think you scared her off." Lu said as he shifted on the couch. His body was hard and ready. "Stay out of my dreams, you know I don't like it."

"Just showing you how it could be." Puca said as he leaned forward pressing his lips to Merrow's neck before he nibbled along his jaw, pulling him awake.

"By trying to scare her away?" Bodach asked.

"No, just showing her how it could be with us. How we would worship her."

"Puca," Merrow gasped as the hand that gripped his cock moved faster, his balls tightening as he spilled his seed.

* * *

Lola stood at the coffeemaker, trying to ignore their conversation and the gasping moans. She bit her lip at the thought of them worshiping her and at the way that Merrow had gasped out Puca's name. She wanted to go in there and pull the sheet off of Merrow, to watch his hips thrust up into Puca's touch. She pressed her thighs together as she grabbed the bag of coffee. Glaring at the coffee pot, she didn't know what to do. She didn't understand how she could feel this way for all of them.

The dream left her craving things she had never felt before. It was going to be a long day. She needed to get away from them for a bit. Maybe that would help her with the need she felt.

Was she broken?

When she had hit her head, had something broken inside of her? Making her crave the fae men that were in her living room.

Shaking her head, she dumped the grinds into the little basket before moving to the sink. Filling the coffee pot with water, she dumped it into the machine.

Coffee would make things better, it always did. Turning around, she pulled out several boxes of cereal. She couldn't help but chuckle as she looked at the Lucky Charms. She wondered what Lu would think about Lucky the leprechaun.

Lola could hear them getting up and moving around in the other room. The soft groan that filtered into the room made her body clench. Closing her eyes, she could only imagine what was happening. What she had seen before seemed like an appetizer, and she couldn't help but wonder what the main course would be like. Scrubbing her face, she let her hands fall to her sides.

With a sigh, Lola reached into the cabinet and pulled out the bowls. Grabbing some spoons, she turned around, heading back into the living room.

Puca and Merrow were no longer in the room. Sitting the bowls on the coffee table, she looked up. Her eyes meeting Lu's and he winked at her.

"Those two are always like that." He said as he stepped closer to her. "Do you need my help?"

"If you'd like to help me, I wouldn't say no." Lola replied as she turned back towards the kitchen, Lu turned to follow her. The scent of freshly brewed coffee beckoning her forward. "Did you sleep well?"

Lola didn't see the way that Lu's cheeks flushed. Or the way the top of his ears turned red at her question. He knew exactly how he wanted to help her.

"I had pleasant dreams. Do you have plans for the day?"

"Um, just for the morning. Then I plan to come home, I'd like to take you guys somewhere later." Lola didn't know why she didn't mention that she was going to see Erik.

"Oh? Where would you like to take us?"

"I know of a pretty place that you guys might like." Lola said, filling up the coffee carafe as she nodded towards the cereal boxes, "If you wouldn't mind?"

"Oh, um. Yes." Lu blushed as he watched Lola grab the milk from the fridge, bumping the door closed with her hip.

Puca returned, followed by a much more relaxed Merrow as

Lu sat down the two cereal boxes onto the coffee table. "What are we eating?" Bodach asked as he sat down in front of the small table.

"Well, you've got your choice of Lucky Charms or granola cereal." Lola answered as she sat the coffee and milk onto the table. "Coffee too, I forgot mugs." She frowned.

"Sit, I'll get them." Merrow said as he breezed past her with a grin. Lola's gaze lingered on him as he walked away. When she looked back at the others, she couldn't help the blush that heated up her cheeks as Puca's eyes met hers.

"Something on your mind?" He asked, his eyebrow raising as he licked his lower lip.

"Coffee, I need coffee."

* * *

Erik stood at the kitchen counter as he arranged cookies onto the plate. The kettle was barely starting to whistle as he went about getting things ready for Lola. He'd made the shortbread cookies last night. Nerves had kept him from sleeping. In the early hours of the morning, he had finally given up.

Baking had been a fun hobby for a while. Something to take his mind off of what he was going through.

He hoped that soon he wouldn't be so worried. That he could take Lola out for a proper date. Having tea together was nice, but he longed for more. To show her the world, he had a feeling she would love the lands of his home.

Erik liked to think that his family would like Lola.

He closed his eyes, thinking about her. The one before Lola.

The way her eyes would shine as she smiled at him. The sun bringing out the shimmering highlights in her wheat colored hair as she looked over her shoulder. Her lavender eyes meeting his. Shaking his head, he set up the teapot.

The whistling of the kettle pulling him from his thoughts. Erik knew that she would have liked the woman that Lola had become.

It was best not to think about her. It always put him in a bad mood for what once was and what could never be.

The bells of the door chimed, pulling him from his depressing thoughts.

* * *

Lola breezed into the shop, the lingering scent of fresh cookies and books filling her senses making her mouth water. It made her feel warm and fuzzy. It was the smell she associated with Erik.

"Erik, are you in?" She called out. The sign on the door had said he was closed. Lola knew he usually didn't flip the sign to open until after lunch on Sundays.

"In here."

Following the delicious aroma Lola walked into the kitchen, she paused when she saw him. Taking in the fact that he had pressed his slacks and he wore a button-up shirt. The sleeves folded up to his elbows, revealing surprisingly muscular arms. She was right, this tea was a date. She was glad she had dressed up and put on some lipstick and mascara.

"Good morning, Lola." He said, glancing up as he picked up the tea set, taking in her floral skirt and pink tank top. The light makeup she had on only added to her beauty. "I thought we could have tea on the back porch since it's a lovely morning."

"I'll get the door for you." Lola said moving towards the door, Erik stepped past her and she felt her heart flutter in her chest at his soft gaze. He looked forward, stepping out onto the covered porch.

Lola had never been back here before. She took in the silver lace like screens that covered the porch. It made her feel like they were still in the house while outside, the breeze and the sunlight filtered in between the swirling designs. She couldn't help but feel trapped, like a bird in a beautiful cage.

Come to think of it, she had never seen Erik outside of his store. She couldn't help but wonder if he lived here. It made sense if he did. The shop had been converted from an older Victorian home, so it had all of the things a home would need.

"What's on your mind?" Erik asked as he set the tray down and moved to stand beside Lola as she looked at the lace.

"Do you live here? I mean, like in your shop?"

"I do. The attic is converted into a small apartment. It's perfect for a bachelor like me."

"I bet it's nice."

"I could give you a tour sometime?" Erik bit his lower lip, his eyes watching the way the sunlight moved through her hair and over the freckled skin of her shoulder.

"Are you asking me up to your room?" Lola asked, turning back towards him with a raised eyebrow.

"In the future, yes." His eyes met hers, his gaze moving to her lips before back up again. "Tea?"

"I'd love some," Lola squeaked out as she moved to sit on one of the wicker chairs that were tucked into a shaded spot on the porch.

The wind chimes clanged together and Lola looked towards the sound. Taking in the strangely drawn symbols, the black iron looked like trailing ivy plants.

"Do you like it?" Erik asked as he handed her a tea cup and then moved to sit across from her.

"It's pretty, the sound is unique."

"I'm glad you like it." Erik said as he took a sip of his tea, his eyes taking in the overgrown backyard. He'd have to call in his gardener soon. He wanted to go out there. To feel the grass tickle his ankles, the dirt beneath his feet.

Shaking his head, he knew that wasn't an option right now. He turned to look at Lola. "How is your friend?"

"My friend?" Lola asked, her brows knitting together as she tried to figure out who he was talking about. Two pinpricks of heat filled her cheeks as she realized he was talking about Puca. "Oh, you mean Puca."

"I do, he seemed…" Erik paused, trying to think of the words he wanted to use, "Different."

"He is, but he's quite nice. A bit of a flirt, but he seems to care a lot for his friends." She said with a shrug, not really sure about what to say about the fae man. How could she tell her friend about him without making herself seem crazy?

"Does he like you?" Lola's eyes widened as her eyebrows shot up. She looked towards Erik again. "I'm sorry if I'm being too forward."

"I, he, he," Lola stammered, trying to search for the right words. "He does like me."

"And do you? Like him, that is?" Erik asked as he took another sip of his tea, his eyes searching hers before she bashfully looked away.

"I don't know." Lola muttered, looking down at the teacup in her hands. How could she tell him that she did like Puca? That she liked him and his friends more than she cared to admit. That her stomach fluttered to life with fireworks at the thought of kissing Puca, of kissing any of the fae men.

"Guess I'll have to work harder on making you fall for me." He said biting his lower lip, pulling her away from her thoughts.

"Erik-" She whispered as she looked back at him.

"It's okay Lola, I'd rather know that I have competition. It would be a shame if I were out of the race, not even realizing I was in one." He leaned over, sitting the delicate teacup down before moving to his knees to crouch in front of her. Taking her hands in his, he ran his thumb across her knuckles. "You're far too precious of a prize for me to let you slip away."

Lola felt her blush spread and her heartbeat hammered in her chest. Her skin felt warm where he touched it with a soft stroking thumb.

"I'm not a prize to be won." She said, a frown marring her face.

"You may not think you are, but any man would be lucky to have you smile at him. To be gifted with your kiss." Erik leaned up and Lola felt her eyes widen as he moved closer. "Can I?"

"Can you what?" Lola squeaked out as she looked down at his lips.

"Kiss you?"

"Yes." Lola whispered.

Erik leaned forward, his lips hovering over hers and she sucked in a breath, his scent filling her sense as she closed her eyes.

His lips pressed against hers, gentle but firm and warm. Erik's thumbs stroked over her wrist as he trailed his hand up her arm. Lola waited for the feelings to move through her.

For goosebumps to pop up as he put a hand on the back of her neck, holding her in place as his lips moved against hers and she responded. The other taking the teacup from her hands and placing it on the wicker table.

Lola moved closer, twisting her legs to the side as he tried to deepen the kiss. Her lips parted with a sigh as his hand moved to her side. Pulling her closer as his tongue touched against hers.

Erik's thumb brushed against the side of her breast and she felt her nipple harden. Lola gasped at the feeling. It wasn't the same as it was with the fae men. The kiss with Erik was nice, almost like putting on your favorite sweater.

Comforting, soothing, but not thrilling.

She pulled back, worrying her lip as she looked into his eyes. Erik slowly opened his eyes. She saw a hunger there she hadn't realized he would feel for her. It was much too soon for him to look at her like that.

"Thank you, Lola." Erik breathed out and she frowned.

Lola wasn't sure how to respond. The kiss hadn't left her breathless and craving more like Bodach's had. It was just nice, not toe curling.

"For what?" Lola asked as she sat, her back straight as he dragged his hand down her arm. Trapping her in the loose circle of his arms.

"For letting me kiss you. How do you feel?"

"I, I'm not sure how I feel?" Lola said, worrying her lower lip. How was she supposed to tell him that it had been nice? Just nice, but it made her think about another kiss. A kiss that had made her toes curl and her body respond in a way that his kiss had not.

Yes, it had been pleasurable. Lola wanted the heat, she

wanted more. Turning she looked at the delicate tea set, she could feel her cheeks heating up.

"I'm sorry, I got ahead of myself." Erik said leaning back he brought his hand up to her cheek, guiding her face so he could meet her eyes.

"It's okay, I like you. I just-"

"I understand, I can wait til you want me like I want you." He said as he moved to sit back down.

"Thank you," Lola whispered as she moved forward to pick up her teacup and take a sip. More to have something to do than to look at the man across from her. She picked up one of the cookies, studying the small square of purple jam.

"It's raspberry, I thought you might enjoy it."

Lola took a bite of the pastry, letting the flavors swirl together as she chewed. It stirred a memory of enjoying the same type of cookie with her mother. Her mother used to bring cookies like these on the weekend after work. She had loved them then. Erik's shortbread cookies always made her think of her mother.

"It's good, thank you. Do you have any plans for today?"

"Just working here, I plan to close early. I started a good book and I can't wait to finish it." Erik said, and for a while they lost themselves talking about books.

* * *

The morning passed easily and they enjoyed their tea. Lola left his shop with another envelope tucked into her bag and a payment. As she walked home, thinking about the kiss she had shared with Erik.

If Bodach never kissed her. Woken that soul clenching

desire in her. She had a feeling she would have been thrilled over her kiss with the handsome shopkeeper. Before that kiss, Lola could have seen herself falling in love with Erik and how comfortable she felt with him.

Like she could be herself for the first time in her life around another person, with a man whom she liked.

Now she had met the fae men, it was a connection she couldn't deny. Even if she wanted to.

Unlocking the door to her apartment, she stepped inside. Her shoes and their boots were sat neatly in the small entryway. She could smell the fresh breeze filtering through the room along with hints of the stew that she had made the night before. The arguing voices made her raise an eyebrow as she peeked into the now tidy living room.

"Look, it connects to something." Lu said.

"Just use the broom." Bodach groaned. "It's easier than trying to figure out that thing."

"You both fight too much, she'll be here soon." Merrow's soft voice chided them.

"You're just jealous I kissed her first." Bodach said, and Lola could hear the teasing tone in his voice.

"Aye, I won't lie. I think we all are."

Lola blushed at Merrow's softly spoken confession as she took off her sandals and hung up her bag.

"You lot do know that she can hear you?" Puca said, Lola froze at being caught watching. Puca's back was turned to her and she could see Lu as he looked towards her. Cheeks reddened, he looked down at the vacuum. Merrow's eyes met hers and he sent her a wink that made her stomach clenched.

This was the feeling that she had wanted with Erik. The way that her body clenched up in anticipation of what could happen.

"Lunch is ready, if you're hungry."

Lola was hungry, just not for food. Now, she just had to figure out how to make things work with the fae men.

If they wanted her as much as she wanted them?

Chapter Ten

*L*ola looked down at the address worrying, her lower lip. This was going to be a drive, and she wasn't looking forward to it. Being trapped in such a small space with Merrow for that time had her nerves on edge.

"Are you ready?" Merrow asked as he leaned against the door frame, his eyes drinking her in. Making her shiver at the thought of being alone with him.

"Yeah, it looks like I'll be driving. I think you'll enjoy it though." Lola said with a sigh as she leaned over, pulling out her cell phone to type in the address.

"Why is that, ghra?" Merrow said as he bit his lower lip, crossing his arms over her chest to keep from going closer and touching her.

"We'll be going in a car and I've yet to meet a man that doesn't love to ride in my jeep."

"I don't know what that means, but I do look forward to spending time alone with you." Merrow said, his voice husky as he watched the way her legs moved when she crossed them.

Glancing up, Lola looked at him. His eyes glued to her bare legs. She sat the phone down on the bed and moved to stand up, stretching her arms over her head. As his eyes slowly dragged up her legs, taking in the swell of her hips, lingering over her pert breast.

His teeth sank deeper into his full lip as she arched her back. Finally, his gaze met hers. He felt his cock stirring to life as he realized that she had stuck her chest on purpose. Letting him take in his fill of the sight of her. He could play that game, if that's how she wanted things to go.

Lola slowly lowered her arms as she stepped closer to him. "Are you ready to go?" She asked as she looked up at him through lowered lashes.

Merrow stepped closer to her. His hands moving to her hips as his thumbs moved over the strip of exposed skin that was left bare after her shirt had ridden up. "I'm alway up to go a round with you."

His voice was husky and made Lola shiver as arousal coursed through her.

"We should get our shoes on then." Lola said as she brought her hands up, resting them on his biceps. Squeezing the muscles through the black shirt that he wore, she had finally got them into real clothing.

Her face heated up as she thought about shopping with them. The images of the men shirtless and moving about the shop as she and the salesgirl had followed them around, flustered and red faced. It was seared into her memory.

It didn't come close to the embarrassment she felt when they passed the lingerie shop. Lu had seemed particularly interested in that store, as had Bodach.

Lu had taken an interest in the sheer white fabrics, his eyes meeting hers as the top of his ears turned red. His eyes glassy as he stammered the words, "T, t, this one," pointed to one that left little to the imagination.

"No, this one would be more fitting." Bodach said as he stepped closer holding up a black lace number as he pressed it against her body making her shiver.

"I'd prefer to see her in nothing at all," Puca had whispered in her ear, his lips touching the tender shell of her ear, making her shiver in anticipation.

"Aye, those could be pleasing. I'd rather see her spread out for me with nothing in my way." Merrow said as he stood beside her.

"What are you thinking of?" Merrow asked as he hooked his finger under her chin, pulling her attention back to the present.

"Yesterday."

"What about yesterday?" He asked as he trailed his thumb over her jaw and Lola felt her breath catch in her throat. "Was it dressing me up any way you wanted too?"

"Yes, and then after."

"I wonder when you can return the favor?" His lips twitched into a smile as he trailed his fingers over her neck, his lips coming closer to hers.

"Are you leaving yet?" Bodach asked from the doorway, startling Lola.

"Soon," Merrow whispered.

Lola had the feeling that he wasn't talking about leaving as he traced his thumb over her lips. She closed her eyes, trying to get her racing heart under control as she turned to peer over at the other man.

"Just need to get my shoes on and then we'll head out."

Chapter Ten

Lola smiled as she stepped out of Merrow's grasp and walked around Bodach.

His hand darted out and, catching her wrist, and pulling her closer, "Careful with that one, acushla."

"Huh?"

Lola looked at the hand on her wrist, his grip loosening as she looked up at him. "Just telling you, Merrow plays for keeps. Once your his, he won't want to let you go."

"I think I'll be okay," Lola replied as Bodach's hand moved up her arm, his fingertips gently caressing her skin.

"I have no doubts about that, just a fair warning." He said, tucking a lock of hair behind her ear.

"Thank you," Lola whispered as she stepped away from him and his hand slipped from her wrist.

"Warning her away?"

"Never said I was. Just returning the favor." Bodach's grin deepened as he stepped closer to the merman. "I remember how you used to leave them."

"None of them ever complained." Merrow said as he took a step closer to Bodach, looking up into his eyes. "Neither did you."

"I've never been too picky about who I give pain to. Pleasure either."

"Aye." Merrow agreed as he thought about the feelings that Bodach was trying to stir to life in him. They were dangerous feelings to have around Lola. He didn't think she could handle a rough tumble.

"Merrow, are you ready?" Lola called out, pulling the two men away as she moved back into the bedroom. Grabbing her purse and her cell phone. She looked up at both men. She could feel the heat in their interaction.

See the challenge shining in Bodach's eyes as he looked at Merrow, who was looking at her.

"Aye." Merrow said as he straightened his shirt.

"Sure you two don't need a moment?" Raising an eyebrow as the words slipped from her lips, she covered her mouth with her hand.

"I like this side of you, acushla." Bodach said as his gaze moved to her and she couldn't help but shiver. "Have fun, but know that my turn with you is coming."

Lola bit her lower lip and nodded up at him, heart hammering in her chest at his words. Merrow stepped closer, grabbing her hand, lacing their fingers together as he pulled her closer to him. "She will, I'll make sure that she enjoys herself." Merrow's voice was low. She didn't know if she should be anxious or thrilled at his words.

Lola couldn't help but feel that the day might not go as she had planned. She didn't think that would be a bad thing, she just hoped she got her job done.

* * *

"What is that?" Merrow asked as he walked closer. He looked from Lola back to the strange unmoving brightly colored object.

"It's my jeep." Lola said pressing the button on the key fob making the lights flash as the doors unlocked. Merrow jumped at the sound.

"We are expected to ride in there?" Merrow asked as he glanced at Lola.

"You can stay home if you'd like." Lola bit her lip as she glanced up at him, "I could always ask Puca to come with me."

"Nay, he and I agreed already."

"What do you mean?" Lola asked as she opened the door and slid into the jeep.

"Just that if the time comes to lay with you, I should take it." Merrow said as he watched Lola start the massive beast that she called a jeep.

"Good to know that I won't be causing problems between the two of you." She said before closing the door. Rolling down her window, she smiled at him. "Are you coming?"

She watched Merrow study the vehicle before he stepped closer, "How do I get inside?"

Lola leaned over to the passenger side door and pulled the handle before giving the door a push. "That should make it easier."

"Many thanks." Merrow said as he walked around the vehicle. The image of Lola bent over as she crawled to open the door, had him wanting to get to wherever they were headed to, soon. He sat in the seat and Lola looked at him with a thin raised eyebrow. "What is it?"

"You need to fasten your seatbelt." She said at his puzzled look. Leaning closer, her Hand snaking up to grab the belt, Merrow couldn't help but breathe her scent in.

The soft scent of her floral shampoo tickled and teased his senses. He snaked his arms around her waist, pulling her against his chest.

"Merrow." Lola said with a gasp as he pulled her into his lap.

"Lola," he groaned out as he pressed his lips to hers. His tongue snaking out to lap at the seam of her closed lips, making desire coil low in the pit of her stomach. She parted her lips, her tongue snaking out to move against his. Coaxing it into her mouth as his arms tightened around her waist, pressing her more firmly against his chest with a low growl.

Lola tangled her fingers in his soft locks as his tongue moved against the roof of her mouth. Tasting and teasing her, he savored the soft moans she let out as his fingers moved over her side. Pulling her shirt up so he could feel the soft skin hidden from his view.

She sucked on his tongue, making him shudder as his cock twitched, "Feumaidh mi mo ghràdh dhut." His words were rough and gravelly as he spoke them against her skin. Kissing his way to her chin, bucking his hips up so she could feel exactly what kissing her was doing to him.

"No idea what you just said, but god it was hot." Lola said as his lips trailed lower, his teeth nipping at her ear lobe making her shiver.

"I need you." Merrow's voice was husky in her ear as he spoke. "Tha mi gad iarraidh."

"Merrow." Lola groaned as his warm breath tickled her skin.

"I want you." He unwrapped an arm from around her waist, slowly trailing his fingers up her thigh as she sat perched on his lap. Pushing her short jean skirt up, he pressed his fingers against her heat. Marveling at the damp feel of the material. "You are already wet for me, ghra."

Lola rolled her hips at the slight pressure, with a low moan spreading her legs open. It wasn't enough as he trailed his lips along her neck.

"Please, touch me." She begged, his deep chuckle made her shiver as he pulled the scrap of fabric out of his way. His fingers moved against her slit and she let out a gasp. He dragged her wetness up, his thumb moving against her clit in a slow circle.

"All you had to do was tell me." Merrow said as he worked a finger through her folds. Thrusting it inside of her, her body was tight as her vaginal walls adjusted to the intrusion.

Merrow rolled his hips up as he worked his fingers in and out of her. Slipping in another as her body grasped his digits. His tongue flicking out to taste her skin as she started to pant his name. Her fingers tightening in his hair as her hips moved of their own accord.

She'd been so ready. So willing, he couldn't help but wonder if she had wanted him as badly as he needed her.

His name slipping from her lips had him ready to take her. Not just the orgasm he planned to give her right now. He wanted to know how her body would feel with her cunt wrapped around his cock as she came. Would she pant his name like he was a God? He hoped she would, even if she quietly shattered around him he knew he would enjoy watching her face as she silently rode out her pleasure.

"I'm going to, I'm so close." Lola panted out, her words incoherent as the low coiling sensation in her body intensified and she could feel herself drowning in pleasure. Her juices lubricating his fingers as he worked them faster. His thumb strumming across her engorged clitoris.

"Just let go, my love. Come for me." He ground out against her skin, sucking it in between his teeth, knowing that it would leave a mark. He worked his thumb faster in a rhythm that had Lola frantic.

"Oh god, Merrow." Lola said with a moan. Her body tensing up as she closed her eyes. Fireworks flaring to life behind her eyelids as her body spasmed around his talented fingers.

"That's it, ghra. Take your pleasure." He said as he released her skin, his movements slowed down as she caught her breath.

He moved his other hand to tangle it in her brightly colored locks. Dragging her face to his so he could press his lips to hers.

"I don't, that was-" Lola said as he pulled his fingers from her.

"We should go and grab the package you need to pick up," Merrow said, before kissing her again. "I'm far from done with you."

Chapter Eleven

❦

*S*hifting uncomfortably in her seat, Lola glanced over at
Merrow. Her cheeks heating up as she thought about
what they had done earlier. How his tongue had darted
out, lapping at his fingers afterwards.

How his eyes had slipped closed as he savored the taste of
her. Making her shiver. She glanced over at him again as he
watched the water come into view.

"The ocean." Merrow breathed out before turning bright
eyes towards her.

"I thought you might like to see it. After I pick up this
package, maybe we could have lunch on the beach? Or go for
a quick walk?"

"Thank you, ghra." Merrow whispered as he grabbed Lola's
hand in his. Weaving their fingers together. He brought it up
to his lips, pressing them softly on the back of her hand.

Lola looked back at the road as he stroked his thumb over
hers, "You're welcome." she sighed, they were nearing their
destination. She wasn't ready to get out of the jeep, to end this

little bubble of just the two of them.

Parking the jeep in the driveway, Lola pulled the keys from the ignition and looked over at Merrow.

"This shouldn't take long," she said as he turned to look back at her.

"Take the time you need, I've missed her so much."

Lola knew that Merrow was eager to get out of the vehicle. She wished that she could share this moment with him instead of going inside. She hoped there would be many more firsts for her to get to experience with him, with all of them really.

Climbing out of her jeep and closing the door, she could hear Merrow doing the same. Only she knew his path would take him to the sandy shore instead of the beach house that she was headed to.

The blue and white house was picturesque, with its charming little seashell wind chimes and its sun-washed purple door. She stepped up onto the porch, looking back to see Merrow, his long lean body silhouetted by the sand and waves.

"Don't just stand there, sit down." A voice called out as she sat on a sturdy rocking chair, her blue eyes watching Lola with a strange, unwavering gaze.

"Hello, I'm Lola. Erik sent me." Lola said as she stepped closer, dipping her head at the woman.

"I figured as much, I don't get many visitors besides those that he fancies." The woman said, tucking a strand of curling gray hair behind her ear. "You're prettier than the last few."

"Um, thank you?" Lola said as she moved to sit down in the matching rocker.

"Take it as you will. Tea?" She asked, tilting her head towards the teapot and cups that sat on the low table beside her.

Chewing on her lower lip, Lola tried to decide which would

be the best option. It was clear to her that this woman didn't get many visitors and would probably enjoy her company. She wanted to get this done quickly so she could spend time with Merrow.

Decision made, she nodded, "That would be lovely."

"Lola, you said your name was?" The older woman asked as she poured a cup of tea.

"Yes, ma'am."

"Ack, don't call me ma'am. It makes me feel old. My name is Annwn." She said as she leaned over, the bracelets on her wrist clanging together as she handed Lola a cup of steaming tea.

"Yes, ma- Annwn." Lola said as she took a sip of the mint tea.

Glancing over, she noticed that Annwn had an eyebrow lifted at her. "Is the package ready?" Lola asked after she swallowed her tea.

"It is," Annwn said, then she called out a little louder, "Hyster, bring the gift."

The purple door to the house creaked open and a handsome young man came out. His high cheekbones would have made Lola jealous if he didn't look so lost. He had an ornately carved box clutched to his chest. Lola figured it was Annwn's grandson by the way she smiled at him. Pushing his sandy locks out of his green eyes, he looked from Annwn to Lola. His gaze finally settled back on Lola as he moved closer. She watched him shift from one foot to the other.

"Host," he said, bowing his head towards Annwn before his gaze moved back to Lola. She realized that maybe he wasn't the woman's grandson. Chewing on the inside of her cheek, she studied the way he fidgeted as he stood in front of her.

"Hyster, it's impolite to stare." Annwn said through clenched teeth.

"My apologies. I've just never seen-"

"That will be all." Annwn said with a growl, making Hyster turn back towards the open door. The box still clutched tightly to his chest. "Leave the chest."

"But Host-"

"I said to give it to her." Annwn said pointedly as she lifted up her teacup and took a sip.

"As you wish." Hyster turned towards Lola with a pained expression as he kneeled down. He extended the chest in his arms forward. His hands shaking, his eyes filled with unshed tears.

"Give Erik my regards." Annwn said as Lola reached out, taking the box in her hands. "That will by all."

Lola wasn't sure if she was being dismissed or Hyster. She stood up and nodded her thanks as the blonde-haired man stood stiffly, making his way back into the house.

"Thank you for the tea and I'll share with Erik." Lola said.

"The pleasure was all mine, I hope we can visit again soon."

Lola hurried to her jeep and placed the chest in her backseat. She looked back towards Annwn and the beach house. From a window, she could see Hyster. His eyes red rimmed as tears flowed freely, his shoulders shook and she realized that he wasn't even trying to hold back his tears.

She couldn't help but wonder why the delicate-looking man was crying so.

"Is your business done?" Merrow asked as he strolled closer, pulling her attention away. His hands shoved into the pockets of his shorts with a soft look in his eyes.

"It is," Lola smiled at him. She'd never seen this side of him, the relaxed way he walked. His shoulders back, his hair was damp and as he stepped closer. The faint traces of salt water tickled her senses. "Good swim?"

"Would have been better if you had joined me." Merrow said as he brought his hand up, running his fingertips over her heated cheek in a soft caress.

"Maybe we could do that later?" Lola asked, looking up at him through lowered lashes.

* * *

Hand in hand, Merrow and Lola walked along the beach. Lunch had been fun, if not rushed with Merrow's excitement to get back to the water. Lola could understand. It was a beautiful day as the sun beat down on them, making sweat trickle down her back even with the cool breeze. She wished she had thought to grab her swimsuit. Or to grab Merrow a pair of swim trunks. It would have saved her a bit of embarrassment.

Merrow stopped their casual stroll and looked out towards the water. Pulling his hand from hers. Lola blushed as she watched him toss his shirt into the sand. He had started to undress earlier. She'd stopped him as he unbuttoned his shorts. Much to her disappointment.

Granted, by the shops where they had been walking, there weren't that many people about. But there were still enough to call the police if he had stripped naked and jumped into the ocean.

No matter how good he looked. Or how much she wanted to kiss a path down his chest to the pale downy hairs that lined his abdomen in a thin strip.

She understood why it was called a happy trail. It made her very happy to think about mapping out his flesh with her lips and tongue.

"Care to join me?" Merrow asked as he toed his shoes off, catching Lola's appraisal of his body.

"I don't have a suit."

"Me either, but no one is around to catch us." He said in a silky, smooth tone that made Lola bite her lower lip as her body clenched up. "You could leave your undergarments on." He said tracing his fingers along the neckline of her shirt.

"Merrow-" Lola flushed at his words. His fingers moved lower, tracing the lace of her bra through her shirt. Her nipples pebbled up under his light touches. She wanted for him to give her more than this gentle, teasing touches.

"Or you could wear nothing at all, I know what I'd prefer." He smirked, his tongue moving along his lower lip before he bit his lip. His eyes on hers as he brought his finger lower, inching her shirt up.

Lola lifted her arms up as his finger scraped across her skin. He bent down to kiss along the skin that was revealed. His teeth gently nipping at her, making her suck in a breath as he pulled her shirt higher before tossing it into the sand beside his. He traced his fingers over her breasts, a question in his eyes as he moved closer to the clasp.

Merrow waited for Lola to stop him as he unhooked her bra. A slow smile spreading across his face as he pulled the fabric free from her body. Dropping the garment on top of their shirts. Lola brought her arms up, her hands covering her breasts.

"Don't hide from me." Merrow said. His voice was different from normal. It did something strange to her body as his eyes searched hers before his hands moved up to pull her hands away. The breeze ruffled her hair, and she shivered as his hands moved to cup her breasts. "Ghra, Lola, my love. You are beautiful."

His thumbs caressed her nipples as his lips crashed into hers. Lola's tongue moved against his as she dragged her fingers across his abdomen. Undoing the button to his shorts and slowly pulling the zipper down to free his semi-erect cock.

Stroking him to full hardness, she smiled at the way he shuddered with a groan. Her name slipping from his lips as he pulled back to let out a pleasure-filled sigh as she stroked her hand up his length. Her thumb brushing over the head of his cock as she pulled his foreskin back.

One hand slid from the breast he was teasing. Slipping lower to shove her skirt down her hips in a swift move as he pushed her hands away. Dropping to his knees in front of her. Merrow slipped her skirt and panties from her legs as he buried his nose in her curls. Inhaling the scent of her arousal.

Lola bit her lip, trying to fight back a moan as she looked down at him. His gaze moved up as he lapped at her soaking slit. His tongue moving easily through her slick folds as his hands moved to her hips, holding her in place as he gently sucked on her clit.

"Merrow." Lola gasped out as she bucked her hips. The delicious pleasure filling her as her body tightened up. His tongue teasing her, she threw her head back, closing her eyes, panting his name.

Her vaginal walls were already starting to tighten with an impending orgasm that was preparing to rip through her when he stopped leaning back on his heels.

"You taste just as good as I thought you would. You can't

come on my tongue just yet, my love." Merrow purred out as he kissed her trembling thigh.

Lola brought her hands to his head. For a moment, she thought about tangling her fingers in his hair and dragging him closer to where she wanted his tongue to be.

"I want you in the water," Merrow said as he leaned forward, working his tongue against her. "I want to lap at you while the sea rocks your body." His words were muffled against her skin.

"In, in the ocean?"

"Yes." He said with a nod.

"But how? Breathing might be an issue."

"Won't be a problem for me, I know what to do." Merrow said, pulling back to peer up at her. "Do you trust me, Lola? I would never let you get hurt. I swear it."

"I trust you." Lola whispered as he kissed his way up her body. His tongue laving across her nipple before he stood. Pressing his lips to hers, she felt his smile. Merrow picked her up, clutching her to his chest, his other arm hooking under her knees. His smile deepened at her girlish squeal and giggle as he made his way to the water.

"I plan to take you afterwards."

"Take me?" Lola asked as the water crashed around Merrow's ankles, slowly going higher the deeper he got.

"Until you can't breathe or think of anyone else." He growled out as the water crashed around their bodies. He unhooked his arm from her legs and let her slip down his body as her lips formed a silent o. "I want to be the only one on your mind this afternoon."

Chapter Twelve

"Get out of her things." Puca chided as he walked into Lola's room and flopped onto her bed.

Bodach was lying sprawled on her bed as he watched Lu. He turned to glare at Puca before looking back towards Lu.

Lu, who was currently in her closet looking at the bookshelf above her clothing. His eyes taking in the shiny restraints, he bit his lip. His cheeks flushing a bright crimson stain as he thought about Lola being bound.

That was more of Bodach's thing, he'd never really been interested in tying a partner down. There was plenty of fun to be had without that. Stepping further into the closet, he let out a groan of pain as his toe found the sharp metal edge of a wooden chest.

"Gabhdán." Lu bit out. Hopping on one foot as he brought the injured foot up and rubbed his toe, checking the damage. When he realized he wasn't bleeding, he put his foot down and leaned over. Pulling the sweater that had been tossed down over it off. His eyes widened as he studied the box.

"What did you find?" Bodach asked as he rolled to his side, pushing his hair out of his eyes.

Puca stood, stepping closer to the closet as Lu picked up the chest. Turning, Lu looked up at the other man with wide green eyes.

"Do you think-"

"Must be, why else would she have one like this." Puca said, taking the chest from Lu's hands and placing it on the bed.

They stood staring at the skillfully etched designs before each exchanging a glance.

"Merrow will be fine, as long as they avoid the water." Bodach said as he sat up, his finger tracing over the waving designs of the box. "And rutting."

"Why don't you tell me not to breathe?" Puca growled out through clenched teeth.

"They'll be fine. I doubt she could hurt him, even if she knew what she was. Or what might be a part of her?" Lu said, then he bit his lower lip, shaking his head. Wishing he had been able to hold his tongue. Glancing over at Puca, he wanted to kick himself as he caught the bleak look on his face as the man opened up the chest.

* * *

Lola gripped his biceps as he kissed her, her chest pressed to his. As he tasted her lips.

"Are you ready?" Merrow asked as he pulled back to look at Lola, his chest moving as he took quick breaths. To calm himself, he wanted to sink his cock into her. First, he wanted her to have an experience that nothing could compare to. The need to taste her was stronger. He knew she would enjoy what he was about to do to her.

She nodded as the water moved about them in gentle waves beneath her breasts. Merrow pressed his lips to the soft skin of her shoulder. She could feel the press of his cock against her abdomen. Vaginal walls clenching in anticipation as she thought about what was about to happen.

Merrow kissed her lower as he started to sink beneath the water. She watched the trickle of bubbles come up to the surface of the clear blue waters as his lips pressed against her stomach. His tongue dipping into the well of her navel, hands trailing over her thighs as he moved one leg over his shoulder. The first touch of his tongue against her made her moan.

Tangling her fingers in his hair, not just to help her steady herself, but to hold him where she needed him to keep his talented tongue. He licked along her folds with steady stokes that had her grinding her cunt against his face. His thumbs moved against her hip bones and she felt the webbing between his fingers. She realized that his body had adapted to be in the water.

His tongue dipped into her channel and Lola bit her lip as his thumb moved from her hip to press against her clit as he worked his tongue in and out of her. Fucking her with it, she let out a whimper as he worked his thumb faster over the bundle of nerves.

Merrow kept up the pace and her body was soon tensing up as she tightened her fingers. Closing her eyes as he moved his tongue faster. The sounds of the ocean made her feel at ease in a way that no other sexual encounter had ever given her. She cried out Merrow's name as she shook her orgasm crashing through her. His movements didn't stop as he lapped at her core. She tugged the wet strands in her fists up, Lola needed him to take her.

Merrow unhooked her leg from around his shoulder and pulled her lower. Sucking in a breath as her head slipped below the water. His lips pressed against hers as he pulled her under. Guiding her to wrap her legs around his waist as he pressed his cock against her pulsing sex.

He moved to stand and Lola enjoyed the weightless feeling as he thrust his cock into her. Gasping as her head moved above the water. His lips didn't leave hers, instead he used the parting of her lips to move his tongue against hers as he thrust deeper into her.

"Never have I felt anyone like you." He panted as he pulled back, guiding her in a pace that would have been brutal if she hadn't been so ready for him. "It feels like coming home when I'm sheathed in you."

Lola dragged her hands along his back. Her nails leaving angry red lines on his skin as she wrapped her legs around his waist. Lola didn't know if it was Merrow, or having sex in the ocean that was causing her to feel the way she was.

Almost like something was building up inside of her as the familiar clenching started low in her abdomen and she knew that although the last orgasm had been good. This one would be earth shattering.

Moving her hips faster, her clitoris rubbed against his pubic bone at just the right angle. His hands gripping her ass were driving her faster as he panted her name against her neck. His teeth nibbling along her skin as his own pleasure overwhelmed him.

Heart thundering in his chest as his hips moved frantically. The feeling of being in the ocean again and the fact that he was sharing it with Lola was driving Merrow closer to the edge. Her nails scraped along his shoulder only heightened his arousal.

"Merrow," she moaned against his shoulder as her lips pressed against his skin, making him shake.

He'd engaged in pleasure in the ocean before, but it had never felt like this. His head spun as his cock throbbed. Lola's vaginal walls fluttered around him and he let out a groan of pleasure.

Glad that she had come, because there was no way he was going to be able to last with the way she was riding him. His balls tightened as he sped up his thrusts, his vision blurring as his head swam.

"Lola," he growled out as he spilled his semen in her pulsing body. Merrow's world faded to blackness as he fell forward, taking Lola beneath the water with him.

* * *

"Merrow, Merrow." She softly called his name, he looked up smiling at her. She always looked so beautiful when the sun shone through her hair like that.

It looked like white, silken webs. Her face glowed as she smiled down at him, her fingers brushing over his face. "I've missed you."

"And I you, deartháir." She whispered as she pushed his hair away from his face and he moved, pressing his ear against her swollen stomach. Feeling the soft flutters of the life that grew within her.

"I just want to hear his heart."

"You can't though, it's time to go back now." The woman

said, as she tucked a strand of hair behind her ear.

"I'll miss you."

"And I you, dearthair." She whispered as she leaned down, kissing his forehead.

* * *

"Merrow, Merrow. Please wake up." Lola cried as she pressed her hands to his chest, trying to remember every television medical drama she'd ever seen as she started doing compressions. "Please," she pleaded as she pressed her mouth to his and pinched his nose before blowing.

Merrow gasped, tangling his fingers into her hair. Holding her in place as he snaked his tongue into her mouth.

Slapping him on the chest, Lola pushed him away. "I thought you were dead." She sobbed, sitting back on her heels, the sand scratching her knees as she brought her hands to her eyes.

"Nay, the sea could never kill me." He said moving to sit, his hands moving to Lola's pulling them away from her face. He watched her shoulders shake as she watched him with bloodshot, tear-filled eyes.

"Then what happened?"

"That was all you," Merrow whispered, his hand coming up to cup her cheek. His thumb wiping away a tear.

"What? I couldn't, I wouldn't hurt you." Lola sobbed harder as he moved closer, pressing his lips to hers.

"I had my suspicions before, but this confirmed it." He whispered, resting his forehead against hers.

"What are you talking about? You passed out after we…" Lola said, trying to shake the image from her mind of the way her body had gripped him. The experience had been earth shattering and then he had fallen forward. Pulling her underwater, trapping her under his weight as she struggled to find her footing. Struggling to pull him up with her.

Lola had clutched his body to her chest, breathing hard as she tried to get him into the sand. She hadn't been sure that CPR would work on a merman, but she had to do something.

Merrow hadn't been breathing and his skin had a greenish tint, as she had slipped her way onto the beach. Dragging him along.

"After we had sex."

"I'd call it more than that." Merrow said as he traced his thumb over her lips, brushing his thumbs over her cheeks as she hiccuped.

"I don't get it, what would you call it then? Besides laying together?" A few things came to her mind besides sex, but she was curious to see what Merrow would say.

"Lola, you are fae."

"No, I'm not, I'm just Lola. Plan boring, human Lola." She said, shaking her head as she placed a hand on his bare thigh.

"No, you're fae." He said pressing his lips to hers between each word.

Shaking her head, Lola pulled away from him. His hands on her wrist kept her from moving away from him. "Merrow, please."

"Lola, I don't know how I could have missed it before." His words were so soft and tender that she looked up at him.

"What am I?"

"Lola, you're a-"

* * *

"Korrigan."

"Nay, she is not." Lu said, shaking his head and pressing his lips together as they looked at the carvings on the inside of the box.

"Hard to deny the truth, the lines are written here." Bodach traced his fingers along her name. It wasn't written in the text like the books he'd seen on Lola's book shelf. The language of man, this was fae. His eyes grew wide as the design lit up with a bright swirling color beneath his touch. "What's this?"

"Seems to be a lock of some sorts." Puca said, leaning forward to get a feel for the magic of the box. He opened the lid, peeking inside, not finding anything of interest.

"Aye, wonder what it opens?" Bodach said, continuing to trace the designs, watching bright colors flare to like.

"Perhaps a false bottom?" Puca stuck his hand in, sifting through all the odds and ends. Tapping on the bottom of the box. "Or not."

"Don't you feel it?" Bodach said as his finger moved.

"Feel what?"

"It feels like being underwater." Bodach muttered, his red eyes unmoving from the box.

Frowning, Puca looked over at his friend, he'd never seen eye to eye with the other man. Boredom and time could bring two people together, and they had been brought together more times than he could count. "Best to leave it be."

"I can't."

"Why not?" Lu asked, his eyes flicking back and forth between Puca, Bodach, and the box.

"I think it's enchanted." His finger still moved over the designs, he knew that he should pull his hand away. Something kept him from being able to do it. It was like his hand had a will of its own, as if it were being guided. His body pulsed with the magic slowly spilling out.

* * *

Lola stomped over to her clothing, well as best as she could through the sand. She tugged her skirt on and pulled her shirt over her head before snatching up her bra and panties and tossing them into her jeep. Turning, she looked over at Merrow as he calmly got dressed.

Leaning against the jeep, she let out a deep sigh. Her brows knit together as she pressed her lips into a thin line. From what the merman had told her, she was some sort of fae creature, or at least a watered-down version of one.

Snickering to herself, she looked up into the sky, watching as the sun dipped lower. How had the day turned into this?

It had started off normal, well as normal as it could with four fae men living in her house. Tea had been nice with Annwn. It left her with more questions than answers. Who was Hyster, and why had he looked at her like she was breaking his heart?

The pain had been clear to her. She didn't understand how Annwn could dismiss him away so easily.

Then what she and Merrow had shared in the water. Her heart beat faster as she thought about it. The sex had felt more right than anything she had ever felt before.

She hoped that it was because of Merrow. Not what he had suggested, that she was at home in the water, just like he was.

"Want to talk about it, ghra?" Merrow asked as he stepped closer to her, his hands coming to rest on her hips and the butterflies fluttered to life in her stomach.

"It's a lot to take in."

"Only because you were not raised with your kind." Merrow said, his fingertips moving over her hipbone as he gave her half smirk. "You won't be without us."

"You don't know that." Lola said, glancing down as she leaned forward to lay her head against his chest.

Merrow arms wrapped around her and he kissed the top of her head, breathing in her scent mixed with the sea. It was the most comforting thing he had ever smelled before. "Yes, I do."

Chapter Thirteen

*H*eart hammering in her chest. Lola pushed open the door to the apartment with Merrow practically glued to her side. The ride hadn't been as fun on the way home. Her eyes and body ached.

"Can you back up a little?" She asked with a glare. Her head was throbbing, and she wanted to crawl into bed. Burrow beneath the covers and fall into a deep sleep. Maybe then her headache would be gone, or at least not nearly as bad.

"I can't help but worry about you." Merrow said as he stepped into the room behind Lola. He wasn't trying to hover. It couldn't be helped. He knew that she wasn't feeling well by the way her shoulders had slumped, the way she had rubbed her eyes after she had parked the vehicle.

"That's fine, you can worry, but I need some space." Lola said dropping her bag and shoes as she moved towards her bedroom. The eerie quietness of the apartment didn't penetrate through to her, but it did to Merrow.

"Lola, wait."

"No, I'm tired. Merrow I'm going to bed." Lola said with a growl as she stormed off to her room. Shaking off his hand as she went. Pushing open her door, she let out a groan at the familiar shining lights that flickered around her room like fireworks.

"Bodach stop." Puca all but shouted. Trying to shove the other man's hand from the box. Lola's head started to throb worse, black spots moving over her eyes.

"What are you doing?" Lola asked, moving further into her room. She looked at the three men sitting on her bed. Bodach's hands on the small chest her grandmother had given her. It had been her mother's. "Bodach, stop. What are you doing?"

Her head throbbed worse and Lola couldn't help but wonder if in all the excitement of today if it had been too much or if she had been hurt somehow.

"I can't stop, I've been trying." Bodach said through clenched teeth. Lola closed her eyes, preparing for what had happened last time a box had done that.

"Lola," Lu said as he moved to stand, "You're glowing."

"It's just the light show, it happened before." She replied without opening her eyes.

"No, Lola. He's right, you are glowing." Merrow said softly and Lola opened her eyes, looking back and forth between both men.

"I think I know what the enchantment unlocks." Puca said as he moved off of the bed to stand in front of Lola. His hands cupping her cheeks as he looked into her eyes.

"It's fine, just leave me trapped here." Bodach said with a growl, pulling Lola's attention towards him and the box.

"What's he doing?"

"He's sucked into an enchantment and now he's unlocking something within you." Puca whispered as he took in the pale glow of her skin and the way her eyes shown. He leaned forward. Taking in her scent mixed with the fresh smell of the sea. "You smell of the ocean and Merrow."

"We took a swim." Merrow shrugged and pushed his hair out of his eyes.

Lola bit her lip as Puca's eyes moved back to hers, "Did you now?"

Nodding her head, "We did."

"What happened?" Puca asked as he pressed his lips together in a thin line. His thumbs stroked over Lola's cheeks.

"I'm fine," Merrow said, stepping forward, resting his hand on Puca's forearm as the light in the room and Lola grew brighter. "I just know what she is now."

Puca placed his lips against Lola's forehead before as the light show started. Lola let out a gasp as she brought her hands to his waist, clutching his body closer to her own. She closed her eyes, revealing in the sensation it was as if her heartbeat to the sound of a babbling brook.

"A korrigan, I shouldn't have been surprised." Puca murmured against her skin as he trailed his lips to her temple. "Such a beautiful creature, will you lure me to a watery grave?"

Sucking in a breath, she could feel the heat, low and pulsing in her core. "Puca," Lola whimpered as she pressed herself closer against him while dragging her hands up his abdomen. Giving into the feelings that were stirring to life in her.

"Aye, you will," he said with a chuckle as he moved his lips over her cheek and towards her ear. Making her shiver as she pulled him closer.

"I removed the enchantment." Bodach pouted as he sat the

box on the bed and crossed his arms.

"What enchantment?" Lola asked as she tilted her head to the side. A rational part of her brain was telling her that she should stop Puca as he peppered her neck with feather-soft kisses. That things were moving too fast. The other side of her felt that it wasn't moving fast enough. That they had too many clothes.

"It's as he said, I'm guessing that whoever laid the enchantment was probably trying to keep you safe or others." Merrow said as he pressed his body against her back, slipping his hands around her waist.

"Why don't we give her a moment to catch her breath, she looked unwell." Lu said as he grabbed Lola's hand and let out a whimper as he too was caught under her spell. "Oh, that's what you meant."

"Come on now, the pull to her can't be that strong." Bodach said, rolling his eyes as he watched Lu lift her hand to his lips. Kissing the pads of her fingers as Morrow's hands moved along her hips. Bodach's eyes were glued to the hands that pushed her shirt up, revealing a strip of pale skin that even without touching her he wanted to bite.

With a long sigh, hating that he would have to be the one to interrupt them. Bodach grabbed the quilt off Lola's bed. If he broke their contact with her skin, he might be able to keep them from mauling her. It was a first feeding, though.

Standing, he shook the blanket out as he moved closer. Puca tilted his head to look at him, his teeth barred. Bodach lifted an eyebrow as he stepped closer, lifting the quilt up.

"I think it was to protect you, Lola." He whispered.

Wrapping the blanket around her, Bodach let out a sigh. Lu was the first to let go. His cheeks stained with a blush as he looked up at Bodach and then away.

"Go raibh maith agat."

"Aye, now get a blanket and help me." Bodach said, trying to push Merrow and Puca back. "Now, I would normally be in for this kind of fun, but-"

"Then join us, mo chara." Merrow said as his hands found the zipper of her skirt. His body thrummed with the need to feel her wet heat on his fingertips. To share her with Puca, with Bodach, with Lu. It didn't matter as long as he got to taste her again, to feel her.

"I'd love to, but I'd prefer it when she's got more control over herself or I do." Bodach chuckled as Lu returned, "Lu, you take Merrow, I'll get Puca."

A gasp slipped from Lola's lips that made Bodach tense up, Puca let out a low chuckle lost in the heat of his desire for her.

"Got him!" Lu shouted as he pulled Merrow away and then let out a groan of pain as he took an elbow to the gut. Bodach threw a punch and Puca stumbled back, readying to launch himself at the other man.

Shielding Lola in his arms he turned his body ready to take the blow if it meant that she was safe. He felt hands on his back and tensed up. Those weren't Puca's hands. They were small and gripping at his shirt, desperate.

"It's okay, Lola. I've got you." He said, trying to soothe her worry as he let himself relax.

"My skin, it feels like-"

"I know, just let me take care of you." Bodach said softly he shifted from one foot to the other. He looked over his shoulder at Puca, "Are you feeling like yourself again?"

"Aye." He replied, his face flushed as he thought about the way her skin had felt under his lips. Even knowing that being with her right now might kill him, it had been worth it. The gasp that Lola had let out had been his breaking point. He wasn't one to lose control. In fact, he very much liked being the one in control.

"Go get the cuffs from her closet." Bodach said as he pulled the quilt away from her face, careful not to touch her skin. He knew that it wouldn't do for him to get pulled into her spell.

Puca stood stock still, his mind still on the kiss he had shared with Lola. The way that she had sounded as his hands had moved with Merrow's, coaxing out more of her warm wetness onto his fingertips. How her nipples had felt through the thin material of her shirt, her breasts pressed against his chest.

"Puca, damn it." Bodach growled, Lola looked up at him with wide, frightened eyes.

The urge to reach out and touch her was one that was all-consuming. As he fought down a groan, Bodach tried to reign in his temper. He glanced towards Merrow and Lu, if they would just work together. He could help her. "A little help?"

Lu dashed around Merrow, heading towards her closet. He snatched the cuffs off of the closet shelf and moved towards the bed, searching for a way to attach them.

"Against the wall, the chains have hooks." Lola moaned, her skin felt hot. Her veins felt like the blood they carried was boiling and she could feel her pulse in her eyes. "What's happening?" She asked Bodach, her eyes locked on his worried red ones.

"Your body… Acushla, is preparing for the kill." Bodach said, helping her move to sit on the bed as Lu attached the cuffs to the silver loops on the wall.

"I don't want to kill anyone, I'm not a killer." Lola panted as she untangled herself from around Bodach.

Looking at Lu, her teeth sharpened as her stomach clenched, her nails lengthened. He stepped back, watching her normal emerald eyes turn a deep shade of red as she leapt forward.

"Oh, no you don't." Bodach said with a growl as Puca pulled Lu out of the way and he knocked Lola to the bed. She lay pinned beneath him and let out a shrieking growl.

"Let me free." Her words were garbled as she spoke, her tongue not used to sharp, elongated teeth.

"Not tonight, my beauty." Bodach purred in her ear. Her struggling made him bite his lip and fight back a shudder of desire. His cock hardened as it pressed against the swell of her ass. He wanted to thrust against her, to feel her squirm beneath him. Shifting to the side, he wrapped his arm around her waist. Pulling her wrist up to one cuff, he secured her and then repeated the action. Locking her into place beneath him, she looked up at him and he could see the roots of her hair turning a glossy white color.

"Bodach, please." She begged, rocking her hips up to grind herself against him.

Standing, Bodach looked towards Lu. As he ushered Puca out the door. Seeing his chance, he took it, knowing that he wasn't likely to get another.

He closed the door behind the other men, turning the lock, he ran his hands over the wood. Enchanting it so they would have the time they needed.

Turning bright, shining red eyes back towards Lola as she withered on the bed. He knew what he needed to do, he just hoped the others would understand. Forgiveness was something that would come with time, and he knew that they had plenty of that.

He just hoped that she would forgive him.

"I can help you, would you like that?" He asked, his tone going lower as he looked at her unbuttoned skirt. The smooth abdomen he had felt under his fingertips as he had moved her into the cuffs burned into his mind. Making it hard for him to think of anything but taking her. "Would you like that, Lola?"

"Please." Lola begged, pulling at the cuffs. The metal clanged loud in his ears. The sounds of the other men on the other side of the door did nothing to change his thoughts on what he was about to do as he stepped closer.

Fingers trailing up her ankle, he marveled at the softness of her skin. The way she shivered, how a moan slipped from her throat.

"I will bring you pleasure, it will come with pain." He said scraping his nail up her thigh, watching as it trembled. "Can you handle it?"

Lola bit her lip as her skin crawled. It was like her body needed something, she just didn't know what. She just knew that Bodach could give her what she needed. "Yes."

Bodach's hand trailed higher and he could feel the heat under his fingertips. Smell the scent of her arousal perfuming the air around them. She panted his name, and he had to fight with himself. He wanted to take her now at that soft sound.

"I shouldn't want you as much as I do. It's like you have me under a spell."

"Bodach my body feels strange, I feel like I should run or, or-"

"Or come?" He asked as he grasped the hem of her skirt and she lifted her hips. Helping him slip it off of her.

"Yes." Her eyes were wide as she looked at him. At that moment, she was the most beautiful creature he had ever beheld in his incredibly long life. Tossing the material to the side, he let out a chuckle that had her body tightening as she closed her eyes. Wishing that he would hurry up and give her the release that she craved.

"So impatient. I can't wait to see how your body responds to me when I have the time to take you over my knee. For now," he leaned forward, placing his hands on the bed as he kissed the arch of her foot. "I plan to give you what you need. It won't hurt me if you loose control, in fact. I crave it."

He dug his teeth into the tender flesh of her arch, smirking as she sucked in a breath. His eyes roamed over her legs towards the glistening curls between her thighs. Soothing the skin with his tongue, he trailed his way further up, nipping at the thin flesh that was stretched over her ankle bone. His teeth breaking the skin as he savored the heady taste of her blood.

Rich, sweet even from the few drops.

Reaching down to the front of his slacks, he adjusted his throbbing cock. Soon enough he would satisfy both of their needs.

He trailed his fingers up her thigh. Watching as she moved her legs further apart to welcome him. He couldn't help but grin against her skin, "Such a greedy thing, aren't you? Begging for my touch."

"Bodach, please."

"I will ease your suffering." He smiled, his warm breath blowing across her skin as he bit into the flesh of her thigh and she cried out. His finger brushed over her nether lips, her honey coating his digits. She bucked her hips up, seeking contact.

Lola tugged at the restraints, feeling the metal of the cuffs dig into her skin as Bodach's fingers made contact with her heated sex. Pushing the back of her head into the pillows as he worked his thumbs through her folds, she bit her lower lip. He spread her apart. She could hear him breathing in the scent of her pussy. She wanted to beg him again. Normally, she'd be all for him taking his time to explore her as he pleased.

Now though, she was ravenous in her need. His lips moved further up her inner thigh as he pressed a kiss against her aching clitoris. She closed her eyes at the sure stroke of his tongue as he lapped at her slit, teasing out more of her juices onto his tongue. Before settling himself more comfortable between her legs and slowly fucking her with his tongue.

She wished she could tangle her fingers into his hair, to drag his talented tongue to where she needed it most. Against the small aching bundle of nerves. His moan made her thrust her hips faster as she tried to take as much control as she could.

Bodach was in heaven, or as close as he ever thought he would get as he listened to her breathless moans. Tasting the sweet yet tart taste of her coating his tongue, her cunt filling his nostrils. The urge to lap at her all night until she was spent was one that he couldn't wait to experience. As it was, he'd settle for the little time he had now to work her into a frenzy as she babbled his name. Begging him, pleading. He moved his hands under her bottom and lifted her hips so he could have better access.

His thumb pressed against the tight sphincter of muscles and he groaned. He couldn't wait to take her there too, dragging his tongue to lash at her clit.

Lola's back arched up at the contact as he sucked the engorged flesh into his mouth. His eyes traveled along her body as he watched her struggle against the restraints. He could already feel the waves of her magic crashing over him. Fighting to pull him under her spell, he didn't know how the merman had survived it.

Bodach had had enough. He knew if he didn't take her soon, he'd spill his seed in his trousers as he thrust himself against the soft bedding. Moving up her body, undoing his slacks as he went. His fingers wrapped around his length and he hissed, rubbing his cock against her soaked slit.

"Is this what you want, my darling?" He asked and Lola pressed her feet flat onto the bed, trying to make him fuck her. She was wanton, and he loved the way she responded to him. "Lola, stay with me."

"Please, please just fuck me."

Bodach thrust into her with one fluid motion. He held himself still as he waited for her to adjust to the size of his long, thick cock. "Gods, you feel so good."

Lola tried to rock her body, but his hands on her hips pinned her in place as he savored the way she fit around him. So perfect, like she had been made just for him. He could still feel the heat of her magic moving through him, caressing against his own.

"Do you feel that?" Lola whimpered as he started to thrust into her.

"It's our magics greeting each other." Bodach purred out as he moved them so Lola's hips were back on the bed. Bracing his forearms on either side of her head, he kissed her. His tongue moving against hers as she moaned into his mouth.

She wrapped her legs around his hips, heels digging into his lower back as she tried to force him to move faster. It wasn't enough, just as much as it was too much. The feeling spread through her as it had before with Merrow. This time stronger, like it was all-consuming. She had the feeling that if she weren't careful, it would pull her under as well.

129

Groaning at the feel, Bodach threaded his fingers through her purple and white strands, tugging her head to the side. She let out a moan, and he felt her body start to clamp around his cock.

"You do like a bit of pain, don't you?" He asked as he frantically thrust his hips, sharp teeth nipping at her chin. Moving his hand, he jerked her head to the side, harder. Teeth digging into her throat as she let out a guttural keening sound.

Bodach moaned at the taste of her, the way her body spasmed around his cock. Pulling him over, the way her magic nipped at his skin. It was all too much. He dug his teeth in deeper. His fingers pulling her hair tighter as he shot his load deep inside of her quivering body.

Lola looked towards the door as she tried to calm her frantically beating heart, enjoying the comforting weight of Bodach on her body. She could hear the other men banging on her door. Biting her lip, she couldn't help wondering why they didn't just come in. There was no lock in place keeping them out.

"I put an enchantment on it earlier." Bodach panted as he kissed the tender skin of her neck.

Moving her legs from around him, Lola realized her head no longer pounded and her eyes didn't hurt. She had so many questions, but she wasn't sure where to start as Bodach reached above her. His hands making quick work of the cuffs.

Lola brought her hands down to rest them on his shoulders as his penis softened within her. Slipping from her body, he brushed her hair from her face. Admiring the way she looked, as long pale lashes fluttered closed over her now normal green eyes. Her hair was slowly returning to its normal purple color. He couldn't help but wonder how she would look with it all pale and glossy as she rode him. Shaking his head, he tried to stomp down the beginnings of his desire for her.

"Do you, is every-" Bodach stammered out. He closed his eyes. He'd never felt as nervous as he did now. "Did you enjoy yourself?"

"I'm umm, better." Lola answered as he settled beside her. His red eyes intently watching her. She tucked herself against his chest. "Why, why didn't it hurt you?"

"Laying with you?" Bodach asked as he bit his lower lip, quirking an eyebrow up at her.

"Yeah, sure let's call it that." Lola said, fighting back a grin as she looked at Bodach.

"You and I, our breed of fae is more suitable to each other. Korrigans and I have a lot in common, you could say." He said, coiling a lock of her hair around his finger before giving it a slight tug to pull her closer. His lips moved against hers and she felt relieved she didn't feel the same as she had before. "The first time is always the hardest feed, with time you'll be able to control it."

"Control what?"

"Your body's natural urge to lure men to their deaths." His lips pressed against the corner of her mouth and she had to fight down a hysterical giggle that tried to bubble past her lips. His tone was so casual, like they were discussing the weather.

Not the fact that her body wanted to kill him, not just him. It had tried to kill Merrow earlier.

"We should open up the door, I'm sure the others are worried." She didn't want to tell him that the thought terrified her. That she could hurt any of the men who were worming their way into her heart.

Bodach placed his lips against Lola's in a kiss that was almost chaste, and she felt her heart clench in her chest. It wasn't just the others that she was beginning to love, but him as well, "Aye, just know that I'm far from done with you."

He watched as the blush spread over her cheeks with a slight smile, before he moved to the edge of the bed. Tucking himself back into his trousers and moving to the dresser to grab Lola a pair of shorts. His fingers grazed hers as he handed them over, and he couldn't help but feel the pinpricks of her magic coursing over his skin.

It had felt nice before, but now it felt incredible. He wanted to lay against her like a lizard with a heat rock. To bask in that feeling, to surround himself in her.

"Bodach, the door." Lola said as she slipped on the shorts and brushed her fingers through her hair.

Looking towards the door, Bodach let out a sigh. He knew he'd have to deal with them sooner rather than later. At least he knew that she wouldn't kill him. She hadn't been his first korrigan, but she would be his last.

He traced his fingers over the thin wooden door. Watching the runes flare to life as he went. Lola stepped closer to him, "Thank you."

"It is I who should be thanking you." He said, tucking a lock of hair behind his ear as he glanced back towards Lola. She couldn't help but smile as she saw the warm look in his eyes.

Looking down at the floor, she shifted from foot to foot as the door opened and Puca came into the room. He shoved Bodach down, and the other man fell backwards, sprawling out over the bed.

"Keep your trickery to yourself." He growled before walking over to Lola, "Are you hurt?"

"Relax my friend, I wouldn't hurt her."

"Wasn't talking to you, fraochÚn a fheileann dá dheartháir." Puca growled, his golden eyes flashing over to the fae man before he stepped closer to Lola. "Are you okay?"

Lola nodded her head slowly as Puca brought his hands up to cup her cheeks.

"About what happened before-"

"I'm sorry." Lola blurted out before he could say anything else. She buried her face against his chest, trying to hide her reddened cheeks.

"Lola," Bodach said as he pushed up onto his elbows, Puca shot him a look that had him rolling his eyes.

"Go halainn cailín. Never feel the need to apologize for something that is beyond your control." Puca wrapped his arms around her, kissing the top of her head. He felt Lola relax against him. He glanced over at Bodach, giving him a slight nod.

He may not like what had happened, but he could understand what the other man had done. It hadn't been just about keeping Lola safe. He had been protecting the others too.

Merrow and Lu both tried to come into the room at the same time. They turned to look at each other, Lu scowled at him.

"I think you already went first." He said before moving into the room.

"Aye, but I won't be last." Merrow responded and Lola rolled her eyes as she pulled away from Puca.

"I meant what I said, it was beyond your control. Which we will help you work on." Puca said his words were husky and Lola couldn't help but shiver. "You should get some rest."

"I should get a shower." Lola said, wrinkling her nose.

"I could help," Merrow smirked, moving closer to her.

The no was shouted by all the men in the room as Lola blushed and hid her face in her hands.

Chapter Fourteen

⸎

*D*ense softly scented, steam filled the bathroom as Lola stepped out of the shower. She grabbed a soft green towel from the towel rack and let a sigh out as she thought about the day. About what had happened and what she had learned about herself.

She couldn't help but wish her grandmother was alive. She longed for someone to be able to answer her questions. Why was the box that her grandmother had left her enchanted? How could they not tell her what she was?

After toweling her hair, she wrapped the towel around her body. A soft knock on the door made her jump.

"Lola, are you okay?" Lu asked in a soft voice.

"I'll be out in a minute."

Lola looked around the bathroom and realized she hadn't grabbed any clean pajamas. With a sigh, she cracked open the door and peeked out at Lu.

"Um, Lu."

"Yes, Lola." He said with a gulp as he realized the only thing she was wearing was a towel that was much too short. His gaze moved to her long toned legs before quickly back up to her face again as he tried to focus on her eyes.

"Could you grab me some clothes from my room?"

His gaze moved to the light dusting of freckles on her shoulders, and he wondered how the skin would feel under his lips.

"Lu?" She said, pulling him from his study of those freckles.

"Sorry, yes. Clothes. I can do that." A blush covered the tops of his cheeks as he turned away from her. Lola opened the door, watching his copper colored curls as he walked down the hallway. Her eyes moved down the toned lines of his body to the shorts that hugged his ass.

Her cheeks heated up. She could hear the soft sounds of the others talking in the living room. Their voices a low mummer. For a moment she had the urge to follow Lu into her room. To close the door behind him and drop her towel.

She couldn't help but wonder if his cheeks would flush as his eyes roamed over her. She had a feeling with him, she would probably have to take the lead. She leaned her hand against the door, pushing it further open. Turning, she moved in the cramped space to the counter. Grabbing her hairbrush and starting working out the knots. The salt water had dried her hair out and as she looked into the mirror, she noticed it would soon be time to touch up her color.

Maybe this time, she would keep it natural. She thought with a smile before sitting her brush onto the counter and picking up her moisturizer.

* * *

Lu looked through her dresser drawer. He tried to ignore the lacy scraps of fabric as he grabbed a random pair of undergarments. He opened the bottom drawer, grabbing a pair of small shorts and a soft cotton top. Turning, he looked towards the box that still lay on the bed.

He couldn't help but wonder who had placed the enchantment on Lola? Why she was here and not with her kind.

Making his way down the hallway, Lu saw the sliver of light from the bathroom. The door hadn't closed all the way, and he watched as Lola through the small opening as he walked closer. She smoothed on some type of lotion on her face and then a different one onto her arms.

Lu let out a sigh as he brought up his hand to gently tap his knuckles on the door. He wished he could watch her doing small things like this all the time. Maybe one day they would have that type of relationship. Lu could still remember watching his parents slow dance in the evening. How his mother would look at his father. He wanted that, he'd rather have her knowing though, rather than watching her like this. The door pushed open and Lola turned to look at him. She had a bottle of lotion in her hand.

"Would you mind getting my shoulders?" She asked, biting her lower lip as she looked at him through lowered lashes.

Stepping into the small space, Lu's eyes met hers. She handed him the lotion and turned around, pulling her hair to the side as she watched him in the small bathroom mirror.

The smell of wildflowers filled his senses, and he breathed in the fresh, clean scent of Lola. Sucking in a shuddering breath, he opened the bottle and poured some of the creamy liquid into his hand.

He sat the plastic bottle down on the counter and rubbed his hands together before bringing them up to smooth the lotion over her skin. His thumbs brushing over the pale dusting of freckles that he had been admiring earlier. Caressing his palms up her shoulders, he let out a gasp as she leaned back. Pressing her towel-clad body against his as she looked over her shoulder at him.

"Thank you." She whispered.

He fought back a groan as she brought her hand up to cup his cheek. She leaned closer and he could feel her breath fanning over his lips. His finger tips trailed along her collarbone as his other hand moved to her waist, pulling her body closer against his.

"Are you teasing me?" He whispered. Moving his nose to trail it over her the smooth skin of her shoulder.

"Just a little." Lola shivered as his lips moved against the bite marks Bodach had left along her skin.

"Two can play that game." He said with a growl against her skin as he spun her around. Moving her so she sat on the counter in front of him, he pressed closer to her. Lu brought his hands up to cup her cheeks, "Is this okay?"

"Very much so." Lola said as he brushed his thumb over the top of her cheek. His lips pressed against hers and she felt a toe curling shock run through her body. Tangling her hands in his long hair, she deepened the kiss, moving her legs so he was pressed flush against her.

Lu let out a moan as his body responded to her, his cock swelling to life. It wasn't like before, where he'd felt the need so ingrained in him. This was gentle, normal.

Lola pressed her body against his, feeling the swell of his cock press against her sex.

"We should stop," Lu panted as he pulled back to look at her.

"We should," Lola agreed, grabbing the front of his shirt and pulled him in for another kiss.

"This isn't stopping." Lu said as he gripped her hips.

"It isn't, but we will." Lola said as she pressed her lips back against his. Her hand moving to wrap in the cotton fabric of his t-shirt.

Lu pulled back, "If we don't stop now, nothing will stop me from taking you."

Lola bit her lower lip, closing her eyes as she let out a little whimper of frustration. She didn't want to stop, but putting Lu in danger wasn't something she wanted to do. No matter how much she wanted to slip her hand between the two of him. Free his hard cock and shift her hips ever so slightly so he could fuck her.

"Lola, if you keep biting your lip like that, I won't be able to help what happens next." Lu said. His green eyes sparkling as he flexed his fingers, enjoying the heat of her body through the towel.

"What if I want you to keep going?"

"Bactha, you tempt me so." Leaning forward, he kissed the tip of her upturned nose. "We will have plenty of time for love-making later."

Lola looked down at his chest, fighting back a smile, "So you want to make love to me."

"Woman," Lu said, tilting her chin up so their eyes met, "I've never wanted anything more in my entire life."

"While that is touching, I don't think either of you are ready for that." Bodach said as he leaned against the door frame. His arms crossed over his broad chest, he pushed his hair over his shoulder as he gave Lu a pointed look.

"I was bringing her clothing." He said picking up the clothes he had set down on the cabinet. A scrap of black material fluttered to the floor, and Lola buried her face against Lu's shoulder to hide the blush as both men stared at her panties. "We'll leave you to get dressed."

"We?" Bodach said in a slow drawl.

"Yes, we." Lu said, moving away from Lola with a lingering glance as he handed her the clothing. He reached down, handing her the lacy panties.

"Thank you," Lola said as she slipped down from her perch on the counter. The towel slipping up the tops of her thighs made Lu's breath catch in his throat.

"Lu," Bodach said in a low voice, and Lola watched the other man's spine straighten.

"I know you like to play games with the others, I don't want any part of it." Lu growled as he moved closer to a now smirking Bodach.

"She likes my games." Bodach said as he turned away, Lola closed the door behind the two bickering men. Leaning against it, she brought her hand up to touch her lips.

She smiled as she thought about Lu's kiss. Each of the men were so different and she knew that if she were asked which was her favorite. Lola wouldn't be able to pick just one of them.

Quickly getting dressed, hanging her towel up and moved into the hallway, making her way to her room. The smell of sex still hung in the air, making her wrinkle her nose.

She moved to the window and pulled it open, looking up at the brightly glowing orb. The moon was full and she could feel it shining on her skin. It was a strange feeling. Fighting the urge to strip down so she could bask in its glow.

Merrow walked up behind her, his arms going about her

waist. "It's beautiful, isn't it?"

"It is." Lola agreed, the sound of fabric rustling pulled her away from her study of the moon. She turned, pulling away from Merrow. Seeing Lu stripping her bedding. "Let me help you."

Grabbing a corner of the sheet and pulling it off of the bed as Lu gave her a half smile.

"I figured we should change the sheets before getting you to bed." Lu said and Merrow let out a low chuckle. "To sleep Merrow, nothing more."

"Aye," he walked over. Taking the sheet from Lu's hands and tossing into the hamper as Lola and Lu made quick work of putting on the fresh bed linens.

"Where are Bodach and Puca?"

"They went to sort a few things out, don't worry about it ghra." Merrow replied as he tucked in the corner of the bedspread.

Lu chuckled as he turned the covers back, Lola's frowned hearing her phone chime. She moved down the hallway towards the front door and pulled it out of her bag. Checking her messages.

Frowning, Lola opened the latest text from Erik.

Erik: The moon tonight makes me think of you, I look forward to seeing you again.

Lola bit the inside of her cheek. She was going to have to talk with him soon about their relationship. Even though, yes she did like him. It was a pale comparison to how she felt about the other men.

The front door rattled on its hinges and Lola took a deep breath as she moved closer.

"I wouldn't, they're just working out some issues." Lu said

as he walked closer to her.

"Issues?"

"Yeah, Bodach likes to think that he's in charge." Lu said stuffing his hands into his pockets, "If we had a leader it would be Puca. After all this time, they're still trying to get things settled into place."

"Oh," Lola said as the door rattled on its frame again. "They're not hurting each other, are they?"

"Consider what they're doing foreplay. That's the way I think about it." Lu said as he held his hand out to Lola.

Looking back towards the door, she bit her lip. The thought of the two men fighting each other for dominance had her wondering just what type of fight was happening in her hallway. She wanted to peek through the peephole and check, worried that it might bother the other tenants. She did want to be on Sam's bad side.

Instead, she slipped her hand into Lu's and he pulled her down the hallway back into her room.

Merrow was settled under the covers, his chest bare and his hair a tousled mess. He patted the spot beside him as he pulled the blankets back. Lola frowned, looking at his clothing on the floor.

"What are you doing?"

"Joining you for bed." Merrow said.

"Naked?"

"No, I have on the undergarments you made me get." He grumbled.

"Good." Lola said, letting out a sigh. She didn't know if she would have been able to take laying beside him all night with his bare skin pressed against her.

"My bed isn't big enough for all of us."

"Nay, but it is plenty big enough for us three." Lu said as he pressed his lips to her shoulder, "It's just for sleeping tonight, if that's okay with you."

Lola blinked as she turned to look at him with wide eyes. She wanted to do more than sleep with the two of them.

"Just sleeping?"

"Just sleeping." Lu repeated as he brought his hand up to touch her cheek.

Lola sat on the bed and moved to scoot beside Merrow, Lu joined her and both men spooned up against her body. Merrow pushed her hair away from her neck and pressed a soft kiss on her heated skin, making her shiver. "Relax my love."

Yawning, Lola nodded her head as she closed her eyes. It had been a long day and she couldn't wait to see what tomorrow would bring.

* * *

Bodach smirked as he looked up at Puca, his cheeks sucked in as he quirked an eyebrow up at the other man. His look was almost daring as he tried to provoke him over the edge..

"Stop whatever game you are playing with her." Puca hissed through clenched teeth.

"Not a game, Tha mi ag iarraidh oirre."

"You don't fancy her, the only one you've ever cared about is yourself." Puca's fist slammed into the front door and Bodach surged forward. Hands moving to the other man's waist to spin him around, pinning him against the wall.

"You and Merrow would have mauled her. She would have killed you, tell me I don't care, mo charaid."

"I saw the way you watched her." Puca said as he pushed Bodach's hands away.

"And I can still smell her on your fingers." Bodach countered, sucking his cheeks in as he lifted his eyebrow.

"So vulgar." Puca grumbled, shoving the other man away.

"Did you and Merrow enjoy the taste you had of her? Does it bother you that it was Merrow who got to her first?" Bodach stepped closer, "That you didn't get to watch?"

"Bodach," Puca growled out, his tone low and dangerous.

"Tell me that the idea of watching Merrow take her doesn't have you hard…" His eyes traveled lower as he bit his lower lip, "Well, harder."

His hand moved to cup the other man's erection through his shorts, "I know how you like to watch, maybe next time I tie her down you can watch."

"Tha mi a 'toirt rabhadh dhut."

"Warning me?" Bodach's grip tightened, "Why don't you just let go? We both enjoy it when you lose control."

With a growl, Puca tangled his hands into Bodach's dark hair. He pressed his lips to the other man's feeling the curve of the smile before they fought each other for dominance. He could taste Lola still on the other man's tongue and he let out a groan, feeling his cock twitch at the teasing taste of her.

Chapter Fifteen

*L*u was lost in a haze. Under his palm was a firm yet soft breast. He could feel the nipple hardening through thin material as he gently massaged the flesh. She let out a whimper and pressed her bottom against him and he let out a gasp, rubbing his growing cock against the swell of her ass.

Her scent swirled around him, and he took a deep breath as he rolled her nipple between his thumb and forefinger. He couldn't remember the last time he had woken up pressed against a soft feminine body like this one. She smelled like Lola. He really hoped it was her as he moved his hand to push her hair away from her neck. Cracking open an eye as he skimmed his fingertips over her neck and down her shoulder.

The morning sunlight glistened over her purple locks. He let out a soft moan as she pressed herself back against him, his fingers slowly moved down her arm, to her waist. Closing his eyes, he pressed his lips against the smooth skin of her shoulder. Trailing his lips up her neck as his fingers moved to the waistband of her pajama shorts.

Fingers threaded through his as she moved his hand into her shorts, past her panties. She pressed his fingers against her wet core and he groaned against the skin under his lips.

"Are you sure?" He asked and Lola nodded her head. He sucked in a deep breath as he brushed his thumb over her clitoris. Working two fingers inside of her, marveling at the tight wet heat that surrounded his digits. Her soft gasping moan made him smile as he worked his fingers in and out of her. Loving the way she moved her body against his.

Merrow's hand moved over Lola's hip, his fingers brushed against Lu's wrist. Smirking he met the other man's eyes, "Couldn't wait could you?"

"Shut up." Lola growled as she wrapped her hand around the back of Merrow's neck and pulled him closer. His lips curled into a smile before she dragged him into a kiss.

Merrow gripped her hips, swallowing her moans as his tongue moved against hers. Her hand holding him in place tightened on the back of his neck as her nails dug into his skin as Lu added another finger. His hips moved as he thrust his cock against her. Grinding himself against her ass as her vaginal walls started to flutter. His thumb circled her clit, making her let out a gasping sob. Merrow brought his hands up to tease her breasts as she moved her other hand past the waistband of his shorts.

Her fists wrapped around his cock, stroking him in a jerky motion. Her body started to shake from the stimulation, and Lu's voice was husky in her ear as he spoke.

"The way ye move against me, Lola-" He said as he thrust against her again, "I cannot wait until the day when I can finally take you."

Lola whimpered against Merrow's lips at the thought of Lu thrusting into her, filling her more fully than his fingers ever could. Her vaginal walls started to spasm and she felt the warm spurt of Lu's semen spill on her exposed lower back as he let out a groan. His thumb never stopped moving against her, as his fingers kept up their pace.

Moving her fist faster as she got closer to orgasm, Lola sucked Merrow's tongue into her mouth and he shuddered. His cum spilling, the warm liquid splashing against her stomach. Lola's body tightened as Lu guided her through her orgasm. Her nails dug into Merrow's neck as she gasped against his mouth and he chuckled, pulling back to watch her face as she came.

"What a way to wake up." Lu whispered in her ear, gently nipping at the lobe as he slowed his movements down, letting her ride out her orgasm.

* * *

Freshly changed and cleaned up, Lola walked into the living room and bit back a smile at the sight that greeted her.

Puca and Bodach lay sprawled together, a tangle of long arms and legs. The slants of sunlight highlighting the muscles on their chest. She creeped closer to the sleeping men, taking a moment to admire their beauty.

It wasn't often that she got to see these two peaceful and not arguing. Though she supposed now that she knew it was foreplay and not actual fighting. It made it more intense as she thought about the fights she had witnessed between them in the brief time that she had known the fae men.

"Want to join them?" Merrow asked as he stepped behind

her, wrapping his arms around her waist.

"Merrow," Lola chided.

"Trust me, when I say they wouldn't mind."

Lola shivered as she thought about his softly spoken words. The idea of being between the two dominant men had her pressing her thighs together.

Which one would take control of her, or of the other one? She could imagine Puca tangling his hands in her hair as he kissed her, his cock thrusting into her as Bodach watched with hungry red eyes.

Or maybe even Bodach tying the other man down, making him give up control. Just for the moment.

Bringing her hand up, she threaded her fingers through his. Brushing her thumb against his palm, the sound of the shower running pulled her from her thoughts.

"I should fix breakfast before I leave." Lola mumbled.

"Or you could not and join them. I like to watch as much as I like to be a part of the fun." Merrow said, he brought his other hand up. Pushing the strands away from her neck so he could trail his fingers over the fading love bites from the night before.

"Merrow, are you trying to get me fired?"

"No, you have your job to do and I have mine." He whispered as he traced his fingertips over the shell of her ear. Smirking as she shivered. "My job is taking care of your needs."

"Tease."

"Am I, though. If it's a for sure thing?" He asked as he moved closer. Sucking the lobe into his mouth and teasing the flesh with his teeth.

Lola tilted her head, giving him better access, "Yes, you are because you know I've got things I've got to do today. After that then I'll be all home all day."

"Lola to myself all day?" Merrow purred as he let go of the lobe.

"Nay," Puca said sleepily as he turned to look up at them. His eyes meeting Lola's, "He had you all day yesterday, I'll be going with you."

Lola bit her lip as Merrow chuckled huskily in her ear, "Looks like one of us will be taken care of by Puca."

"When has he ever left you wanting?" Bodach asked as he tossed an arm over his eyes. "It's too bright in here."

"Oh, he leaves me plenty wanting." Merrow said as Lola looked between the two men and the tented sheets that covered their morning erections.

"You could always sleep in my room." Lola said, and Bodach moved his arm. Turning to look up at her with a slow smile.

"Inviting me to your bed for another round?" Bodach asked as he licked his bottom lip.

"Yes, well, no. I mean, it's not as bright in my bedroom as it is out here." Lola said, stepping out of the loose circle of Merrow's arms.

"You scared her off." Merrow said with a pout as Bodach turned over and pushed up to his hands and knees. The sheet falling to the floor as Lola clapped her hands over her eyes.

"You've already seen all of me, acushla." Bodach chuckled as she peeked through her fingers.

"There are others-" Lola stammered out.

"This isn't something they haven't seen before." Bodach teased, running his hand down taunt abs.

"Bodach." Puca said with a growl as he sat up. Reaching over, he popped the other man's ass with an open palm.

Turning to glare down at Puca, Bodach let out a growl.

"See, Foreplay." Lu said as he walked into the livingroom and flopped onto the couch.

Lola's face felt hot under her palms as she scurried to the kitchen, away from the chuckling Merrow.

* * *

Lola smiled at the woman who opened the door to Erik's shop as she walked in. Puca following close behind her. His arms full with the chest that she and Merrow had picked up yesterday. Lola gave her thanks at the woman as Puca sat the chest down on the counter.

"Hello, Is Erik not here today?"

"He's always here. He'll be down in a moment." The woman said as she studied Lola. Puca turned back to look at the woman. He stepped closer to Lola.

Lola dipped her head before turning to look at Puca as he pulled her closer to him. His fingers tangling with hers.

"Are you friends with Erik?" Lola asked.

"You could say that." She said, pushing her blonde hair over her shoulder as she looked to Puca and Lola's clasped hands with a slight smile. "I'm Callie."

"It's nice to meet you, Callie," Lola said with a smile, "I'm Lola."

"I know," she said, pushing her blond curls out of her eyes. "I've heard a lot about you."

Puca's fingers tightened around hers and she glanced up at him, wondering if Callie's words were making him jealous.

"Sorry to have kept you waiting." Erik said as he walked down the stairs.

"It's no bother, we were just talking to Callie." Lola said. She tried to pull her hand from Puca and he tightened his grip.

Erik's eyes moved to their hands with a frown as he looked towards Callie. "I thought you had somewhere you needed to be."

"I just wanted to stay to meet your... Friend." She said with a smile that was anything but friendly.

Erik nodded at her, "Til next time then."

"You won't be going anywhere." Callie turned towards the door and Lola caught the grimace that graced her lips as her hand connected with the doorknob.

Lola didn't say anything as she watched the woman leave, but she could feel Erik's eyes on her. Not so much on her, but on the two of them.

"Erik, would you mind if I used the restroom?" Lola asked, finally pulling her hand free.

"By all means," he said, gesturing down the hallway, his eyes locked with Puca's golden gaze.

* * *

Lola exited the small half-bath and walked down the hallway, an open doorway catching her attention. She'd never been in this part of the shop before, and her curiosity got the better of her as she pushed the door open.

Taking in the small, open roll-top antique desk. Running her hand over the smooth, polished wood. She wondered if this was Erik's office. Picking up a letter, she read his name to herself before sitting it back down. She knew she should just turn around and respect his privacy. A framed photo tucked into the corner caught her attention and she moved closer.

It was a photo of her mother sitting outside of the antique

shop. The wind ruffling the hem of her floral sundress as the sun shone down on her honey-blonde wavy hair. Lola bit her lip as she picked up the mother-of-pearl frame for a closer look. Her mother was smiling in the picture and Erik stood behind her in the doorway of the shop. A soft smile playing across his lips as he looked at her.

The look in his eyes was soft and loving, it was the same way he looked at her. The strange thing was, he looked as if he hadn't aged.

If she hadn't known it was her mother, she would have thought it was a recent photo. Setting the picture back down on his desk, she looked at the notebook that lay open.

It was the one she had written her number in before. She flipped through the pages, looking at the strange, swirling symbols. They were like the ones that were on the box she had bought. Like the ones that were on the chest she had hidden in her closet. She couldn't help but wonder.

Did Erik know about the fae?

Was he one of them?

* * *

"What are your intentions with Lola?" Puca asked, pressing his lips into a hard line as he took in the other man.

"I'm courting her." Erik said as he crossed his arms over his chest.

"It is a wasted effort on your part." Puca said, his lips twitching into a slight half smile.

"I doubt that," Erik said, stepping closer to the taller man, a challenging look in his cold steel eyes. "I'm not out of her mind yet."

"Not yet, but when she's with me. I will be the only man in her thoughts."

"We shall see." Erik said, a hard glint in his eye.

"What are you guys up to?" Lola asked as she walked back into the room, her eyes moving back and forth between the two men.

"Just getting to know each other." Erik said, looking over at her with that same soft smile that she had seen in the photograph.

"I was just letting Erik know that we have plans for the day. So, we wouldn't be able to stay for much longer." Puca said as he moved to closer to Lola. A glare shot at the other man as he wrapped an arm around her waist, pulling her flush against his side.

"Oh, um, okay. I guess I'll see you Monday unless you need me sooner." Lola said as Puca guided her towards the door. He hesitated for a moment before turning the iron doorknob and stepping out.

"Thank you Lola, I look forward to seeing you then." Erik called out as Puca pulled her into the street.

Erik watched them leave the store with a frown. He hadn't realized that he was going to have competition with that man. Things would not be as easy as he'd hoped.

Pressing his hands together, he moved forward to look at the chest that Lola had brought to him. Running a hand over the wood, admiring the craftsmanship that went into making such a piece. Erik hefted it into his arms and carried it up the stairs.

As he walked, he dug a heavy key from his pocket. Stopping in front of the locked door, he slid the key in, listening to the lock tumble as it opened. He pushed the door open, walking inside the vast room that was lined with shelves. The room practically hummed with old, forgotten magic. Desperate to be set free, he walked inside. Pausing for a moment as the ward brushed against his skin. Once the tingling feeling passed he walked deeper into the room, past all the shelves that were filled with boxes of various sizes.

Erik passed an enormous cage that sat in the corner of the room, as he searched for a vacant spot to put the chest.

The door chimed beneath him as he found an empty spot. Erik turned, rushing out of the room. One day he would be out of here. His term would be complete. Til then, he hoped to find someone to help him share his burden. Longed for the day when he would have help. It was a lonely task. At least he had the shop to keep him busy.

Until that time, he would keep guarding them until it was time to release these creatures back into the world. There were others like him, none truly as cursed as him though.

Trapped for a time to watch over their charges. In his long life, he hoped that it would pass by like the blink of an eye and he could forget about his time as warden. As a prisoner.

Erik knew one day his confinement would be up. Then he would do what he had been waiting to do for so long. He would take Lola to meet his family.

After all, a bride should get to know her in-laws before the marriage and he was sure that they would love her.

Chapter Sixteen

"What happened between you and Erik?" Lola asked Puca as they strolled towards her apartment. She'd caught him shaking his hand again. She hated that he had chosen to get himself hurt rather than just let her open the door for him.

"Just letting him know where he stands?"

"What do you mean?" Lola asked. She had hoped to have a minute to talk with the handsome shop owner.

"Lola, he cares for you." Puca said, stopping to turn, his angry gaze meeting hers. "He'd keep you for himself if he could."

"I know, I'd like to let him know that I'm-" She stopped, unsure of how to say it. How would you tell someone that you were interested in four men, that you were okay being shared between them? More than okay, that you longed for it with every fiber of your being.

"That you are what?" Puca asked, bringing his hand up to the back of her neck and moving closer to her.

"That I'm with you."

Puca lips slowly spread into a smile at her words and he watched the blush spread across her cheeks, "Well, I'm with all of you. I need to talk with him about that and well, I found a picture of him and my mom. I have so many questions and I'm not sure what to do."

"Why would he have a picture of your mother?" Puca asked with a frown.

"I don't know, but that's not the weird thing. He looks the same as he does right now and that's-" Lola looked up at him, her emerald eyes shining with unshed tears "My mother died almost twenty years ago. There is no way he should look like he's in his early thirties."

"Lola, I don't think he's human."

"Then what is he?" Lola asked, worrying her lower lip as she brought her hands up to tangle them in the front of his shirt.

"I don't know." Puca said as he pulled her closer to him. His thumb caressing the soft flesh under her ear.

"Why did he have my mom's picture?" Lola whispered as she rested her cheek against his chest. His strong, steady heartbeat giving her strength.

"We'll figure it out, go halainn. Let's get you home."

* * *

Lu diced the carrots and then added them into the pot to simmer with the potatoes. He picked up one of the spices from the spice rack and twisted off the small metal lid.

It had a picture of a garlic clove on the front. It smelled nothing like fresh garlic he frowned, adding a quick shake of it to the stew. He hoped it didn't mess up the taste. Glancing over, he looked at Merrow as the other man kneaded the dough on the floured surface of the counter. A smear of flour dusting the top of cheek.

"You've got something…" Lu said, gesturing to his face before turning away from the merman.

"Are you going to get all weird about what happened this morning?"

"Wasn't planning too. I mean, you and Puca have shared women before." Lu said as he pulled the meat from the fridge. "The relationship is different, that doesn't have to make it awkward."

"Yet here it is, all awkward." Bodach drawled as he leaned against the door frame, watching the two men cook together.

"Was going fine until you got here." Merrow said with a shrug as he put the balled up dough back into the bowl, carefully placing a dish towel over it before moving to the sink.

"Are you sure?" Bodach said with a half smirk, "I know your type is any port in a storm. Lu, Lu needs the feelings, the connection."

"Hey now, I feel something for Lola." Merrow said.

"Lust isn't what I'm talking about."

Lu wished he was anywhere but here right now as he tossed the cubed stew meat into the mixture.

"She isn't Gwragedd. You and she were close."

Lu tensed at the mention of Merrow's sister's name.

"You don't get to bring her up." Merrow said as he turned to look at the other man his teeth barred. "She's my kin."

Lu moved to the sink to wash his hands with the full intention of slipping out unnoticed. So these two could have their little spat.

"It's your fault that I was away from her. That she went through the birth of her child with none of her kin by her side."

"If you think that it's my fault, that is your problem. You chose to come with me that night. The allure of being with a succubus pulled you from her side. No one forced you." Bodach said as he pushed away from the wall and Lu slipped past him. Hoping that their fighting wouldn't ruin the meal that the leprechaun was trying to make for Lola and the others.

He sat on the couch, not even bothering to turn on the television. There was already enough drama going on right now. He hoped they resolved it before Lola got home.

A smile spread across his face as he thought about what had happened this morning. He hoped he got plenty more mornings waking up with Lola. It really didn't bother him that Merrow had been with him. Sure, he would have preferred to have her to himself. Lu wanted to take things further than they had, but he didn't want her korrigan to arise and feed off him and Merrow. He'd heard that it would be a pleasurable experience, if you survived.

"Can not blame me for everything thusa asal a ghoid sonas." Bodach's booming voice filled the small apartment, followed by a loud thwack as a fist met flesh.

Lu leaned over, peaking into the kitchen. The loud sound of a pot falling to the floor made him cringe as he dragged a hand over his face. He needed a drink. He needed several. It had been so long since he'd had a real drink.

Standing, he frowned as he made his way back into the small kitchen. He saw the mess they had made. Bodach was holding his blistering arm under the faucet. The remains of the stew were scattered about the floor.

"Had to ruin our nice meal, didn't you?" Lu growled out, "We can't have anything nice with the two of you, can we?"

Merrow looked away from the other man as Bodach looked at his arm, "Sorry Lu."

He turned, leaving the others to clean up the mess before Lola and Puca got home. He was going to get that drink.

Walking down the hallway, Lu dragged his fingers through his curls. He was stressed, his emotions were all over the place. He walked onto the sidewalk, tilting his head to the side. Closing his eyes, he let his feet guide him in the direction he hoped would lead to a strong drink.

Lu pulled open the heavy steel door open with a grimace. Lu didn't know how his kind functioned in a world like this? All the steel and iron everywhere, it hurt. The unfamiliar stench of cigarette smoking making him scrunch his nose. Under that scent was the smell he longed for. Alcohol of all different kinds. He stepped inside the dimly lit bar with a frown.

He could feel the magic of shifters sweeping over him. There weren't that many right now at this early hour. The lingering presence was still there, moving over his skin. The call of ale was greater than his fear as he took in the bar. The bottles that lined the shelves behind it. Moving closer, he sat on one of the barstools.

"What can I get for you?" The bartender asked as he wiped down the counter.

"I'll have. Hmm, what do you recommend?"

"You smell like a whiskey kinda guy." The green-haired man said as he pulled out a bottle and set up a crystal tumbler for the man.

"Wouldn't be wrong, my friend." Lu said with a smile. His

mouth watering at the thought of a good, strong drink.

"So are you passing through or staying for a bit?" He asked as he poured the amber-colored liquor.

"Passing through, well I hope to be passing through. Depends on if she will come with us when we find a way home or not."

"Lady problems?" The man asked as he resumed wiping down the counter.

"Not so much. Things are good with her. It's the menfolk."

"Oh, my alpha has multiple mates. I've heard that it can be… Trying."

"What breed are you?"

"Wolf," The man shrugged as he peeked up at the red-headed man. "I've never seen a fae creature like you, what are you?"

Lu shook his head as he took a sip of the whiskey. He always hated this question. Hated that people always treated him like he was a drunkard or a thief after they knew the answer.

"I'm a leprechaun."

"No shit?" The wolf smiled, "Man, I know some vamps that would be super excited to meet you."

"No thanks, I've heard we're tasty to them."

"Best to avoid those, they have a newly turned witch with them."

"I'll keep my distance. Are they nearby? I need to warn my family."

"No, their clan is pretty nomadic. Last I heard, Charles and Ciaran had taken their girls back to Europe." The man said as he reached for the bottle and refilled the tumbler.

"I doubt we'll be going there. Thank you for the warning." Lu said as he lifted the glass up and took a long drink. "What's your name, friend?"

"I'm Dev," The shifter said as he poured another glass.

* * *

"We're home," Lola called out as she and Puca stepped inside of the apartment. The cool air making goosebumps rise across her skin as she kicked off her shoes and hung her purse up.

Bodach walked up and pulled her into his arms to spin her around, his lips pressing against hers. Lola couldn't help but let out a girlish giggle.

"What was that for?" Lola asked as he sat her back onto her feet.

"Just missed you."

Lola brought her hand up to his cheek. She wasn't used to this kind of carefree behavior with Bodach.

"He's just trying to distract you." Merrow said with a frown. "Lu is gone."

"Gone?" Lola asked, moving her hands to grip Bodach's bicep.

"Yes, gone." Bodach said and Lola looked between the two men with a frown as she pulled away from Bodach's arms.

"Where are you going?" Merrow asked as he moved closer, he'd intended to give her a greeting. She was moving back to her shoes. She grabbed a pair of flats. Slipping them on.

"To find Lu, he doesn't know what it's like out there." Lola said, panic filling her voice,

"It will be okay, Lola. Lu's probably found a tavern already." Puca said, trying to comfort Lola.

"How do you think he plans to pay for those drinks? He has no money." Lola said, her voice rising as she stomped out of the apartment. Slamming the door behind her as she went.

Pulling out her phone, Lola let out a sigh. She didn't know what had happened to make Lu run off. It had to be something big. He was the calmest out of the four fae men. From what little she knew of them.

Lola searched for local bars and let out a sigh as Merrow caught up with her. He looped an arm around her shoulders, pulling her closer, and she glared up at him.

"I've come to help you search for him."

"What happened?" Lola asked as she pressed her lips together, not looking at the merman.

"Just a bit of a scuffle between Bodach and I. We messed up Lu's dinner plans." Merrow admitted, glancing away as Lola looked up at him.

"Why were you fighting?" Lola said as they walked closer to the brick building.

"He brought up my sister." Merrow said, dropping his arm from around her shoulders as his jaw clenched.

"You've got a sister?"

"I do." Merrow said, shoving his hands into his pockets.

"Do you want to talk about her?"

"No."

"Okay," Lola said with a long sigh. She turned towards the first bar on her list and moved closer to the doors. The fading crescent moon painting on the door read 'Moonlight' as she pushed the steel door open. Shaking her hand as she stepped inside.

It hadn't seemed like the door should be as warm as it was.

Standing still, letting her eyes adjust. Lola heard the soft strains of the guitar filling the air as a band setup on the stage. She looked towards the sound, taking in the twin women standing in front of the stage. One talking to a woman with bright multi-colored hair and a man with sleek long hair. She turned, looking towards the bar. Lu's wild curls caught her attention and she let out a sigh of relief.

They had found him and he seemed okay. He was talking to a man in a tailored business suit and a bartender with bright green spiked hair.

Lola walked forward with Merrow following closely behind her. His eyes moving about the room as he tried his best not to bring the attention of the vampire to Lola and himself.

Walking up to the bar, Lola felt her heart clench at the laugh that Lu let out. It was deep and full, more carefree than she had heard before from him.

Merrow's arm brushed against hers and she glanced at the other man. Watching the tense way he held himself as he looked between Lu and the other patrons.

"Lu," Lola said as she stepped closer to him. He turned, she could see the flush of his cheeks and she wondered how much he'd had to drink.

"Ah, there she is. Mo nighean bhòidheach." He said with a wide smile, Lola stepped closer to him and he snaked an arm around her waist pulling her into his lap.

Lola sat stiffly perched on his knees as she looked between him and the bartender.

"I was worried about you."

"Nothing to worry about my love," Lu said as he brought a hand up, brushing her hair out of her eyes. "Just needed a bit of refreshment."

"Lu, let's take our girl home." Merrow said as he wrapped an arm around the man's shoulder. His eyes moving to the man in the suit and then back to Lu.

"Has dinner been sorted?" Lu asked as he brought his hand

up to trail his fingers through Lola's hair. Not noticing the way that the vampire was studying Lola's neck. Or how sharp teeth sank into his lower lip.

Merrow noticed, he noticed with the keen sharp interest of one predator meeting another.

"Owen, are you okay?" Dev asked as he looked at the vampire. He took in the ridges forming across his forehead and he let out a nervous laugh. Merrow glanced over at him, watching the way he twisted the rag in his hand. The way his other hand moved under the bar and he couldn't help but wonder what the man was reaching for.

"Enjoying a pleasant drink with some new friends, this is Dev." Lu sang, his words slurring.

Merrow moved to stand in front of the Lu and Lola. Golden demonic, glowing eyes glared up at him. Eyes that sent a thrill of fear up Merrow's spin. He didn't understand how Lu could be causally drinking with a creature like this one mere feet away.

How he could have Lola pulled into his lap? With a jovial laugh as he nuzzled his nose against her neck.

Sure, he was good for a brawl. But there was no way Lu would be able to protect Lola in the state that he was in.

"Fine."

The words were said with a slight rumble that made Merrow's fist clench at his side. His muscles tensed as he prepared to get Lola and Lu out of danger should he need to.

"You don't seem fine." The Dev said as he waved over the dark-haired man who was strumming his guitar.

"Eli, why don't you take Owen up stairs, Candy, Abby, and Annie can finish setting up with me." Dev said as he sat down the rag he had been using to wipe the counters down. His other hand coming to rest on the smooth surface.

"Sure, no problem man," Eli said as he looped an arm over Owen's shoulders, pulling him off of the bar stool. "Why don't we head to Drake's office for a quick… Chat."

Turning to look at the three creatures, Dev let out a sigh of relief. There was no doubt in Dev's mind that they were all fae and very much in danger.

He nodded towards Lu and the girl perched on his knee, "Let's settle your tab and get you three on your way."

Lola gave a nervous smile to the man. She didn't know what was up with this bar. She had a feeling that these beings were about as human as she and the fae were.

Merrow relaxed as Lola hopped off of Lu's lap. He glanced up towards the stairs that the vampire and Eli had walked up as he moved to help Lu stand.

"Um, can you repeat that total for me?" Lla asked and Merrow Looked over at her as Lu swayed beside him.

Dev rattled off the total and Merrow watched Lola worry her lower lip as she dug through her bag, pulling out her wallet. She handed over the small card and he couldn't help but feel guilty.

Merrow knew taking care of them must be expensive, and she was a woman by herself. He wished that he could take her to his realm, so she wouldn't have to worry about things like this. So that he and the other men could take care of her, pamper her like she should be pampered.

Turning towards them, he watched as she tucked her wallet back into her bag with a grimace.

"Ready my love?"

"She's ready, I'm ready, you're always ready." Lu sang out and Lola nodded her head towards Merrow. Grabbing Lu's other arm to lead him out of the bar.

Dev shook his head as they left. Hoping that things wouldn't be so complicated for him with his mate.

* * *

"Lu," Lola said, her voice soft as they walked, "Are you okay?"

"A 'dèanamh math," He said with a chuckle. "Does it ever rain here? Haven't been in the rain in ages."

"He's just a bit drunk." Merrow said, "Let's get him home to sleep it off."

"I'm not just drunk." Lu said as he moved his arm wrapping it around Lola's waist pulling her flush against his body. "It's all my fault really, Merrow won't say it. But I know he blames me for missing the birth of his sister's child."

"Lu, that's enough."

"Bodachs right is all. I need the feelings. The night that we went to see the succubuses. Is it sucubi?" He slurred out before shaking his head. "I begged Merrow to come with us. I need the feelings, he's always been my friend. I knew it would make things easier. It's not like with you, I feel so much for you."

"It's okay Lu. Let's get you home and into bed." Lola said, trying to hurry him up before he said something that Merrow didn't want her to know.

"Not okay, he's been my best friend for as long and I can remember. I shouldn't have dragged him with us." Lu said, pulling his arms away from Lu and Merrow.

"What's done is done. I don't blame you."

"You say that, but I saw how mad you got with Bodach earlier."

"Bodach was just trying to get me to lose my temper. You know how he is, he just wasn't done pushing everyone." Merrow said, reaching for his friend as the man staggered forward.

"I'm sorry about Annwn." Lu said, falling to his knees,

Biting her lip, Lola tilted her head to the side, "Did you say Annwn?"

"Yes, my sister's name is Gwragedd Annwn."

"We need to go back to the beach." Lola said moving closer to Lu. She held her hand out to him and Lu lifted his hands. Wrapping them around her middle and burying his face against her stomach as he let out a mournful sob.

"I don't think now is the time for a trip to the beach, ghra."

"That's not what I meant, the woman yesterday. That gave me the chest. Her name was Annwn." Lola said as she patted Lu's shaking shoulders.

Merrow Moved closer to Lu, gently prying his arms from around her.

"My friend, did you hear what Lola said?"

"My kin is alive."

Chapter Seventeen

*P*ulling the blankets over a softly snoring Lu. Lola smiled before leaning over and kissing his forehead. Standing, she moved to pull the curtains closed, blocking out the bright afternoon sun. Worrying the inside of her cheek, she thought about the sob of relief he had let out at Merrow's words.

His sister was alive. She truly hoped that the older Annwn was his sister and not someone with a similar name.

Softly closing the door and letting out a sigh, she rested her head against the door. She couldn't remember the last time she'd had a quiet moment to herself.

"What's on your mind?" Puca asked as he moved down the hallway, filling up the narrow space.

Walking up to him, Lola brought her arms up to wrap them around his waist. Her cheek resting against his chest as she breathed in his scent. Letting it wash over her. She didn't know what it was about Puca that soothed her. That made her feel like she could let go.

But he did. She felt herself melt against him as his arms moved around her. Fingers brushing her cheek as he stroked her hair.

"You should get some rest, go halainn."

"No time for that. I need to drive Merrow to see Annwn." Lola said, pulling away from his chest to look up at him. "I'll rest later."

"Aye, it will do him good. Help heal things between him and Bodach." His fingers moved over her cheek and her breath caught in her throat as he leaned forward. His warm breath fanning over her lips and she leaned closer. The kiss was firm, commanding as he teased her lips until she parted them with a sigh.

Tangling her hands in the back of his shirt. She felt the low coiling in the pit of her stomach, dancing up her spine as his tongue moved against hers. His hand cupped the back of her head, the other hand moving to her hip.

"Puca," Lola moaned out as fingers tightened in her hair. His hand moving to massage her ass as he kissed his way down her neck.

"The way you say my name. Gràdhaich an dòigh anns a bheil do bhodhaig a 'brùthadh an aghaidh mise. Mar a bhios tu a 'gearan m' ainm." Puca panted against the skin of her neck, "Makes me so hard for you."

Lola whimpered as he moved his lips back to hers. She wanted to undo his jeans. To feel the hard length in her palm instead of pressed into her stomach through the layers of clothing that they both had on.

"Puca-"

"Soon enough, Lola. I want you to be in control when I take you."

Lola's heartbeat sped up as she thought about riding Puca. The image of him sprawled beneath her as she rode him had her biting her lip and looking at him through lowered lashes.

Puca let out a growl, "If you keep looking at me like that I won't be able to help myself, beautiful."

"What if I don't want you to stop," Lola asked. The tip of her tongue darting out to run over her lower lip.

"What my lady wants."

"She will get later." Merrow said as he bounced down on the balls of his feet. "I want you two to lay together, but Lola and I have more pressing matters."

Puca let out a sigh as he looked back at Lola with a sigh, "He's right. Go, but come back to me safely. Both of you." He said glancing over at Merrow.

"Aye, we'll be back before you know it. Til then you can keep Bodach busy."

"I'm standing right here." Bodach said, crossing his arms over his chest as he leaned against the wall further down the hallway.

"I know," Merrow said with a slow, wicked smile spreading across his face, "Maybe they fight. Maybe they find other things to keep them busy."

"Merrow." Lola whispered. If he kept up his teasing. She didn't think she would be able to keep from jumping one of them. Or all of them.

"I jest." He said holding his hand out towards Lola.

Glancing up at Puca, her eyes met his, and he nodded before letting her go to the other man. His golden eyes moving to Bodach's. They had a score to settle before the fun began, and Puca had the feeling that the other man needed to work out his frustrations as well.

Merrow pulled Lola towards the front door, Bodach's hand shot out to grab her wrist.

"Oh, come on now." Merrow grumbled, letting her hand go as he turned around to glare at Bodach.

"I'm just saying my goodbyes." Bodach said as he gently pulled Lola closer,

"Bodach, I'll be coming back."

"I know, just remember what I told you. Let's get you under control first. Don't let Merrow tempt you away." He said, his thumb stroking the inside of her wrist as he gave her a look that had so many emotions Lola didn't have a name for.

"I won't." Lola whispered as he let her hand go and she looked away from him, feeling her cheeks heat up. Merrow's eyes met hers with a wink before he turned away, his hand clasping hers. Pulling her towards the front door.

Slipping on her shoes, Lola turned to Merrow as he held open the door for her. They had a bit of a trip to make and he all but dragged her down the stairs towards her jeep.

Closing her door, Lola moved into her seat. Clicking the seatbelt. She glanced over at Merrow as he rubbed his hands together. She could practically feel the nervous energy pouring off of him.

"What if it's a different Annwn? Is that a common name?" Lola asked as she put her key into the ignition and started the car.

"It's her, it's got to be her." He said as she pulled the car into the street.

"I don't know Merrow," Lola said, worrying her lower lip. "The woman was old, she didn't... She didn't look like you."

"Lola, we are fae. Time works differently for us. If she looked older. It's because that's how she wanted to appear to you."

"What do you mean?" Lala asked as she drove.

"We have many different forms, many gifts. Annwn and I... And you, we are water fae." Merrow said, taking his hand into her.

Rubbing her other hand over the leather covering on the steering wheel, Lola couldn't help but think about his words and Bodach's. If she were a water fae as he said. Then what had Bodach meant when he had said that they were suitable for each other?

* * *

Lola pondered Merrow's words as they pulled up to the beach house. The sun was fading beyond the waves of the water. Painting the waves of the ocean in hues of orange and purples.

She turned off of the keys and this time Merrow was out of the jeep before she'd undone her seat belt. This time he was half-jogging towards the cozy-looking beach house.

Sighing, she pulled the keys from the ignition and slid out of the jeep. Closing the door behind her, she walked over to the passenger and nudged it closed before she headed up to the porch where Merrow stood staring at the door.

"Are you going to knock?" Lola asked as she touched his forearm, pulling him from his thoughts.

"What if she is mad at me still?"

"Won't know until you knock." Lola said, her voice low and soothing. "You guys are family though, I'm sure she's forgiven you."

"Aye, in some ways it's easier not to know."

"It is, but it's family." Lola said linking her fingers with his, trying to lend him some of her strength. "I'd offer to knock, but this feels like something you might need to do."

"Aye." Merrow breathed out as he brought his hand up, his knuckles tapping on the sun-washed purple door.

After a brief moment, the door swung open and a much younger Annwn stood looking up at them. Her soft white blonde hair pulled back into a braid, showing off her delicate features. Her earlobes held simple pearl earrings, and Lola was shocked by how much she looked like Merrow.

"Halò, a bhràthair."

"Aye, Piuthar beannachdan." Merrow said, and Lola could see the shine of his eyes from unshed tears as he tried to keep his emotions in check.

"Lola," Annwn greeted as she stepped to the side, letting them come into her home.

"You, you look-"

"I told you, we can appear how we want." Merrow said as he stepped in, pulling Lola with him. He dropped her hand, stepping closer to Annwn and pulling her into a hug that pulled her feet off the floor.

"Merrow," she giggled, her bangles clashing together as she held onto him. "I've missed you so."

"And I you,"

Lola pushed the door closed. Trying to give Merrow a moment with his sister as they spoke softly to one another in a language that she couldn't understand. Looking about the room, she saw a shelf filled with small carvings made out of driftwood. Stepping closer, Lola studied the small carved pieces. They were small figurines of people no more than three to four inches tall.

"Do you like them?" Hyster asked softly and Lola jumped,

spinning around to look at him.

"I do, they're very... Detailed." Lola said, looking from Hyster to the small carved figurines. One of them, a fisherman, caught her attention. She leaned in closer, studying the way his clothing almost looked like it had moved in the breeze.

"She makes them." He whispered, and Lola couldn't help but wonder at the sadness in his voice.

"Why were you crying?" She asked as she looked over at the handsome, tanned man.

"It's my own fault."

"What is?" Lola asked, turning to look at him.

"Lola, you shouldn't meddle in things you don't understand." Annwn warned. Lola jumped and spun to look at the no longer old woman.

"I'm sorry, I was just-"

"Interfering where you shouldn't be?" Annwn asked, crossing her arms over her small breasts.

"Piuthar ghaolach." Merrow sighed, moving to stand closer to Lola. "Lola is still learning our ways. She's just showing concern for another."

"Concern will get her killed. The unseelie has taken an interest in her."

Merrow let out a snarling sound that made the hairs on the back of Lola's neck stand on end. Slowly, she looked at him. Lola wanted to let back a shriek at the sight of her lover.

His normal sea-green eyes seemed luminescent, his teeth were like sharp points. It reminded her of an angler fish. Luring its prey closer with that bright light in the darkness, those sharp teeth ready to take a bite out of someone.

"Merrow." Lola whispered, her eyes wide as she brought her hand to her mouth.

"No one will hurt you," He said, closing his eyes, and Lola could see the struggle as he tried to rein his emotions under control.

"That fire is good, you'll need it. Just don't be too rash and fall into any traps." Annwn said, patting her brother's arm as she moved to sit on the couch. The soft breeze from the open windows ruffling the loose tendrils of her hair as she pushed back a strand of hair behind her ear.

"What do you mean? Fall into any traps?" Lola asked.

"Sit, Hyster will make us some tea. Or I guess, coffee would be better." Annwn said, motioning Lola and Merrow towards the love seat.

"Yes host." Hyster said as he turned away from Lola and moved into the compact kitchen.

Lola sat down on the edge of the love seat, her fingers gripping the cushion beneath her. Muscles stiff, like she was ready to run away if she should need to.

"Oh relax, Merrow is only showing his true side because he's worried for you. He falls more towards the Unseelie side of things so he knows what they're like and the danger that you are in."

"What do you mean?" Lola asked as Merrow sat down beside her.

"What she means is that we will fight dirty to keep that which we believe is ours." Merrow said, prying her hand from the cushion and taking it into both of his.

"I don't belong to anyone." Lola said, pulling her hand away. "I'm my own person, yes I like you. But belonging to you?"

"You may not know it, Lola. You are ours. I knew it the moment that you unlocked the box and I laid eyes on you. You were meant to be ours. Just like we were meant to be yours." Merrow said softly and Lola felt the butterflies in her stomach.

It was too soon for her to be feeling this way. Yes, she had admitted to herself that she was falling for the four men. Hearing it out loud, though, that she belonged to them caused the modern women in her to bristle up.

The other side of her, the hopeless romantic, swooned. Wanting very much to belong to the fae men. To bask in their affection, to see what being with all of them would bring. How it would make her feel.

"You two can sort that out later," Annwn said, her lips curling up into a slight smile. "We have much to discuss and the night is young."

Hyster came back into the room, handing Lola and Merrow a mug of coffee before he moved back into the kitchen carrying one for himself and Annwn.

Nodding her head as she accepted the black coffee, Lola took a sip of the black liquid before grimacing at the taste. It was bitter, and she couldn't help but wonder if Hyster had ever made coffee before. Given the amount of grounds, she doubted it.

"What happened to the child?" Merrow asked.

"Which one?" Annwn said with a soft smile, before she accepted her mug from Hyster.

"You had more than one?" Merrow asked. Lola could hear the sadness in his voice that he had missed this time with his sister and her children.

"I birthed a healthy, beautiful boy." Annwn answered before she sat her mug down and reached towards the coffee table, grabbing her phone.

Looking over at Merrow, Lola saw his frown as he watched

his sister swipe open the small device. She leaned closer, handing it to him. Three men stood with their arms wrapped around each other's shoulders. Their skin was bronzed with a healthy tan and their bright eyes, eyes like Merrow's sparkled in the sunlight.

"My boys." Annwn said proudly as Merrow studied their faces, looking for hints of their parents.

"When can I meet them?" Merrow asked, looking up from the picture. His sister had a family. Something he'd never thought she would be able to have given her curse.

"I'll tell the younger two to come home so you can meet them."

Hyster let out a choked sob as he escaped to the kitchen.

"Is he okay?" Lola asked, looking from Annwn to the small kitchen where she could hear rasping sobs.

"He will be." Annwn replied. "My oldest, he is imprisoned for the time being."

"What where?" Merrow demanded as he moved to stand.

"What happened?" Lola asked, pulling on Merrow's hand. Trying to get the fae man to sit down, she felt a sinking feeling in the pit of her stomach.

"Hyster is his partner. His sentence is to stay with me until his love returns."

The sobs got louder and Lola couldn't help but want to go to the other man. She could only imagine how he must feel.

"And their father?" Merrow asked, his hands fisted at his sides.

"Twice and I left, if he had struck me again. It would have been his death, just like my eldest son's father." Annwn said with a sad smile.

Merrow's jaw clenched. He moved to his sister, dropping

to his knees in front of her. "I am sorry, I should have been here to help you raise them."

"Brother, you know my curse. It's okay, I was meant to walk alone." Annwn said as she brought her hand up to cup his cheek. "It hasn't always been lonely. I've had plenty of partners to keep my bed warm."

"Aye, but I should have been here with you to help you with your children. You were alone."

"Not for long, brother. I just wish I hadn't cursed my children with my gift. No one should laugh the way I do, or have tears that can cause such violence."

The sobbing increased in tempo.

"Is he really okay?" Lola asked, looking back at Annwn. She didn't understand how the other woman could ignore those heart wrenching sobs.

"He will be, you can't strike one of us three times. Or you will suffer, Hyster and my son are paying that price." Annwn said.

"Like the fae or just you?" Lola asked, worrying the inside of her cheek.

"Just me and my children." Annwn said, picking up her coffee and taking a sip before her nose crinkled. "Long ago a curse was placed on me, I had hoped it wouldn't be passed to my children."

"No worries, if you'd like to spank me." Merrow said, squeezing Lola's knee as he leaned forward handing the phone back to Annwn.

"Still the same Merrow." Annwn said with a chuckle. Watching as Lola's cheeks turned a lovely cherry red.

"With Lola it's different." Merrow said as he leaned back. Wrapping his arm around her shoulder and pulling her closer.

"She's different."

"I can see that." Annwn smiled at Lola, who kept looking towards the kitchen.

"When you say that the unseelie are interested in me, what do you mean?"

"I mean that you've caught his eye. He wouldn't haven't sent you here to collect my so- the prisoner if you hadn't caught his interest."

"His eye, do you mean Erik?"

Annwn pressed her lips together as she looked between Lola and Merrow, "I cannot reveal who it is."

"So it's Erik." Lola asked, quirking her eyebrow up.

Annwn pressed her lips together as she raised an eyebrow at Lola. "You don't listen very well?"

"I try, but not really." Lola answered honestly.

"She can listen very well." Merrow purred out as he dragged his nose along her cheek and Lola felt her blush spread to her hairline.

"Yes, still the same Merrow." Annwn muttered to herself, looking towards the kitchen.

Clearing her throat, Lola pulled away from Merrow. Scooting to the far end of the love seat.

"If Hyster is being punished, and he's your oldest son's partner..." Lola said, her eyes darting towards the kitchen where she could still hear the other man crying.

"Yes, the box you took yesterday." Annwn sucked in a shaking breath before speaking. "Contained my son."

Chapter Eighteen

*W*orrying her lip, Lola glanced over at Merrow as they drove. Her mind on what Annwn had told her. Merrow's nephew was trapped in a box. She had taken that box to Erik's shop with Merrow and Puca's help.

How the other woman had hinted that Erik was fae. Lola wasn't quite sure what that meant, but she intended to find out. She and google had a date tonight, well if she could get free of her fae men.

"You okay?" he asked, and Merrow looked over at her with a sad smile.

"I am, I just wish there was something I could do to help my sister and her child." Merrow said with a sigh. "I know I can not interfere, that good things would not come from it."

"I wish I could help you Merrow, I don't understand how things work with the fae." Lola said as she pulled the car into the parking space in front of her apartment.

"Lets get you in so you can get some rest." Merrow said. One day she would understand their ways. Til then, he knew he'd work on teaching her. He still wanted to take her to their home so she could relax and let them take care of her as she had been taking care of them.

* * *

Bodach flopped onto the couch with a sigh. Puca lay sprawled beside him, his body relaxed as he looked out the window towards the dark starlit sky.

He was glad that the other man had given into him. He always enjoyed taking a whip to him on the rare occasions that Puca gave up control. The way that he'd suck in a breath through clenched teeth, how he'd fight him. Made Bodach anticipate the experience of taking Puca once more.

He was able to get the other man in that state, and it was one that he always treasured. He'd never tell anyone, Bodach knew that Puca wouldn't be able to admit that he secretly loved giving up control.

Leaning forward, he swiped the remote control from the coffee table. The plastic smooth and strange in his hands as he pressed the soft button. Watching the television flare to life, Lola had already shown him and the others how to navigate onto what she called the Netflix.

He scrolled through the movies, looking at the pictures. Finally, coming across one that looked interesting. The dark cover featured a man with a hat and blood on the screen.

Bodach pressed play and leaned back as the opening credits started.

"Previously on the Walk-"

"Why are we watching this?" Puca asked as he rolled his head across the back of the couch, looking at Bodach.

"It looked interesting. Lola likes it."

"Can't we just enjoy the silence?" Puca asked as he stretched his legs out.

"You didn't get enough quiet in the box?"

"The box didn't have Lola. Just sitting her in her home, it's enough. In our prison, I couldn't escape you or the others. Now I'm afraid to be without you." Puca said, dragging his fingers through his hair. "I know that I'd never be without Merrow, but you and Lu."

"Lu won't be going anywhere."

"And you?" Puca asked.

"I'll follow Lola wherever she leads. I guess that means your stuck with me." Bodach said with a wide grin. Watching the way the other man relaxed, his hands resting on the cushion beside Bodach's legs.

The door opened and Bodach looked towards the sound as Lola and Merrow stepped inside the apartment.

"You started it without me." Lola said with a pout as she kicked off her shoes and hurried to sit on the couch between both men. Puca moved his arm to the back of the couch and Lola relaxed against him as Bodach took her hand in his.

"Not fair." Merrow said with a pout as he crossed his arms over his chest, flopping into the chair by the window.

"You've had her all day and most of yesterday." Puca said as he twirled a strand of her hair around his finger, giving it a gentle tug.

"Doesn't mean I have to like it." Merrow grumbled, turning to look at the screen, as zombies attacked the main character. "On that, I'm heading to bed."

"It's not real." Lola said as he walked by.

"Doesn't make me feel any less... Creeped out." Merrow

said, chuckling as he shed his clothing before walking back to Lola's bedroom.

She looked back to the screen, "Oh, some popcorn would be nice." Lola said, pushing herself to stand. Moving into the kitchen. Bodach looked over at Puca, his hand snaking out to touch the other man's bare chest.

"Are you trying to start something?" Puca asked, raising an eyebrow.

"Maybe I am." He said with a smirk as he looked back towards the screen. Bodach scrapped his nail over Puca's nipple, smirking as the other man drew in a breath as he plucked at the hardened peak. He pulled his hand away as Lola came back into the room, a fresh bowl of hot popcorn held in her hands.

She sat between the two men, grabbing the remote and unpausing the show. Lola reached down and grabbed a few of the buttery kernels and popped them into her mouth. She looked over at Puca as he leaned closer, "Did you want some?" She asked.

He nodded, his gaze flickering from the popcorn to her lips, and she wasn't sure which he wanted. Her kiss or the salty buttery goodness.

Lola picked up a few of the kernels and held them out to him. His fingers trailed up her wrist as he dragged them closer to his mouth. His tongue darting out to take one of the offered puffed kernels.

Shivering, Lola looked up at him as he chewed the fluffy morsel. The way his Adam's apple bobbed. She was filled with the desire to nibble on the delicate flesh of his throat. Her throat tightened as she felt a coiling sensation low in the pit of her stomach.

"I think Bodach would like some too." He said, his voice a husky whisper.

Biting her lip, Lola turned and looked over at Bodach and picked up a piece of popcorn. The butter oil making her fingers slick as she held it out to him.

His pupils dilated as he held her wrist, much like how Puca had done. His teeth nipped at her fingertips as he took the offering into his mouth. Lola felt her vaginal walls clench in anticipation.

"Tastes good?" Puca said as he moved the bowl from Lola's lap and pressed his body against hers. "Doesn't it?"

"Mmm mm, I know something that tastes better."

"What's that?" Lola asked, feeling the heat of her blush spread across the tops of her cheeks at the closeness of both men.

"You." Bodach's words were gravely as he pressed his lips against hers. His hand snaking to her thigh, giving it a sharp squeeze.

Lola gasped against his lips as she felt Puca trace his fingertips up her other thigh. She didn't know if she wanted to clench her thighs together or open them further. Both men dragged their fingers closer to her core with a teasing slowness. Bodach released her lips and she panted. Drawing in a gasping breath. Puca's other hand moved to her chin, guiding her lips to his.

His warm lips moved against hers as his tongue snaked out teasing against her bottom lip before his teeth nipped at the soft flesh. She moved her hands to grip both of their thighs, feeling the flex of muscles under her fingertips as Bodach's hand pressed against her heated sex. She could feel her panties getting damp with the slick coating of arousal. His fingers moved to the waistband of her shorts, unsnapping the button. His teeth and tongue teasing against the outer shell of her ear as Puca's hand brushed past his. Sharply tugging at the curls between her thighs.

Making Lola groan low in the back of her throat as his fingers dipped past her panties, slipping between her folds. Finding the sensitive bundle of nerves and circling with his middle finger before delving further into her slick, wet heat.

"Mar a tha thu a 'faireachdainn paisgte timcheall mo chorragan, a' toirt m 'anail air falbh.."

"If you think she feels good. You should taste her." Bodach said with a smirk, his words spoken against the shell of her ear making her shiver. "Would you like that, Lola, for Puca to taste you."

Lola gasped as Puca's finger moved inside of her and she nodded her head.

"Acushla," Bodach chuckled, "He needs your words."

"Yes."

"Yes, what?" Puca asked, his lips twitching as he pulled back to look at her.

"Yes, I want you to taste me." Lola said, and then she was on her back. Puca tugging at her shorts before she was done uttering the words.

Bodach smoothed the hair away from her face as Puca moved between her thighs. His warm breath painting across her lips as he breathed in the scent of her sex.

Rubbing his cheek across her thigh, Lola moaned as he placed an open-mouthed kiss over her sex.

"Mm-mm, you were right. She does taste nèamhaidh." Puca growled, making Lola curl her toes as he moved closer. His tongue lapping at her slit. Lola went to move her hands to tangle them in his long locks.

"No, you don't m 'aingeal." Bodach growled as he grabbed Lola's wrist with one hand, pinning her in place as she let out a breathy moan. His other hand slipping inside of her shirt, pushing her bra down so he could cup her breast.

Lola's back arched as Puca sucked her clitoris in his mouth and Bodach plucked at her nipple. Puca's hands moved to place one of her legs over his shoulder as he lapped at her core. Making her close her eyes as she struggled against Bodach's grip as he plucked at her nipple.

"Do you like the way his tongue is moving inside of you?" Bodach growled as he gave her nipple a sharp tug.

"Yesss." Lola hissed out, Bodach's fingers moved to her other breast repeating the action and Lola bit her lower lip.

Puca lifted her hips higher, his tongue moving against her asshole. He smiled as her thighs shook around his head before moving up to focus at her core. Fingers moving to her press against her clitoral hood.

"Puca." Lola panted out and Bodach moved to his knees beside her. Freeing his throbbing cock from his slacks. Lola turned her head to the side. Engulfing his cock into her mouth, moaning around him as Puca moved his tongue in and out of her. Fucking her until her eyes rolled back into her head and she let out a strangled scream as his thumb moved at a faster pace, circling her clit.

Bodach tangled his fingers in her hair, guiding her mouth faster. He threw back his head, savoring the feeling of her mouth on his cock. He'd taken care of Puca's needs earlier but hadn't seen to himself. It wouldn't take him much with the way she brought her hand up and twisted it around the base of his shaft. Her other hand snaking out to fondle his sac.

"Lola." He growled out as he thrust faster into her mouth. She was perfect. He loosened his hold on her as she moaned around him. The vibrations making his testicles tighten and he tried to warn her. To pull himself from her mouth, but she gripped him tighter.

Working her hand faster as he let out a strangled gasp, his cum spilling down her throat.

Puca lapped at her center as he looked up Lola's body, his cock throbbing painfully. He didn't stop his gentle teasing as he moved his tongue in and out of her channel. Loving the way that her body shook as Bodach pulled his now flaccid cock from her lips.

Lola let out a whimper as she moved her hand to grip the back of the couch as Puca kept up his onslaught. He watched how Bodach leaned down, his thumb catching the spilled cum on bottom lip before he pressed his lips to hers.

The small groan that slipped from the other man's lips made Puca shiver. He moved back up to her clit, pulling out another orgasm from her.

Lola panted his name, a begging whimper as he gently nibbled the engorged nub. She tangled her other hand in her hair. Pulling at the strands as Bodach trailed kisses across her sweat drenched skin.

"One more," Bodach said as he pulled her shirt out of his way and bit at her shoulder. His eyes meeting Puca's "Can you handle that?"

Blinking slowly, he dragged his hand from her thigh, roughly massaging himself through his jeans. His lips moved roughly over Lola's clit and she let out a sobbing sound before she panted his name.

"I don't think she can't take much more, aon stòlda."

Puca closed his eyes, focusing on the sounds that she was making. Hating the way that Bodach tried to take control of everything. Yet he loved it at the same time. The way that Lola quivered beneath him, panting his name like he was god.

Her legs shook as she let out a keening sound, fingers roughly tugging at his hair. Her other hand moving to Bodach's as he kissed her breast with closed mouth, teasing kisses.

Bodach pulled back with a smirk, "I'm going to get cleaned up."

Puca planted kisses along her inner thigh as she caught her breath. Everything in him wanted to take her, and he wanted to demand that the other man come back in here. So he could bend him over the couch. He didn't want to risk hurting Lola, if he took her the way that he wanted to right now.

"Lola?" He asked, his voice thick with arousal.

"Hmm?" She asked, licking dry lips as she adjusted her shirt.

"Did you enjoy that?" He asked in a growling tone that made her eyes widen.

She bit her lower lip as her eyes met his hungry ones. They were luminescent in the dim light. She nodded her head as he mouthed her thigh, nipping at the soft flesh. Lola let out a moan as he moved to stand.

She brushed her hair away from her face as she looked at the bulge in the front of his slacks. "Puca."

"Yes, go halainn?"

"Did you, umm, did you want me too?" She stumbled over her words, trying to get them out. She didn't know why she couldn't say it after what they had just done.

"Why don't you and I go clean up?" Puca asked, the tip of his tongue peeking out between his lips as his lips twitched into a slow smile. He heard the door to the bathroom swing open and the soft slap of Bodach's bare feet as he walked towards the bedroom.

Nodding her head, Lola slipped her hand into his and he pulled her flush against his body. Enjoying the way her breasts felt pressed against his chest. The way her cheeks heated with a blush as she felt the heat build back up between them.

Puca turned, pulling them towards the bathroom. He turned the water on and turned back to face her. His fingers moving against her stomach as he dragged her shirt up and over her head. Lola brought her arms up as she shyly looked up at him.

"Lola, do not hide from me." He pressed his lips against hers. She sighed against his lips as she dropped her arms. His hands moved to the clasp of her bra and he undid the hooks. Dragging the material down her arms and letting it fall to the floor.

His thumbs brushed over her nipples and the flesh hardened into sharp points that he dragged his fingertips over them.

"I love the way you respond to me." He whispered against her lips as his hands moved down. Mapping out her flesh as his hand moved lower to her tender folds. "Undress me."

Lola shivered as his fingers pressed against her and she moved her hand to the front of his jeans. Fumbling with the button as she tugged at it with shaking hands.

"Slowly." He whispered, working a finger in and out of her wet core.

Lola let out a shuddering breath as she stilled. Enjoying the way that he was building her body back up. She undid the button and slowly pulled down the zipper. Freeing his thick cock, she brought her fist down to caress his shaft. Dragging the foreskin back so she could run her thumb over the glistening tip. She moved her finger through his pre-cum and brought it to her mouth.

Puca brought his finger to his lips, savoring the heady taste of her honey.

Her eyes on his as she took the digit in her mouth, her tongue swirling around her thumb. Tasting him as he pulled his fingers from his mouth.

Puca tangled his hands in her hair. His lips pressed against hers as he backed her up until her ass pressed against the sink. His lips, hungry and devouring her with a soul consuming need. Lola brought her hand to his penis, marveling at the soft yet hard felt feel of his skin in her fist as she guided him between her folds.

"Ah ah ah," he teased. His hand moving over hers as he moved the head of his cock against her clit. "I've already said how I want you to fuck me, and this isn't it." His other hand moved to her breast as he tugged at her nipple.

"Puca." Lola gasped out as he stroked his cock against her. She tried to tilt her hips, so he'd penetrated her. He let out a dark chuckle. Her body clenched up and he smirked down at her.

"Let's take a shower."

Chapter Nineteen

P uca turned, stepping into the narrow shower stall. He looked back at Lola, holding out his hand to her as she looked up at him.

Her eyes flicked over to the running water and back to Puca. She was afraid of what might happen in the shower as her toes sunk into the plush bath mat.

"Are you joining me?" He asked, his tone commanding yet giving her the chance to say no if she wanted to.

"I'm afraid to."

"Nothing will happen. I know you fed will with Bodach." Puca said, bringing his hand up to run his fingers over her cheek with a feather-light touch that made her eyes flutter shut and her heart thud quicker in her chest.

"Nothing will happen in the shower?"

"Oh something will happen, but Lola…" He said with a long pause. His thumb moving over her lower lip as she opened her eyes. Looking up at him through hooded eyes. "I meant what I said, control is very important to me."

"Are you sure?"

"Very much so," he said. His thumb caressed her lip one last time before he stepped back into the water. The warm streaming water soaking into his hair, making him look like something from a dream. Lola followed him into the compact space. Her hands coming to his waist as she stepped into the shower's spray.

Puca's lips moved along her jawline as he reached over. Grabbing the bar of soap and lathering it into the large, puffy sponge that Lola had hanging on a hook. He dragged it up the side of her body. His fingertips touching her skin, trailing up a path that left her heated from such a simple touch.

He nipped at the soft flesh beneath her earlobe, before he leaned back, soaping up her neck. His other hand braced on her hip and Lola could feel his hard length pressed against her stomach. She leaned closer to him as he ran the puff over her breast.

Eyes glued to her nipples as they hardened into sharp peaks at the mesh material scraped over them. Lola's breathing was fast as she watched him bite his lip, his other hand coming up to her breast to tease the nipple.

Rolling it with his thumb and forefinger as he soaped up her other breast and repeated the action. A soft moan escaped her lips and he looked up at her as he trailed the puff down her stomach to the apex of her thighs. Cleaning the juices from her, before dropping the puff to the ground.

His fingers moved over her slick sex and she shivered, looking up at him. Puca spun her around, so she was directly under the spray of warm water. Her back to his chest as he watched the suds rinse off of her skin. His hands moving her hips to hold her in place as he bent his knees, bringing his cock between her legs.

He knew if he angled himself right, he'd be inside of her wet, tight heat. He wanted that. The thought tempted him, but he'd told her how he would take her. She shifted her hips, letting him slip through her folds, and she let out a strangled sound as his ridged shaft rubbed against her sensitive clit.

The heat of her cunt seeping into his skin. He leaned down mouthing her flesh as he rocked his hips slowly, fucking her without penetrating her. Lola braced her hands on the wall as he moved, feeling the tightening coil of arousal flash through her. Hot and intense, as he moved his cock, she leaned forward. Trying to angle herself so she could take his cock inside of her.

"No, my love." Puca growled as he leaned over her, his teeth digging into her shoulder as he fought with himself.

"Please." Lola begged as she bucked her hips, the friction on her clitoris making her legs shake. Finger tangled into her hair as he thrust his hips. The feel of her heat was too much. He dragged the head of his cock against her core. His head pressing against her soaked vaginal opening.

"Do not beg me, love. I can not stand how much it makes me want to give you want you need." He said with the barest of thrusts. Letting her feel the head of his cock. Teasing against her, he felt her slowly thrust back against him.

"Puca," Lola panted as his fingers flexed into her hips, sure to leave bruises. She didn't care as she struggled to try and impale herself on his dick

"I'll give you what you need." He said with a growl as he kissed his way down her spine. Taking his time to map out her flesh with his tongue as the water beat against him. He nipped at the rounded globe of her ass as he got down on his knees. His hands coming up to spread her cheeks apart as he worked his tongue against the puckered hole. His other hand snaking between her legs so he could work two fingers in and out of her body in a fast rhythm. That had her sobbing his name, her fingers scrabbling at the slowly warming tile.

She leaned her forehead against the shower's wall and sobbed. Her legs going weak as he penetrated her anus with his tongue. His thumb moving across her clit as he added a third finger.

"Puca I'm-" Lola bit out, not even getting to finish her sentence. Her body clenched up around his fingers and she felt the flood of slick wet heat leave her body as she came in a great gush of fluid.

With a growl, his mouth was replacing his fingers as he tried to swallow up as much of her essence as he could. Marveling at the taste of her cum.

She stood on shaking legs as his tongue slowed its movements, letting her ride out the feeling before he moved to stand behind her. The head of his cock pressing against her opening and he let out a groan as his semen coated her throbbing, twitching sex.

"I think I should finish cleaning you up." Puca said against her neck as he peppered her skin with small closed mouth kisses. He lifted her up carefully and turned her to face him, feeling the way she weakly gripped at his shoulders.

"Yeah, I-" Lola said, panting as she tried to catch her breath while he cleaned them both off. "I don't think I can handle anymore."

* * *

Moving about the room, Bodach let out a content sigh as he

pulled the couch out. He'd figured out that it folded into a bed earlier today. Now he was putting fresh linens on.

The idea of sleeping with Lola wrapped around him did strange things to his heart. He couldn't wait to feel her soft curves against him as she sleepily snuggled into his side. He fluffed up one of the pillows he's stolen off of her bed and tossed it onto their makeshift bed as he pressed his lips together. Trying not to think about it the way he felt about her.

A sharp keening sound pierced through the air, making him smile. He knew that he would need to feed into Lola's fae side soon. He could trust the others with her as long as he kept her stated until she could control it better.

Til then he would keep doing his part, to help her learn control. Hearing the water shut off, he turned off the light and slipped under the covers. The cool cotton sheets brought goosebumps up his bare flesh.

He could hear the soft padding of bare feet and he looked back towards the hallway. Lola's bed was much too small for her and Puca to sleep in with the other two, and he hoped that they joined him soon.

Lola rested her head against Puca's shoulder as he carried her cradled against his chest. The pale light from outside the window painted the other man with shadows and seemed to make Lola's skin glow in the darkness.

How anyone could think Lola was anything other than fae was beyond him. He shifted to his side, pulling the covers back so Puca could lay Lola down in the center of the bed.

"But I'm naked." Lola said, stifling back a yawn.

"So are we." Bodach chuckled, running his nails down the curve of her hip.

"What if there is a fire?"

"Then we will all be naked together, acushla. We will protect you." He said, his hand moving to hers so he could bring her hand to his lips. He softly kissed each of her fingertips, laying his head on the pillow and pulling her to rest her head on his chest.

"Puca, are you coming to bed?" Lola asked sleepily.

"In just a moment."

His eyes were transfixed on the street below. He could have sworn that he saw someone out there. He closed the curtain and turned back to the others, slipping between the sheets. Puca pressed his body against Lola's back. Biting his lower lip at the way she pressed back against him as her breathing evened out.

Tonight was going to be a long night, testing his fragile grip on his control.

Bodach watched Puca as he dragged his hands through her hair.

"Are you okay?"

"Aye." He said, closing his eyes as he buried his nose into Lola's damp hair. Breathing in the crisp smell of her.

"Were you able to stay in control?" Bodach asked, and Puca let out a sigh as he opened his eyes and looked over at the other man.

"Just barely, something about our leannan. Is very tempting."

"Aye, that she is." Bodach said as he kissed her forehead. "I am trying to wait to see how long she can put off feeding."

"May want to let the others know. I don't know how long Merrow will be able to resist."

"Just Merrow?" Bodach asked as he raised an eyebrow.

"No, not just him. All of us." He whispered, not liking the

way the other man was calling him out on his need for Lola.

"Soon she'll have the control she needs and we won't have to worry. We just need to make sure she doesn't kill one of you first."

"I can only heal so much." Puca said tiredly.

"Let's hope it doesn't come to that. Rest my friend."

With that Bodach closed his eyes, Lola's soft snores lulling him and Puca into a deep sleep.

* * *

Merrow pressed himself into the soft round curve. He was dreaming of Lola. The way that she fit so perfectly against him, how she responded to him and his touch. Sleepily, he kissed the back of her head, feeling the springy curls of her soft hair. He thrust his cock against her again, letting out a moan as her scent tickled his sense.

Whiskey, he frowned. As the soft curved pressed back against him. Lola didn't smell of whiskey,

He rolled his hips once more, gripping the hip under his fingers. Before trailing his hand to the front of his bed partner. Smirking as he gripped the hard dick in his hands. Roughly massaging the other man's length as he thrust himself against his ass.

Merrow didn't care about who his bed mate was, as long as they both got to come. He cracked an eye open, smirking as he remembered crawling into bed with Lu.

He'd hoped that Lola would join them. Waking up with her and Lu had been heaven. One that he wanted a repeat of as many times as he could get. Til then, he was happy to wake up with Lu.

The other man let out a strangled cry as Merrow slipped his hands past the waistband of his shorts. His thumb spreading pre-cum over the head of his cock as he moved to stroke his length.

Merrow thrust against him again, enjoying the friction Lu's ass gave him as he pressed it in between the other man's cheeks. Rubbing the underside of his cock against him.

One day he'd take his friend, show him exactly how good it could be. Til he was ready though, this would be an enjoyable distraction.

Lu's hips jerked forward as he opened his eyes. His balls tightened and he let out a groan. Feeling his release soak through the fabric of his underwear and shorts. The masculine groan in his ears and the splash of warmth he felt across his lower back made his eyes widen. He realized that it wasn't Lola's hand jerking him off.

He looked over his shoulder, worrying his lower lip as his eye widened and he looked at Merrow. Sure they had laid together before. He had figured it had been due to their confinement. Not that the other man actually wanted him.

"Good morning, mo charaid ùine mhòr." Merrow said, his hand trialing up Lu's abdomen as he dragged his hand up to cup the other man's cheek. Before pressing his lips to Lu's.

Lu's eyes widened before slipping closed, his tongue tentatively moving against Merrow's parted lips.

Merrow smiled before snaking his tongue into the other man's mouth with a groan.

Chapter Twenty

*ola stood in the kitchen, looking at the loaf of crusted baked bread that Merrow had made yesterday. An idea forming, one that she hoped her men would like.

Reaching under the sink, she pulled out a wicker picnic basket and sat it on the cabinet.

She moved to the knife block and went about slicing the bread before turning to the fridge. Pulling out the items she would need to fix sandwiches. Lola had a plan. Today she'd take the fae men on a date to one of her favorite places. She just hoped that they liked it as much as she did.

She went about fixing the sandwiches and wrapping them in waxed paper before placing them into the basket.

Turning to the fridge, she grabbed a carton of strawberries and blueberries. She turned towards the sink as she kicked the fridge door closed. Moving to the sink she opened the containers she turned the water on and rinsed the berries off. Letting them drain and transferring them to a container and snapping the lid on.

Arms wrapped around her waist as she jumped as Lu moved his lips over her cheek.

"I am sorry about yesterday." He whispered into her ear, Lola shivered as his warm breath fanned over her ear and neck.

"It's okay, I just-" She paused, trying to sort through her words. "I was scared for you. It felt strange in that bar and I was worried-"

He cut off her babbling, laying a kiss on her bare shoulder. He slipped the strap of her tank top down. Tracing a freckle with his tongue. His time with Merrow had woken something in him, and he longed to share it with Lola.

"You need not worry about me, Lola." He whispered as he rested his head on her shoulder.

"I know, but things are not the same as you're used to."

"Like the werewolves and the vampire at the bar?"

"What?" Lola asked as she spun in the loose circle of his arms to look up at him. "Werewolves and vampires?"

"Yes, that's what those creatures were."

"They're not real. Is that why-"

"They are. Did it feel like your skin was crawling, like you weren't safe? Like you wanted to run away?"

Lola nodded her head as he brought his hands up, cupping her cheeks.

"That's good." His green eyes flitted over hers before they moved down to her lips. "I missed waking up with you."

Lola's cheeks flushed as she thought about waking up with Lu. How her body had clenched up on his fingers and she felt the wetness start to pool at her core.

She pushed forward, wrapping her hands in the front of his shirt as she pressed her lips to his. He gave a low moan in the back of his throat as their lips moved together. His hand trailing down to the back of her neck to hold her close as he pinned her against the kitchen counter. His other hand moving to her thigh to lift her leg to his hip.

A low chuckle pulled them from their kiss, and Lu rested his forehead against Lola's with a sigh of frustration.

Turning his head, he shot a glare at Bodach as the man leaned against the door frame. The bulk of his body blocking the opening.

"Seems you two are having fun." He said with a slow smirk.

"We were." Lola said as she rested her hands on Lu's chest.

His heart did a strange clenching feeling at the fact that Lola wasn't pushing him away to go to Bodach. He caressed the thin strip of flesh over her hip that wasn't covered by her shirt. Smiling when she shivered at his touch.

"You don't have to stop on my account. Watching is more of Puca's thing, but I can enjoy the pretty picture you two make." He said with a chuckle.

Lola's eyes traveled down to his trim waist. She could see exactly how much he was enjoying watching the two of them.

Turning back to Lu, her eyes meeting his as she raised an eyebrow in a silent question. He dipped his head and she leaned closer. Pressing her lips against his jaw and tracing the skin with her teeth and tongue.

Her hands moving lower to lift his shirt up as she traced her fingers over his toned abdomen.

Lu didn't know how to respond as this little minx teased and tortured him. He didn't know how he felt about Bodach watching him. In all honesty, he didn't always see eye to eye with the other fae man.

Lola's fingers traveled higher up his shirt, scratching her

blunt nails over his nipples, and he shook. How could she make him feel this way?

He had the feeling that he was slowly becoming addicted to her. Grabbing her wrist, he leaned forward, pressing his lips to hers. His tongue thrusting into her mouth as she let out a whimper. His cock pressed against her and he rocked his hips as he let go of her wrist to tangle his hands in her hair.

"Seems he does have some spirit left in him." Bodach chuckled as he turned back to the living room. He was glad that Lola had woken before Puca. Given how the man was prone to fighting or fucking in the early hours.

Although Bodach wasn't opposed to either of those options. He could only imagine what it would feel like to have Lola pinned between them as they both fucked her the way that she deserved to be taken.

He moved to the windows, pulling back the curtains and letting the light spill into the room as Merrow came out of the bathroom.

"I'd give them a moment." Bodach said as he sat down on the foldout bed.

"But I'm hungry." Merrow said with a pout.

"She and Lu are making up after yesterday." Bodach smirked as he looked over at the other man.

"They are, are they?" He asked as he stepped closer towards the kitchen.

"Merrow." Puca said as he rolled over. "Let them be."

"Fine, spoil all my fun."

* * *

Standing beside Lola's jeep, Puca looked over at Merrow with a raised eyebrow. This had to be a trick.

"Aye, you've got to get in." Merrow said with a chuckle as he opened the door and slipped inside.

"If you say so."

"I do," Merrow said as he climbed into the back seat. Leaning forward, he smiled at his lover, "Just get in."

"I will wait." Puca said, pressing his lips together as he rested his hand on the door.

"Lola's coming down." Lu said as he slipped past Puca and sat beside Merrow. His cheeks glowing with pinpricks of warmth as the other man rested his hand on his thigh.

"Really?" Puca asked, his lips twitching into a smile as he looked at Merrow and Lu.

"Aye." Merrow said with a chuckle, watching the blush spread over Lu's cheeks. Puca was glad that the two men had reconnected. It would good for both of them.

"Just one happy family?" Bodach grumbled as he came down the steps. Basket tucked under one arm and a quilt in the other.

Frowning, he looked at the others and then backed up to look at the jeep.

"An aon smuaintean, a charaid."

"I guess you should get in." Puca said as he stepped back. Bodach looked from him to Merrow one last time.

"I don't know how we shall all fit."

"You'll fit just fine, it'll be cramped. What are you guys waiting for?" Lola asked as she breezed past them. She opened the driver's side door and slipped inside. Closing the door as she put the keys into the ignition. She looked over at Puca and Bodach with a raised eyebrow. "Would you rather stay home?"

"Nay," Bodach said before passing the wicker basket to Puca

and climbing into the back seat. His lip snarling as he folded himself into the tight space in between Lu and Merrow. Puca gulped as Lola smiled at him.

"Okay." He said, sliding into the seat and closing the door before he looked at Lola. A nervous smile on his lips as he clutched the picnic basket closer.

"You've got to buckle the belt." Merrow said cheerfully, making Puca frown. As he looked for the belt that the merman spoke of.

With a smile, Lola leaned over, placing her hand on his thigh as she grabbed the seatbelt and dragged it over. Clicking into place.

"Now, we're ready." She said, before leaning back into her seat and buckling her own belt. She turned the radio on as she rolled the windows down and pulled out of the parking spot.

Lola navigated the quiet highway with ease, guiding the jeep towards one of her favorite walking trails. The drive didn't take long. Soon she pulled the jeep into the parking lot and turned off the car.

"We're here." She chimed, looking over at Puca with a smile.

"Where is here?" Bodach asked as he leaned forward, looking out the front window. His face was paler than normal.

"It's a walking trail, I want to take you guys on a date." Lola said, her cheeks heating up with a blush as she thought about what she'd like to happen after the date. Or during, her fingers gripped the steering wheel tighter as her heart beat quicker.

Merrow leaned forward and pressed the button on the seatbelt. Making Puca jump and try to scramble out the open window.

"Merrow." Lola chided as she rested her hand on Puca's

forearm.

"Just a bit of fun." He said, a smirk playing across his lips as he winked at Lola.

Frowning, she got out of the car. This wasn't how she had wanted to start things. With Puca being afraid. She walked around to the passenger side. Opening the door and Puca uncurled his legs, moving to stand beside her.

"Was it really that bad?" She asked, worrying her lower lip.

"It was, it was faster than I'm used to moving. Unless I shift." He said, clutching the basket to his chest.

"Huh?" Lola asked as she tucked a strand of hair behind her ear.

"I'm a trickster fae, go halainn."

"So, like how Annwn was able to look old and young?" Lola asked.

"I have an animal form, I'm not the same as the wolves you met. I lure travelers on adventures." Puca said with a chuckle as he tried to force himself to relax.

"He's a horse, well sometimes he is." Lu said as he got out through the driver's side. Looking up into the sky, he smiled and stretched his arms. "It wasn't that bad."

"Says you." Bodach grumbled, pushing the other man out of his way.

Lola bit her lip, looking at both Bodach and Puca. She didn't like that neither of them had liked the drive over. She watched as both men stalked towards the trails.

"Don't mind them, ghra." Merrow said as he looped an arm around her shoulders, planting a kiss on her cheek. "They'll get over it."

"Are you sure?" She asked, looking up at Merrow as Lu came over to them.

"Aye, let them pout for a bit. They'll be fine." Lu said as he linked his fingers with hers. Pulling her towards the trails. "You wanted to show us your favorite place?"

"I did, I hope you guys like it." Lola said as they made their way into the wooded area. The paved concrete felt odd to Merrow as he stepped into the treeline.

"Is it all like this?"

"What do you mean?" Lola asked as they walked at a comfortable pace.

"The ground?" Merrow said, "It seems like everywhere we go it's smooth."

"The beach wasn't like this." Lola answered.

"I know, but it seems like man has made the woods his own." Merrow said as he let his arm slip from around Lola's shoulders.

"I guess it does feel that way, but we won't be staying on the trail for long." Lola replied. "I wonder where Puca and Bodach went."

"They'll find us." Lu said as Lola pulled him along the trail, his thumb brushing over her knuckles.

"They won't get lost, looking for us?"

"Nay, both of them are excellent trackers." Merrow said as he Lola stepped off the trail, guiding them further into the trees.

"Only if they can keep up." Letting her hand slip from Lu's she raced forward with a giggle. Her hair streaming behind her.

"I think our girl wants to play." Lu said, looking back at Merrow.

"As our lady wished." Merrow said with a chuckle before he darted off after her.

Lu smiled as he watched Merrow. Knowing that seeing his sister had helped settle things between them.

Merrow let out a chuckle as he leaped over a fallen tree branch. His eyes locked on Lola as she looked over her shoulder at him. He was close to catching her.

His lips twisted into a smile as he saw Lu dash forward from the corner of his eye and he pushed himself faster, knowing it was useless.

You wouldn't know it by looking at the leprechaun, but he was just as fast. If not faster than the others. Lola let out a peel of breathless laughter as Lu wrapped his arms around her middle. Spinning her around as he caught her.

Merrow slowed his pace, watching his two lovers. He could hear Puca and Bodach as the two men walked towards him.

Lu sat Lola's feet back onto the soft earth as he held her close. Merrow couldn't hear the softly spoken words, but he could see the tenderness in the way that Lola and Lu looked at each other.

"Better?" Merrow asked as he heard a twig snap behind him.

"Aye, leannan." Puca asked as he watched Lola push up on her toes. Rewarding Lu with another kiss, he loved how affectionate she was. How freely she gave herself to them.

"Good," Merrow said, reaching over and taking the basket from Puca. Looking over towards Bodach, "Is she okay to test?"

"Merrow." The other man tilted his head, looking at the merman as he rolled his eyes.

"We will need to know."

"Aye, but not today." Puca said as he started walking towards Lola and Lu.

"If not today, then when?" Merrow asked with a sigh.

"Soon." Bodach smirked as he moved forward, Merrow watched as he seemed to blend into shadows of the surrounding trees.

"No, wait. That's not an answer." Merrow frowned as he watched Lola take off again, making his way towards his friend. He watched Lu as he stood, watching Lola. "Enjoying yourself?"

"Aye," Lu said, looking over at his shoulder at the other man. His cheeks flushed and his lips swollen. Stepping closer, Merrow smirked as he hooked his fingers into Lu's belt loop. Pulling him closer so he could press his lips against the other man's.

Merrow let out a moan, the taste of Lu and Lola mixing together. Lu pulled back, his eyes meeting the other mans.

"She's getting away."

"The others will catch her. Plenty of time for me to steal another kiss." Merrow said with a smirk as he pecked the others man's lips before heading in the direction of Lola's giggles.

* * *

Puca let loose a howl of triumph as he spun Lola around. Her back pinned against the tree as he caged her in. His eyes moved to her heaving breasts as she sucked in great gulps of air.

"I've caught you." He growled. Leaning closer, his hips pressing against her's as he brought his hand up to trace her jawline with his fingertips.

"So you did." Lola smirked up at him as she pressed her body against his, "Now what are you going to do, now that you have me?"

Puca's lips twitched into a dark smile as he dragged his fingers lower, down her neck, into the valley between her breasts. His eyes glued to her lips as she bit them.

Lola batted her long eyelashes up at him and he let out a groan.

"Something wrong?" Lola asked as she wrapped her arms around his waist, an innocent expression painted on her face.

"You have no idea what you do to me, do you, my love?" His fingers tangled in her hair as he held her in place.

"What do you mean?" Lola asked. Her breath coming in short pants that had nothing to do with their earlier game of cat and mouse.

"You test me, more than anyone I've ever known." He said as he leaned down, kissing her forehead.

"I do?" Lola asked as she curled her fingers into his hair.

"Mmm hmm," He said as he clacked his teeth together in front of her nose. "I could eat you all up."

Lola gasped at his words, knowing exactly what he meant as she tangled her fingers into his hair. She pulled him closer to her, pressing her lips to his as she savored the sound he made in the back of his throat.

Looking up at him as she pulled back to catch her breath, Lola bit her lower lip. "We could do that too."

"What's that?" Puca asked, his voice low and seductive as he brushed his thumb under her ear.

"The umm, eating me up thing." Lola answered with a blush, thinking about what had happened between them in the shower.

"Naughty little thing, aren't you?" He said, giving her another kiss, his tongue moving against hers.

"Not giving anyone else the chance to catch her?" Bodach

chided as he seemed to bleed out from the shadows.

"Plenty of time left." Puca grumbled, not wanting his reward to be cut short so soon.

"I'd suggest you run." Bodach said as he stalked closer. Puca stepped away with a sigh.

Lola's heart thudded in her chest as she watched the way he prowled closer to her. Her feet rooted to the spot as he stopped, keeping her just out of reach.

"You don't think you'll need a head start?" He asked with a smile that promised things that made things low in the pit of her stomach tighten.

"I don't know that I want to run away from you."

"What if I want to chase you?" Bodach asked. "It's half the fun."

"Are you sure the fun isn't in being caught?" Lola asked, shivering as a cool breeze ruffled her hair.

"Why don't we find out?"

Lola turned, darting further into the forest. Running from the others had felt like a buildup. Something about the way that Bodach looked at her. The way he spoke to her made her realize there was more to the game that they were playing than she realized.

Lola moved over a fallen tree trunk, her hand coming to rest on the damp bark as she launched herself over it. Her breathing was loud in her ears as she pressed on.

Dodging low hanging limbs and tree roots, she felt lighter than she had in so long.

"Lola." Her name whispered in her ear, startled her and she lost her footing, crashing into the ground.

"Lola."

She snapped her head to the side as she tried to find the

voice. It whispered again and she felt a thrill of fear shoot up her spine.

Pushing up onto her scrapped knees, Lola looked around as she moved to stand. "Bodach?"

"Lola..." The voice whispered again, and Lola felt like the air was being sucked out of her lungs as the colors seemed to bleed from around her.

"Bodach!" Lola gasped out, feeling panic rise within her as she stumbled forward.

Out of the corner of her eye, she saw movement and turned. Barely missing the thing that darted behind a tree as it whispered her name again.

"Lola."

"Who are you?" Lola asked as she backed up, trying to figure out where the person was that was just out of the line of her sight.

"I am many things, girl." The voice whispered, seeming to come from many directions at once.

"Lola." A familiar voice said, pulling her attention away from the whispering voice. "Not enough time..." Lola's eyes darted about the trees as she turned around trying to find the source.

* * *

"Lola, Lola." Merrow said from outside the ring.

"Come on, acushla." Bodach whispered as he stood outside of the fairy circle. His heart clenching in his chest as Lola looked wildly around her. Eyes unseeing them as she called out his name.

"Of course, she calls for you." Merrow said with a frown as

he walked around the circle.

"I was the closest to catching her." Bodach said before he called her name once more. His heart twisting in his chest as she called his name again.

"What has happened?" Puca asked as he walked up to the others.

"She is trapped." Merrow said, moving to stand beside his lover.

"But why?" Puca asked. The magics that surrounded the circle felt familiar, like the first day of fall or the first rays of dawn's light on your face.

Puca looked towards Lu and the other man nodded his head, recognizing the feelings of Holy Court.

"She's being tested and tried." Lu whispered as he stepped closer to the circle. Lola was close enough for him to touch, and he wanted to bring his hand up. To touch her skin, quiet her worries. He knew it was useless though, as long as she was trapped in the fairies ring. "Lola," he whispered, his face dropping as she called out his name, her hair whipping about her shoulders as she spun around towards a sound that only she could hear.

"What do we do?" Merrow asked.

"We could wait until the enchantment is done?" Puca said, even knowing as he spoke that that was not an option.

"Nay," Bodach said as he walked closer to Puca. "We can pull it down."

"We can not," Merrow grumbled, crossing his arms.

"We've done it before."

"It didn't work in the box." Lu chimed in, remembering all of their failed attempts to escape their prison.

"It's different now." Puca said, his golden eyes meeting

Bodach's red ones.

"It's Lola." He said with a nod.

"It won't hurt her?" Merrow asked as they dropped the picnic basket and the quilt.

"I wouldn't risk it and neither would Puca." Bodach said as he held his hand out to the merman "Remember that time with the banshee?"

"We broke her wailing."

"Aye." Puca said as he linked hands with the others. "Hopefully, this hurts less."

"I hope so as well. It took weeks for my ears to heal." Merrow said. He could feel the ring in front of them. Feel the old magic lingering in the air. "Bodach, you are up."

"Aye." he said, as he watched the air shimmering with sparks of light. Pressing his lips together, Bodach focused on the swirls that it created in the air. Following at it as he had with the box in Lola's room.

"Are you locked in?"

"Aye." Bodach said, feeling the cold sweat beaded up on his forehead. He sucked in a deep, shuddering breath.

"Lu." Puca said.

"Aye, I've got it." Lu said. He could feel the tendrils of trickery floating around him. Snatching one from the air, he let out a growl as he tugged and tested the strand.

Merrow glanced over at Puca, "Are we not needed."

"Nay, my friend. Just let them pull from your strength. Let Lola pull from it when she's able to, we do not know what is in there with her."

"I do." Lu said, pressing his lips together as he worked on the knot that the others couldn't see.

"We can't be sure." Puca said, trying to deny the truth.

"If the Unseelie are interested in her, then so is the other side." Merrow said. Feeling the hot stinging in his hands as his companions pulled what they needed from him.

"You are right." Bodach said through gritted teeth, "I can feel her in there."

"Her?"

"Yes, I can feel it the same as before." Bodach said, his gaze traveling along the circle as mushrooms started to spring from the ground. Small lights started to flicker in the air as he neared the end, trying not to pull too much magic from the others as they worked. He didn't know if they would need it when the circle fell and he'd rather be safe than sorry.

"Lola," Puca whimpered. He watched the way her eyes filled with terror. How her body shook. It was clear that whatever she was going through was terrifying her. His eyes were glued to her as he watched her fall to her knees. Her hair hiding her face as her shoulders shook.

* * *

It was dark, so incredibly dark. The type of dark that you couldn't even see your hand in front of your face. The voice was the only thing tethering her to reality.

At this point, Lola didn't even know if this was real. Her fear was.

"Great danger..." The voice whispered across her skin, closer this time, and she fell to her knees. It didn't matter where she ran. Or how loud she called out for her lovers. She was alone and it was dark.

She felt small and helpless, the memory of being trapped in the darkness as a child overcoming her. She let out a hiccupping sob. Her shoulders shaking as she tried to hold herself together.

The teasing whisper was coming again, and she brought her hands up to her ears. Trying to block out the sound, it was like it reverberated through her as she curled up on the ground.

"Be careful of the choices you will make."

"I don't understand, please let me go." Lola said with a sob, closing her eyes. Trying to think of anything but the overwhelming darkness that surrounded her. "Please." She pleaded again.

"Our time draws to a close as they figure out my enchantment. Think about the things I've said to you." It said, the sound of the disjointed whispers whooshing about her.

Arms wrapped around her and pulled her against a firm chest, and she let out a choked sob. Hands moved through her hair, pushing it away from her face, but Lola was afraid to open her eyes.

What if it was still just as dark as it had been before? What if this was some type of trick?

"Lola." Puca's voice filled her ears as he stroked her back, "You are safe, go halainn."

"Open your eyes, my darling." Shaking her head at Bodach's words. She wrapped her hands in Puca's shirt, burying her face in the soft material.

"Lola, I promise you it's okay." Merrow said and she felt a hand touch her calf, giving the muscle a gentle squeeze.

Cracking open an eye. Her body still shaking, the faint traces of light filtering in from her peripheral view.

"What happened?" Lu asked as he trailed his fingers through her hair. His voice was low as he tried to soothe her.

"It was dark and there was a voice. Not one, but many. I

couldn't get away." Lola bit out, trying to pull herself together. "It didn't matter how much I called for you guys. I couldn't get to y'all."

"It's okay, you are safe." Puca said as he brought his hand up to her face, rubbing her tears away with his thumb.

Chapter Twenty-One

*L*ola sat under the quilt that Bodach had wrapped around her shoulders. She couldn't seem to get warm. No matter how much Lu and Bodach pushed themselves against her.

Merrow and Puca sat in front of her, matching worried looks on their handsome faces.

"You think it was her?" Bodach asked.

Lola could feel the rumble of his body through the blanket. She wasn't sure who they were talking about. The voice had sounded neither male nor female. She could still feel the magic moving over her skin.

"I don't know who else it could have been." Puca said, "It felt like her, ask Lu. I know he could feel it."

"It did." Lu agreed, nodding his head slowly. He tightened his arm around Lola, not liking that he and the others hadn't been able to protect her in the first place. Lu couldn't help but blame himself, if they had just been closer to her.

"I don't understand, who was it?" Lola asked as she looked

at the men around her. Not liking the way they wouldn't give her a name. Not liking the way they were talking about her like she wasn't there.

"It was our, the seelie Queen." Bodach said, catching himself on his words. He could no longer say that she was their queen. She may govern the Holy Court, but that didn't mean that they would serve her as they had in the past.

Not after she had attacked one of theirs.

Scrubbing her face with her palms, Lola sucked in a deep breath. She knew that she couldn't fester on the fear that she was feeling. That her lovers would protect her the best way that they could.

"So if Erik is the Unseelie, then who is the queen? Does that make him like a bad guy?" She asked, wishing that she had gotten the chance to look up what these terms meant instead of walking blindly into this conversation.

"Sort of," Merrow said as he leaned back into the soft grass looking up into the clouds, "We are governed by two courts, the Seelie and the Unseelie. Good, bad, the lines blur with the fae. It's more like day and night."

"I, we don't know if Erik, who Erik is exactly." Puca grumbled as he glanced over at Merrow, lifting an eyebrow at him.

"Why would it make a difference who he is?" Lola asked, rubbing her hands together, Lu pulled her closer and pressed a kiss to her temple.

"How about we get some food in you and we'll talk more about this when we get home?" Merrow said, sitting up and reaching for the picnic basket.

"I don't think I can eat." Lola grimaced. She wasn't hungry, she felt like she had run a marathon and her body ached.

"It'll make you feel better." Merrow said as he started passing out sandwiches. "You went through all of this trouble for us. Let's not let her spoil this date you've planned."

Slowly, Lola nodded her head and let out a sigh as she realized that Merrow wasn't going to let up. His fingers brushed against her as she accepted the sandwich and she felt a warmth shoot through her.

It was such a strange feeling to feel after the fear that she had felt. She bit the inside of her cheek as she settled back against Bodach's chest. His cheek brushed against the top of her head and the warm feeling intensified.

If she didn't know any better, she would say it was love. It was much too soon to be feeling that even if she knew it was how she felt. Earlier, had made those feelings clear.

She loved four men, four fae men. Lola didn't know what that would mean for the future, but she couldn't help but hope that it was good things.

"Maybe she is coming around to try to take us home?" Lu said as he looked down at the food in his hand.

Looking over at him, it felt like her heart stopped beating. She'd never thought of them leaving her. "Take you home?" She asked as she picked at the crust of her sandwich.

"Maybe. Our realm differs greatly from yours." Puca said before taking a bit, chewing it thoughtfully.

"Those that have served their time are often granted the choice to come home. It comes with a price." Bodach said.

"It would be good to go home." Lu muttered and Lola felt her heart drop at his words. She hadn't realized that they may not choose to stay with her. Hadn't realized that they weren't from this realm, that they would have a choice to go somewhere that she could not.

Yes, she knew they were fae. Finding out that they had their own realm was a shock to her. She took a bit of her sandwich, peeking up to look at the men as they chatted around her.

Relaxed and carefree as they spoke of Lu's parents. Bodach's clan and Puca's home, Merrow was the only one not talking as he sat studying Lola.

He smiled as she caught him watching her, and Lola felt better. She watched as he pulled out a container of fresh berries and popped the lid open.

"Come here," He said, biting his lower lip and crooking his finger at her. Lola moved to stand, letting the quilt fall from her shoulders as she walked to sit beside Merrow.

He picked up a strawberry, taking a small bite out of the berry. Juice clinging to his lips as he brought the fruit to her lips,

Lola opened her mouth and he pulled it back, "No." He chided and Lola closed her mouth, looking up at him. "Just wait, ghra."

Dragging the berry over her lower lip, painting her flesh with its juices. Merrow leaned closer before sucking her lower lip between his teeth with a moan.

Lola let out a whimper. Letting herself fall into Merrow and the way that he was making her feel as he let go of her lower lip. Moving his lips against hers with a kiss that said so much.

Merrow slid his tongue against Lola's trying to take away the worry he had seen in her eyes earlier. He hadn't brought up the things that he missed from their realm because she was everything he needed.

Yes, seeing his sister had made him feel whole. He was glad that she was in the mortal realm, but all he needed was this with Lola. He cared for the others, loved them in fact, but Lola was his air.

No, not his air. That was Puca.

Lola was his ocean.

It was hard for him to think of a time when she hadn't been with them. Without even knowing that he was searching for someone like her. Lola completed him in so many ways.

He tried to show her that with his kiss. Her breathy moan made him smile as he leaned back, feeding her the strawberry that he had used to paint her lips. She grabbed his wrist, lapping at his fingertips that were coated with juice.

Merrow let out a groan. She was going to be the death of him.

Puca watched Merrow and Lola kiss. He couldn't help but think that the two of them fit together to make such a pretty sight. The clash of Merrow's white blonde hair and Lola's brightly colored locks.

He watched as Merrow pulled back to feed her another berry. Pulling the wax paper wrapped sandwich from her hands. Sitting it off to the side. Grinning as she nipped at Merrow's fingers, making the merman growl low in the back of his throat.

Puca liked the way that she challenged them. He ran his hand up Merrow's thigh as the other man brought his hand to the back of Lola's neck. Pulling her to him for another kiss. Her fingers grazed Puca's as she rested a hand on Merrow's thigh, trying to balance herself.

His lips twitched into a smile as she moved her fingers to weave them with her own as Merrow pulled her into his lap. Puca couldn't help but kiss her fingers, trailing them up to the inside of her wrist.

"Merrow," she panted, pulling back to look at him as Puca

ran his thumb over her knuckles.

"Lola," Merrow smirked as he moved his hand so he could drag his thumb along her collarbone.

"We're in the woods."

"So we are." He smirked before kissing her again.

Puca smiled as he resumed mapping out her flesh with his lips. He glanced over at Lu and Bodach as they sat, red eyes watching Lola. Lu pushed off of the ground to come closer to them.

He crouched down behind her, pushing her hair away from the other side of her neck. Smirking as she shivered, her low moan trapped by Merrow's lips as he teased her with gentle love bites.

Leaning back, Merrow grabbed a plump blueberry, biting it in half and painting it across Lola's lips. "Give Puca a kiss, darling."

Lola blushed as she looked over at Puca. His teeth sank into his bottom lip as she leaned closer to him. Pulling him closer as he kissed the inside of her wrist. His lips moving to the crook of her elbow.

Merrow's hard length pressed against her center and she bit her lower lip. Slowly rocking her hips as Puca dragged his lips up a path to her lips. His tongue snaking out to catch the juice from the berry, making Lola close her eyes as she tried to calm her racing heart.

"Mmmm, my favorite, sweet, juicy Lola." He moaned as he brought his hand up to stroke her cheek.

"Can I have a taste?" Merrow asked with a smirk, and Puca let out a chuckle that did things to Lola's libido that she very much liked.

"I think you've had a taste already." Lola whispered and

Chapter Twenty-One

Merrow's smile deepened.

"I meant from Puca."

Lola's cheeks flamed as she watched Merrow pop a berry into his mouth. He leaned closer to Puca, a teasing light shining in his eyes.

"If you insist." Puca smirked before he moved in, devouring the other man's lips with his own.

Lola gasped as Merrow thrust his hips up, rubbing his cock against her. The friction making her shake as arousal pounded through her. Lu chuckled against her neck, his lips moving along the heated flesh as his hands moved to her hips.

"It's a lovely thing to watch, isn't it?"

"Yes," Lola hissed out as he moved her hips faster. His fingers flexing into her as he worried her earlobe with his teeth.

"I know something I'd like to watch more." Bodach said, and Lola jolted. She didn't know how she could have forgotten that he was watching them, but she had.

"What's that?" Lu asked, his hot breath fanning over her ear as he released the tender lobe. His tongue tracing along the delicate shell as Lola let out a sob.

"Lola finding her release." Bodach said as he moved behind Merrow and Puca, his eyes meeting hers.

"Mmmm, one of my favorite activities." Lu purred into her ear and Lola let out a breathless moan. "Where do you want her?"

"Strip your clothing." Bodach ordered in a tone that made things tighten low in the pit of her stomach. Lu gave her neck one last peck before he moved to stand. Shedding his clothing, Lola felt something rise within her. Almost as if she were waking up.

"I don't-" Merrow's thumb moved over the side of her throat

223

as he pulled away from Puca. His lips pressing against hers as he cut off her words.

Lola tangled her hands in the front of his shirt as he pulled her closer. Wrapping her legs around his waist as he moved onto his knees. Lola let out a sound in the back of her throat.

"He won't let you fall, my love." Puca said with a chuckle as he Merrow laid her onto her back in the soft grass,

"Merrow, I want you to undress her." Bodach said, his tone firm as the other man pulled back to roll his eyes.

"Always so bossy." Merrow grumbled as he locked eyes with Lola. His fingers moving to the hem of her shirt as he pulled it over her head. Fingers moved down her rib cage, lower to her stomach.

Her breath caught in her throat as his fingers skimmed down her abdomen to the front of her shorts. She wanted to tell them to stop, but the words were stuck in her throat.

"Lola?" Merrow asked as he moved to the button, and she shook herself from her stupor.

"We need to stop. I, I don't want to hurt any of you." She whispered and looked back at Bodach.

"You won't, I'll stop you. Feed you if it gets to that point." Bodach said, his tone soft. Much different from the one he normally took in the bedroom.

Lola nodded her head as she looked back at Merrow, and he leaned down, pressing his lips to hers. His fingers making quick work of the buttons on her shorts. Leaning back, he pulled them down along with her panties.

Puca snagged a berry from the container as he laid down beside Lola. Sucking her nipple into his mouth. Teasing the bud into a tight peak before pulling back and taking a bit of the berry.

It's juice trickling down his chin as he pulled it from his mouth and moved to paint her nipples with its juice. Before repeating the action again.

"Lu, you may join them." Bodach said, smiling as Merrow let out a sound of frustration.

Merrow sat back on his heels, watching as Lola withered on the ground. Puca teased her nipples into taunt peaks and he smirked. Loving the sounds she was making, loving the way that his lover was enjoying her.

"Merrow." Bodach said, pulling the man from his study of Lola and Puca.

"Aye." Merrow said as he moved to rest at Lola's other side. Pulling his shirt off as he watched Lu take his place between Lola's legs.

"Why don't you paint our girl's lips, Merrow." Bodach's words moved over his skin and he bit his lower lip. Hating that he enjoyed him taking over almost as much as he enjoyed it when Puca did.

He leaned over Lola, kissing her skin as Puca handed him an overly ripe strawberry. Tracing it along her lips, he chuckled as she let out a soft sob as Lu settled between her thighs. Planting kisses on her inner thighs.

"Only time I'll ever tell you this, but take a bite, ghra." Merrow said, placing the fruit between her parted lips. Lola did as he told her too, her thighs shaking as Lu got closer to her throbbing center. His feather-light kisses were making it hard to think of anything but wanting him closer.

Merrow pulled the fruit back, moving to trace it along her lips when Bodach's voice stopped him. "Not those lips."

"But-" Lola gasped out as Merrow quirked up an eyebrow, Lips twisting up into a smirk that made her heart flutter.

"Do you want us to stop?" Merrow asked as he trailed the berry lower. Leaving a red stain on her skin that he moved forward to lap up. His eyes locked with hers as Puca chased her nipple around his mouth.

"N, no." Lola stuttered, watching as he traced the berry over her nipple. Then lower still as he nodded his head. Swooping down to take the sensitive bud in his mouth as he trailed the strawberry to her nether lips. Painting her throbbing sex with its juices.

"Now taste her." Bodach said, the sound of him undoing his pants was loud in the quiet forest. The clank of his metal belt hitting the button on his jeans and his zipper made Lola whimper.

She couldn't help the sound that left her mouth as Lu's tongue moved about her vulva. Cleaning the strawberry off of her skin as he lapped at her skin with a groan of his own as he savored her.

Pure and unfiltered as the scent of her cunt surrounded him. He worked his tongue into her hot slit, moaning at the rush of her slick arousal coating hitting his tastebuds. Closing his eyes, he took his time, Lapping at her, relishing in every gasp and moan she let out. His own cock twitching at the sound, he dragged his hand down to gripping himself.

Opening his eyes, peering up her body, watching as she panted out his name. No, not just his name. Their names slipping from her lips, like a mantra or a prayer to the long-forgotten gods of old.

In that moment Lu decided that there was no other place he'd rather be than between her thighs as he moved his tongue over her swollen clit. Paying special attention to the sensitive bundle of nerves as he glanced over at Puca and Merrow.

Both men still teasing her breasts with their hands and mouths. Lu could hear Bodach panting harshly behind him as he worked his cock with his fist.

"I want you to take her." He said through clenched teeth and Lu smiled against her cum slick flesh. Tasting her had been amazing and his cock bobbed against his stomach as he moved up her body.

Trying to keep himself from pouncing on her, he didn't want it to be over before it really began.

Lola panted as she tried to catch her breath. Lu's eyes locked with hers, silently asking her a question, and she gave a brief nod. She could see the fight that he was having within himself. She was glad the other two men were leaning back and letting her have this moment with him.

Their sweet torment of her breast had been comparable to heaven. Two different mouths working her body as Lu lapped at her sex, making her body clench up with her orgasm far quicker than she had been ready for.

Lu was on her, his lips pressed against hers, and she could taste herself on his lips as his tongue thrust into her mouth. She brought shaking hands down to his cock. She would have loved to have taken the time to explore his body as he had done hers, but right now she needed him.

Moving his member over her slick, pulsing heat as she pushed his foreskin back. Lu let out a low groan in the back of his throat as the head of his cock pressed against her entrance.

Lola could hear the sounds of Bodach, Puca, and Merrow. Her focus was on Lu as he slowly pushed himself inside of her pussy, sweat beading on his forehead. She could tell that he was trying to be gentle with her, but that wasn't what she wanted. What she needed.

Hooking her ankles around his waist, she drove him deeper, her lips leaving his to pant his name out. As he shook above her, his teeth gritted his eyes screwed shut.

"Lu, look at me." Lola whispered. He opened his eyes and Lola could see a mix of emotions flashing within his green depths. She brought her hand up to his cheek. "Don't hold back with me. I can take it."

"Lola," he choked out her name as she rolled her hips up, forcing him deeper. "Lola."

Pulling back slightly, he thrust into her. Pace quick with his need as he tangled his hands in her hair. Sealing his lips to hers, drowning out the sounds of their lovemaking as their bodies slapped together.

"By the gods," Lu said, pulling his lips away from hers. Holding her close and rolling them over so she sat astride him. Lola braced her hands against his chest. Rocking her hips faster as his hands trailed down to her hips. Guiding her at the pace they both needed.

Lola panted as her body clenched up around his cock, a keening sob leaving her lips as she twisted her eyes shut. Stars blinking to life behind her eyelids.

Lu didn't stop moving her hips as he worked her up and down on his cock. Her head fell to his chest as she gasped and panted his name. That sound was his undoing as he let out a strangled sob. His fingers digging into her hips as he spilled his cum inside of her.

Lu ran his hands up Lola's back, softly caressing her skin as he tried to catch his breath. His heart raced in his chest and he felt dizzy, the clouds swirling above him.

"Lu?" Lola asked, her voice barely above a whisper as she moved her hands to his sides, listening to his struggle to breathe.

"Yes," Lu gasped out, his chest felt heavy, like he was drowning. "Just give me a minute, my love. I'll be ready to go again. Or you can start and I'll just lay here." He said with a strangled laugh, bucking his hips.

Lola pushed herself back so she could look at Lu's pale face. She couldn't help but wonder if she'd hurt him, even if he was joking around.

"Are you sure you're okay?" She asked, watching as his eyes fluttered closed. His cock still hard inside of her even though he'd just come.

"Could not be better." He whispered as his hands fell to his side.

"Bodach," Lola said, looking up towards the fae man, whose eyes were glued to her as Merrow stroked his cock. She felt Lu go limp beneath her. "Help me."

"Damn e don fho-thalamh. I got distracted." He said, pushing Merrow's hand away from his dick. Bodach scrambled over to them, his hand moving to Lu's neck as he checked his pulse. "It is weak, Puca."

Clapping a hand over her mouth, Lola let out a sob as she scrambled away from them.

"Lola, wait." Bodach said, his tone commanding as he moved behind Lu. Pulling the other man into his lap as Puca came closer to him. Lola moved to her clothing, pulling on her shirt as she watched Puca crouch down beside Lu and Bodach.

"He's going to be okay Lola, I can heal him." He said, looking over to Lola as he grabbed Lu's hand in his own.

Her red eyes met his, and he glanced over at Bodach and then to Merrow. The other man was straightening his clothing as he moved closer to Lola.

"Lola, it will be al-"

"No, it's not." Lola said, cutting Merrow off, "I hurt him, I could have killed him."

"Lola."

"No, don't 'Lola' me." She said, her hair moving about her as she backed up a step from him. She didn't want him to touch her. She didn't want any of them to touch her. She could still feel the desire swirling through her and she didn't want them to get sucked into it.

"She is showing good control." Bodach said as he stroked Lu's hair away from his forehead.

Frowning, Lola looked back at Lu. She needed the focus to be on him. Looking over at the other men as Puca ran his hands over him. A bright light coming from his hands as they met his skin. It was almost blinding in its intensity.

"Puca will take care of him."

"What about the time after that?" Lola asked, her voice small. "Or the next time."

Merrow turned back to her, picking up her shorts as he stepped closer. "You will get your fae side under control."

"You don't know that, Merrow." Lola replied, everything in her wanted to go to him. To let him wrap his arms around her and let him comfort her.

"I do, you are strong Lola." He said holding the shorts out to her with a determined look in his eyes.

"No, I'm not," Lola grumbled as she tugged her shorts on, "I'm not as strong as you and the others think I am."

Looking back to Lu, she worried her lower lip. His cheeks had some color, but he still hadn't opened his eyes. She didn't know how she was going to get this under control, but she knew that she had to find a way.

She couldn't keep hurting them. Closing her eyes, she could still picture the way that Merrow had looked as he gasped for air at the beach.

How was she supposed to be with them if she couldn't control what would happen?

"Lola, stop worrying." Merrow said as he watched Lu let out a cough. Water spurting from his mouth and into the air as he took a deep breath, "We fae men can handle more than you give us credit for."

Lola bit the inside of her cheek. How could he tell her to stop worrying? This was their lives. She picked at the hem of her shirt as she watched Bodach lean over and grab the quilt before wrapping it around Lu's trembling form.

She had done this, she'd hurt her sweet Lu. Shoving her hands into her pockets, she told herself that she wouldn't let this happen again. She'd find a way to get in contact with the queen and send them home. At least there she knew that they'd be safe from her.

Because if they stayed here. There was no way that she would be able to stay away from them.

Shoving her feet into her shoes, she moved closer to the men sitting on the ground. Lola knew that she would have to tell them goodbye. The thought made her heart twist painfully in her chest.

She'd never felt more like she belonged than in her time with them. Lola knew she had a long road ahead of her to get the fae home. Then she could mourn for them. There was no way she was willing to risk their lives for her own pleasure.

"Lola," Lu said, a soft smile on his face. She felt the guilt flood through her as she stayed out of arm's reach of them.

It was easier to think if they weren't touching her, if she

weren't touching them. She was glad they had each other, that they were all so close.

That was good though, they'd need each other when she ended things and they were back home.

Chapter Twenty-Two

***

*L*ola stepped out of her room, bare feet barely making a sound as she crept down the hallway.

She didn't want to risk waking them. Grabbing her shoes and her purse, she turned the lock and twisted the doorknob, pulling the door open. Slipping into the empty hallway. Shutting the door softly. She prayed that it didn't wake the others. Her heart thudding in her chest as she let out a breath that she hadn't realized she'd been holding.

Resting her forehead against the cool wood of the front door, she took a moment to breathe before slipping on her shoes. Lola walked past the elevator with a longing glance. The entire time she'd lived in the building it had never worked, and she wondered if the handsome, blond landlord would ever get it fixed.

She opened up the door to the stairwell, quickly rushing down the steps. Once she was outside, she turned her face up to the morning sun and took a deep breath. She could do this. She was strong.

Or at least, that's what she was telling herself.

A part of her wanted to go back up the stairs. To slip back into bed between Lu and Puca, to let them take away these thoughts.

Lola knew that she could not do that. Last night she had dreamed of what had happened with Merrow. Only in her dream, he hadn't woken up. A similar dream of Lu followed, his eyes slipping closed as she worked her body above his. Watching him struggle to breathe as water poured from his lips.

Walking down the sidewalk, she tried to shake the dark thoughts from her head. There was only one person she knew that she could go to about this, she just hoped it wasn't a bad decision.

Picking up her pace as she got closer to Erik's shop, she pulled her hair into a loose bun. Hoping that this wasn't a horrible idea she pushed the door open. The tinkling bells announcing her arrival.

"Lola, it's so good to see you. I was just getting ready to text you." Erik said as he looked up from the front counter, a coffee cup in his hand.

"Erik." Lola said, biting her lip as her eyes moved about the antique store. "I, um, I wanted to talk to you about the Fae."

Sitting his mug down on the glass counter, he looked down before looking back up at Lola. A strange glint in his steel-gray eyes. He dragged a hand over his mouth and down his chin. Biting his lip as his eyes met hers.

"What did you want to know?"

* * *

Puca moved his hand along the cotton sheets. They still held the warmth of Lola's body. He listened to the quiet apartment with a frown as he heard the front door click closed.

Where did his *go halainn* think she was going?

Opening his eyes, he looked at Lu. The other man needed all the rest he could get, so he wouldn't be waking him. Puca rolled off the bed, tugging on his jeans and shirt as he went. His feet barely making a whisper of a sound as he moved down the hallway towards the door.

Grabbing his shoes and slipping them on as he went out the front door. He didn't know where Lola was headed, but he knew he was going to find out. She may not realize it, but he'd always be able to find her.

Exiting the building, he saw the flash of her purple wavy hair as she turned a corner. He jogged a bit behind her, trying to stay out of her sight. He could see from the way she moved her hands together that something was bothering her. He wished she had just woken him to talk about what it was.

Frowning, he watched as she got closer to Erik's store. He had a bad feeling about this. The world around him started to shift and he let out a growl of frustration. He didn't have time for this. Looking at the color fading from the trees and grass around him, he let out a sigh of annoyance. The antique shop turning a muted color as the violet shades of Lola's hair did the same as she stepped into the building.

Puca scanned his surroundings, knowing that as long as he was in this trap he wouldn't be going far.

"Cén scéal?." Puca called out as he circled around, waiting for her to show herself.

"Coinnichidh tu ri do sheann charaid, Puca." The blonde woman stepped out from behind a tree, her curls moving in a breeze that Puca couldn't feel as her autumn eyes studied his.

"Your Majesty," Puca replied. Dipping his head as she moved closer, trying not to get pulled in by her hypnotic gaze.

"You are getting caught up in something you know nothing about. Do you think that she will choose you?" She asked, her lips twisting up into a cruel grin.

"Lola, is ours." Puca said, his fists clenching at his sides as he looked down on the lithe creature in front of him.

"Are you sure?" She asked, running a hand over his chest, "I could send you home. If you will just leave her be."

"Lola is my home." Puca said through clenched teeth, catching her wrist in his grip as she pouted up at him.

"Pity, you were always so much fun." She said, pulling her hand away from his, "I suppose you think that you are going to charge in there and save the girl?"

"That is my plan." Puca said, his hand dropping back to his side as he watched the queen turn away from him.

"I do not think I like that idea. It spoils my plans." She smirked back at him, raising her delicate hand. Bright light enveloped Puca and he let out a scream, trying to move forward. Knowing that he needed to stop her. "You're now part of them."

Knowing that it was too late as he found himself trapped in a cage in a dark room that buzzed with old magic. He moved towards the bars, grabbing them in his fists.

Hissing he pulled back, looking at his scorched flesh. He was trapped in an iron cage and Lola was out there. In far greater danger than he had thought if the queen was against her.

* * *

"I want to know how to send them home." Lola said as she clenched her hands by her sides. She wasn't going to cry. This would help keep them safe. It was what she had to do, she knew this. It didn't make the pain in her heart any easier to deal with.

"Are you sure about that?" Erik asked, a slow smile spreading across his face. She could see the excitement in his sparkling eyes. She frowned, not understanding why he looked like he might start bouncing.

"I am," Lola said, nodding her head. She knew that if she backed out now, there would be no way that she could do this again.

"How did you figure it out?"

"Figure out what?" Lola asked as she unclenched her hands, smoothing over her hips. Watching as Erik moved back towards the kitchen.

"Who, or I should say what I am."

Lola was taken back to all the times she'd watched him make tea for the two of them and it felt oddly intimate.

"Annwn." Lola said as she leaned against the counter watching as he pulled out the kettle and moved to the sink to fill it.

"Really, the host told you?" Erik asked, sitting the kettle on the stove. He turned on the burner before he opened the cabinet, looking through all the boxes of tea before finally picking one.

"Well, not in so many words." Lola said. She wished he'd hurry up. The sooner that she got Lu, Merrow, Bodach, and Puca home. The safer they would be. The quicker she could work on with trying to learn to live without them.

"She doesn't like to involve humans in our business." Erik

chuckled as he stepped away from the tea that he'd fixed. His hip propped against the counter as he waited for the water to boil.

"No, she doesn't." Lola said, remembering her meeting with the fae woman and her words to Merrow.

"But you're not human. What did she tell you about me?"

"That you're the Useelie. I mean, she didn't come out and say it or what it means. Only that you were interested in me." Lola said, looking towards the window as she felt her palms start to sweat and her heart beat faster in her chest.

"Well, that I am. You already know that though." He smirked as he moved closer. Pulling his glasses from his face and sitting them on the counter.

"Erik," Lola said, pressing her hand against his chest. Stopping him from kissing her.

"Yes, Lola." He drawled, studying her lips before his gaze met hers.

"What are you?" Lola's voice was low as she spoke. She wasn't sure how to go about this. "I mean besides the unseelie."

"I thought you would have already figured it out." Erik said as he brought his hand up, pushing a piece of hair that had fallen from her bun out of her eyes. "I'm the King."

"What does that mean?" Lola asked, worrying the inside of her cheek as his fingers moved over her jaw. "And why didn't Puca know, I mean. He's met you before right?"

"Just that, I'm the fae king. I can take many forms, I knew him but he didn't recognize me."

"So you can send them home?"

"For a price." His hand moved lower. Trailing down the side of her neck, and she let out a shiver. This one wasn't a pleasurable touch, even though he meant it to be. It made her afraid of what he was about to say.

"What's the price?" Lola asked, feeling her throat tighten and a cold chill sweep over her.

"You." Erik smirked as breathed the word out.

Lola's lips formed a circle as her eyebrows shot up. She didn't know how to respond, what to say to that. That she would be the price for her lovers to go home.

"What does that mean?"

"Just that. I want you. You would choose me over them. I'd grant them safe passage for your heart." Erik said as his hand moved to the back of Lola's neck.

She couldn't help but wonder if he meant her love or to sacrifice her in some strange fae ritual.

The kettle started to whistle and Lola let out a breath as he let her go. Watching as he moved to the stove, pulling the kettle off and pouring it over the tea ball.

"They would be safe, nothing would happen to them?" Lola asked, needing to make sure.

"You have my word." Erik said as he turned back towards her with the teacup in his hand.

"Why don't we move to the back porch so we can discuss this deal in depth. I'll go grab my coffee and meet you out there."

Lola nodded her head as she moved to the back door and Erik headed into the front of the shop.

Callie stepped into the shop with a smile on her face as the bells rang, and Erik shook his head. He didn't have time for her games.

Freedom was so close right now.

"You have one of them upstairs, waiting for you." She said as she walked closer to him.

"I'll deal with that later," Erik said as he flipped the sign to closed. "I have a feeling that soon you will have a wedding to attend, and I shall be free."

"I don't know about that." Callie said with a smirk as she moved towards the stairs. "It's still early in the game and I don't think anyone is ready for you to be set free."

"Calista, don't interfere." Erik growled, his eyes flashing at her. The outline of his horns peaked through as he tried to get his emotions under control. It wouldn't do to scare Lola away.

"Now, why ever would I do that?" Callie said, as she ran her hand up the stairs bannister. "Don't you like being a guardian.

Erik's answering snarl at her made her let loose a giggle.

"So much fun to tease, dear friend."

* * *

Lola ran her hands over the screen covering the porch and pulled it back with a hiss. Looking down, she frowned at her hands.

Hands that were red and burnt like she'd grabbed a hot stove.

The door opened behind her and she heard Erik move to sit down. The creaking of the wicker furniture loud in the quiet. "I wouldn't touch that if I were you."

"Little too late," Lola said, moving to sit beside him, "I have a question."

"What is it, my sweetling?" Erik asked as he took a sip of his coffee, handing her the cup of tea. Not noticing her wince as she shifted the cup in her hands.

"You have a picture of my mother in your office. Why?"

Lola asked as she pressed her lips together,

"That's easy Lola, I loved her. Like I love you, like I've always loved you."

"What do you mean?" Lola asked as she picked up the teacup. Inhaling the warm, nutty, fragrant steam of the tea. Trying to let it soothe her frayed nerves as she tried to get over the ick-factor that Erik had loved her mother. That he loved her.

"I loved your mother. I know you probably don't remember, but she used to bring you to visit me. It broke my heart that she couldn't love me back. Then I fell for you, as you got older." Erik said as he looked out into the sun-dappled yard before turning to look back at Lola.

Lola shook her head. She couldn't remember exactly when she had met Erik. Just that she had known him for as long as she could remember. Trying to think of a time where he looked different than he did now. In her memories.

He was just a blur. His presence was faceless. Just the vague notion that she had always found him handsome, or that she used to. Now, when she closed her eyes, Lola couldn't help but think of Lu and the way he would smile as he spun her around. Or how Merrow's eyes would twinkle with mischief as he leaned closer to her to steal a kiss. How Bodach would pull her body closer to his so he could pull her into a kiss that would leave her toes curling. Or Puca and the way his hand would snake around her neck as he pulled her closer to him, his intentions clear.

Lola shook her head, trying not to think about what she wanted. What she was giving up. This is what they needed.

"Is that why you look the same as you did in the picture?" She asked, bringing her attention back to Erik.

He nodded, sitting his coffee cup down to cross his legs as

he put his hands in his lap. "You and your mother are a lot alike, I chose this form because it was what she liked. Would you like me to change it?"

"What? Why?"

"I want you to like how I look Lola." Erik said and Lola took a sip of her tea, unsure of how to respond. "We will be spending a lot of time together in the future."

It was too much information to take in. That he had loved her mother. Swirling the tea around her mouth, she gulped it down, finishing it off.

"I like the way you look Erik." Lola said looking away, trying not to let him see the lie on her face. She didn't notice the way his face fell at her words.

"It's okay if you don't love me yet, Lola. We will have all the time in the world for me to make you love me like I love you." Erik said as he moved closer to her, sitting on the edge of his seat.

He took the teacup from Lola's hands, sitting it onto the coffee table. He moved to his knees to crouch in front of Lola, "I will send them to the fae realm if you give me this one thing."

Lola's heart thudded in her chest and she took a deep breath as his thumb stroked over the back of her hand. She knew she couldn't do this, she couldn't give herself to him. There had to be another way.

"Erik, I-"

"You don't have to say it." Erik said, placing his finger over her lips and she felt heat spread across her skin. "I already know what your worried about."

Her eyebrows scrunched together as she tried to shake the feelings that were starting to build up inside of her. Feelings she knew she didn't have towards Erik.

"I know you're worried about hurting me, but I'll show you that you can't."

Lola pulled away from him, pressing her lips together as she looked back over at the teacup. "What did you do?" She asked, panic filling her as she tried to push herself away from the unseelie king.

"I gave you something to help you relax." Erik said, resting his hands on her knees. "I could see that you were tense. Just a tea to help you with your desires."

Pushing his hands away, Lola moved to stand. "I need to get home."

"Lola, I don't think that's a good idea. I can take care of you." Erik said as he rested his hand on her forearm, halting her in her tracks at his soft touch.

"Erik, what are you doing?" Lola asked, trying to pull her arm away as he moved closer. His hand coming up to cup her cheek.

"Lola, I love you." He said, leaning closer. Lola squeezed her eyes closed as she brought her knee up.

Erik let out a huff of air as he felt the wave of nausea sweep over him. Pain radiating from his aching testicles.

Backing up towards the door, Lola didn't dare take her eyes off of her once friend.

"Lola," he growled out as he stood straighter. She turned the doorknob, cursing when she found it locked.

"Erik, please."

"We can do this the easy way, or the hard way." Erik said with a growl, "I could worship you as my queen, or you'll be locked up until you can learn to love me. I won't force you to want me. But you will eventually give in." His eyes were cold as he spoke. Lola couldn't help the fear she felt as her eyes met

243

his gaze. "I couldn't force your mother. It drove her to make a deal with that bitch."

"Erik, I could never love you." Lola said with a sob as the heat spread through her body, her eyes turning red as she looked up at his harsh smile.

"We shall see." He said with a snap of his fingers and they were inside the shop. His fingers digging into her wrist as he pulled her towards a room she hadn't been in before. She could hear someone yelling, feel the sweep of magic over her skin as she took in all the boxes that she now knew held fae creatures.

"Erik, what are you doing? Let me go." Lola said, trying to tug her wrist from his grip. "Please."

"Taking you somewhere where you can rethink your decision." He said. Lola chose that moment to kick the back of his knee. Trying to get him to loosen his grip, she dug her nails into his wrist and pulled her other hand. She had to get away. Her body thrummed with arousal and shame.

"Now sweetling," He said, turning to look back at her as if she had barely touched him. "Don't make me hurt you."

"Erik." Lola sobbed as he jerked her body closer to his.

"My friend has brought you a gift. Be a good girl and I'll let you say your goodbyes." He growled out as sharp horns sprouted around his forehead and Lola bit back a scream.

"Oh, she makes you lose your temper?" A melodic voice said from deeper in the room, and Erik turned with a snarl. "How fun."

"Not now, Callista."

Lola looked at the woman with a frown. She knew her.

Looking past Callie towards the cage-like cell, Lola let out a gasp. "Puca."

Chapter Twenty-Three

P uca caught Lola in his arms as Erik pushed her into the cell. Glaring at the unseelie king and seelie queen as the locked clicked shut.

"He won't be a problem much longer." Erik said as he straightened his shirt, his features returning to normal. Taking a deep breath, he smiled softly at Lola, "Be glad I'm giving you this time. Not many would get it. If you had just agreed with me…" He said, trailing off as he pressed his lips together.

"What a pity." Callie pouted as she eyed the two. "He did have a choice, and he chose to stay with her. She reminds me so much of her mother, that spirit that she has."

"That she does. Why don't you join me for a drink?" Erik said, turning away from them. Callie took a moment to watch the tender way that Puca held Lola in his arms. She bit her lower lip, pressing her hands together as she moved to follow Erik.

Puca looked down at Lola. She was shaking in his arms. Her red eyes glassy and filled with need as she looked up at him.

He pressed his lips together. Leaning down, he breathed her in. Smelling the tea she had been given, he let out a low growl.

"I'm sorry Lola, sorry I couldn't protect you." His words were barely a whisper as he leaned his forehead against hers, letting his eyes slip closed as he felt the gentle tendrils of her magic pulling him under.

"Don't be Puca," Lola said as she wrapped her arms around his waist. She could feel the tension in his muscles as he fought to control himself. His warm breath moved over her skin and she closed her eyes. Waiting for his lips to press against hers. Trying to stamp down the pulse of heat that swept through her, stronger this time now that she was in his arms.

This wasn't right, it wasn't how she had wanted to be with Puca. She knew she shouldn't be feeling this way, but whatever Erik had given her had worked.

"Puca." She sobbed as she opened her eyes. Not wanting to give in, but she could feel sparks moving along her skin. Feeling the need for him coiling through her body stronger than it had any other time. "Please."

"I can't." He whispered, not opening his eyes. He didn't want to see the need that mirrored his own. Dragging his hand up her back, he cradled the back of her head as he breathed her in. His nose skimming along her skin as he trembled.

Lola repeated his name as she leaned up on her toes. Closing her eyes as he drew closer to her lips, her breath coming in short pants as his lips met hers.

Fingers tangled themselves beneath her bun as he moaned against her lips. His other hand moving to her hip to pull her body flush against his.

Lola's hands moved up the back of his shirt, tracing the sharp muscles in his back with her hands. Nails scratching at his skin, making him shudder.

Both of them knew this wasn't the time or place for this, and it wasn't how Puca had wanted things. Her powers moved over him, he knew there was nothing he could do to fight the desire that moved along his skin. Sinking into him, pulling him under like the currents of the Merrow's beloved ocean.

Tasting and teasing, promising him of things that were to come. He moaned when her tongue moved over his. Kissing Lola was something he didn't think he'd ever get tired of.

Lola dug her nails into the skin of his back as she pulled his shirt up his back until she reached the skin. Leaning back to pull it off of him and dropping it to the ground as he made quick work of her sundress. He pulled back, finally opening his eyes to look at her.

Watching the way her breasts moved, encased in the peach-colored lace material of her bra, down to the thin scrap of fabric that hid the neatly trimmed tight curls that covered her sex. He felt his cock twitch in his jeans as she ran her hands along the waistband of his jeans. Needy and desperate as her fingers shook as she gently touched him.

He moaned her name out. She was going much too slow for him. With her light teasing touches, he needed more. With a growl that struck something primal in Lola, he lifted her up. Her legs encircling his waist as he walked them back against the far wall of the cage, away from the iron bars.

Lola moaned at the rough texture of the wall combined with Puca's desperate kisses. Desire flowed through stronger now, and she gripped his shoulders. Rocking herself against his hard length, needing more from him.

Puca's hand slipped between their bodies as he kept her pinned in place. He popped open the button on his jeans and pulled the zipper down, freeing his aching cock.

Lola panted as he pressed his cock against the damp fabric of her panties.

Whimpered at the sound he made low in the back of his throat, "Go halainn, you're so wet. Losgadh mi le do theas." He nipped at her collar bone, teeth, lips and tongue trailing over her skin. The sounds she made, feeding into his need. Making him want to pound her against the wall.

"Please." Lola panted, she couldn't think. Words were becoming harder to form as he teased her clit through her panties with his fingers. "Plese, I need you."

His fingers hooked into the crotch of the fabric, pulling sharply as he ripped them from her body. Puca moved his fingers through her folds, smiling as she bucked her hips.

"I plan to savor this time with you." He said, pressing two of his fingers into her tight wet heat. He didn't want to tell her that he was afraid he wouldn't survive their time together. Didn't want her to feel guilty over something that neither of them could control.

He was already under her spell. Her magic wrapping around him, caressing him. Feeding into his own need, just as it looped into hers.

His thumb moved to her engorged clitoris as he circled the bundle of nerves. Pulling back to watch her as he added another finger. Her eyes were screwed shut as she panted his name.

Lola panted as she fucked his fingers. She could already feel her body pulling from his life essence. He leaned in to kiss her. She turned her head to the side. Hoping that if she didn't kiss him, they would have longer together.

His hand moved to her chin, his thumb caressing her lips as

she felt her inner walls fluttering around his fingers.

Lola took his thumb in her mouth, sucking on the digit as his other hand moved faster. She dragged her nails over his shoulders, watching as his eyes slipped closed and his lip curled into a snarl.

The sound made her body tighten as her orgasm swept over her and she let out a sob. It was wonderful, but she knew that they were far from done as he moved his finger from her body. His eyes meeting hers as he pressed the head of his cock against her pulsing sex.

Lola rolled her hips, whimpering at the feeling of Puca's cock as he worked it into her. It was a feeling that border lined on pleasure and pain as his cock stretched her channel wider than she had been prepared for.

"Knew you'd feel so good." Puca said in a growling, rasping tone that reverberated through Lola. His warm breath tickling over the sensitive skin below her ear. "Even better than I had imagined." He moaned low in the back of his throat as he thrust his cock deeper inside of her. Lola couldn't help the moaning gasp that escaped her lips.

His hands gripped her thighs as he thrust himself full into her, savoring the warmth that enveloped him. Holding himself still as he tried to allow her the chance to adjust to his thick cock.

"Are you okay?" Puca panted as he pinned her against the wall. His hands gripping her thighs as his body shook, his teeth clenched. He didn't want to hurt her, but gentle lovemaking wasn't what either of them needed.

Lola nodded her head as she rolled her hips, making him groan against the skin of her neck. He pulled his dick out of her before thrusting back into her. Lola sobbed as he started to take her with a fast pace. The rough wall scratching the skin of her back as she threw her head back. Enjoying the rough way that he was fucking her. She leaned forward, her hot breath panting against his neck as she wrapped her arms around him, hanging onto him like he was her lifeline.

"Puca," she panted, her breathing harsh as he kept up his pace. Things with him wouldn't be gentle, and she could understand what he had meant about wanting her to be in control when they finally slept together.

If she hadn't been as needy as she was now. Her body wouldn't have been able to handle the rough way he was taking her. How he gripped her hips and thighs. She knew that she'd be bruised for days.

"Gods, Lola, I need you." Puca said, moving his hands from her thighs to let her legs slip down his body as he pulled back. Smirking at the whimper that Lola let out as he spun her around. Placing her hands on the wall, smiling at the way that she arched her back, ready for him.

"Tell me that this is what you need." He ordered as he moved his dick through her folds, teasing her, dipping into her wetness. A chuckle escaped his lips as she pressed her ass against him. Biting his lip, he thrust into her, a short stroke that left her wanting more.

No, not wanting more, but needing more.

"Tell me." He growled against her shoulder as his hand slapped her bottom.

"Puca." Lola panted, shocked at the sound of his hand meeting her skin. She pressed back, trying to force his cock deeper as he gripped her hips. Holding her in place.

"Tell me." He growled out as he pulled his cock from her again. A gentle thrust that wasn't nearly enough was his all he gave her. His palm swatting against her ass again, making her shudder.

"I need you, Puca." Lola moaned out as he rocked his hips. His hands moved over her arms. To pin her hands to the wall, as she scratched her nails against the wall paper. Feeling the aged paper peel up under her fingernails as he threaded his fingers with hers. He kept up the pace until Lola let out a sobbing moan. She was almost there. She just needed more.

"Please touch me," Lola sobbed out. She was so close, her body tight felt tight, like she was about to fall over the edge.

"Where?" Puca said nipping at her earlobe. "Here?" He asked, untangling his hand from hers and scraping his nails up her arm.

Lola shook her head as she bit her lower lip, trying to contain her moan as goosebumps covered her skin. "Lower."

He thrust into her, dragging his nails along her spine, loving the way she shook. "Like this?"

"Puca, I need you." Lola moaned as his hand moved over her hip. Nails scratching along her skin as he went. His cock moving inside of her as she kept her hands braced against the wall.

"Here?" He asked, his finger moving through the trimmed curls at the apex of her thighs, giving them a sharp tug that made her gasp out his name.

"Touch me." Lola all but begged as she pushed herself back against him. Rotating her hips as his he fucked her. His teeth nibbled along her throat as he moved his fingers in a circular motion around her clit.

"I am. I want you to come for me." He growled out as his finger strummed over her clit. His voice was gravelly and low, pulling at something deep inside of her, and she knew that she wouldn't be able to hold out much longer.

Pinpricks of magic danced along her skin. Seeking, searching, and feeding. She felt drunk as her body clenched up around his cock.

"Lola," Puca panted out, feeling her vaginal walls fluttering around his dick. Speeding up the movement of his fingers, he hissed in her ear. "That's right, I want you to come. Know that I'm not done with you. That I will never be done with you. That I'll always make you feel this way."

Lola's body stiffened. She screwed her eyes shut. Feeling the waves of her orgasm crash through her.

"Puca." She moaned out.

"That's right Lola, I love you." His words were spoken with a groan as she felt his semen spill inside of her.

Chapter Twenty-Four

꧁ꕥ꧂

Merrow gripped the soft, cotton sheets as he let out a low moan. Semen shooting from his cock in great ropes as his eyes shot open. His body responding to a stimulation that wasn't happening to him, but to his lover.

"Dreaming of something good?" Lu asked as he stretched his body out beside the other man, smirking at Merrow's moan as his body shook.

"It's Puca." Merrow said, his voice groggy with sleep as he tried to catch his breath.

"You dreamed of Puca?" Lu asked, as he moved to lay on his side. Propping up his head on his hand as he watched the other man, a tired smile on his face.

"No, I could feel Puca coming and my body was trying to catch up to his." Merrow said as he grimaced, looking down at the semen that pooled across his lower belly. "I wonder what they're doing to make him lose control like this?" He closed his, straining to hear anything. He yawned, rubbing his eyes. He knew that they'd slept well, but he couldn't seem to pull himself out of his lethargic haze.

"We could go find out?" Lu cocked an eyebrow, his lips twitching into a grin.

"I like the way you think my friend." Merrow chuckled as he kicked the sheets away. Trying to force himself out of the bed with little success.

Lu climbed off of the bed, his lips pressed together as he turned back to look at his friend. He was moving slower than normal, as if he'd been in a brawl that hadn't gone in his favor. Heading towards the bathroom, Lu grabbed a towel. The soft sounds of Bodach snoring filling his ears. Making him frown as he stepped back into the bedroom, handing the towel to Merrow.

Walking through the hallway he caught sight of Bodach sprawled across the sofa bed, Lola may have slept with them last night. She wasn't there now, and it was clear neither she nor Puca were with Bodach either.

His stomach tightened as he wondered where they could be if they weren't in the living room.

Lu could remember laying down with Lola. Her body pressed between his and Merrow's as she twirled a lock of his hair around her finger. It had been a tight fit, with Puca pressed against Merrow's back. He had still hoped for many more nights like that.

"Bodach, where are they?" Lu said, shaking the other man awake.

The thud from behind him pulling his attention away as he turned to look back at a dazed Merrow.

* * *

Puca took a slow, deep breath. He could feel the tightening in his chest. His eyes closed as he tried not to succumb to the pull of Lola's magic washing over him. Her hands were braced on his chest as she worked her body up and down, moaning as she took his rigid member inside of her.

He had been with plenty of fae creatures. None had ever pulled him under their spell as Lola had. He didn't know if it was the realm they were in or if Lola was just that powerful. She rotated her hips, panting out his name, and he opened his eyes. Taking in the sight of his goddess, her purple and white hair shimmering in the sunlight.

Red eyes unseeing as she worked them both higher. Puca knew that the next orgasm that he could feel tightening up inside of his testicles was going to be the most powerful one yet. He was glad he had the stamina to make it this far with her, to give her the magics that she would need for whatever was coming.

He couldn't help but wish they were in his realm so he could pull magics from the earth to heal himself so they could keep going. Pleasure was his favorite thing to give, and it seemed like he had finally met someone who could handle all that he could offer. He wanted to be the one she craved.

The one that she sought out, whether consciously or not. His fingers dug into her hips as he felt her walls flutter around him, and he knew that she was getting closer as she let out a soft sob.

His thumb moved over her hip bone, before going lower to circle her sensitive clit. She cried out his name, as she had more times than he could count.

He'd never get tired of hearing his name fall from her lips. He only wished that it wouldn't be over so soon. He was getting weaker by the minute and he hated that afterwards.

Afterwards, Lola would blame herself if he didn't make it.

He just needed to hold on for a bit longer, he'd pulled from Merrow's magic. Easily finding it shimmering around him as strong as his own and used that as safely as he could. He'd left him alive, and it would give the other fae a connection to find them.

He just hoped they found them in time.

Puca watched the way her body tensed up above his. Trying to scorch the image to his memory, he never wanted to forget Lola.

Never wanted her to forget him. He rolled his hips up, thrusting his cock deeper inside of her. His cum spilling inside of her again as she fell against his chest.

Forcing his hand up, he ran it over her back. "Tha gaol agam ort, mo chridhe." He whispered.

"Puca," Lola said in a soft voice as she propped herself up. Her chin resting on his chest as her eyes met his. "I love you."

She moved forward, pressing her lips against his as his hand moved to cradle the back of her head. His eyes slipped closed and Lola felt something pulse over her skin as he struggled to stay conscious.

If she had looked over her shoulder, she would have seen the runes on the wall glowing beneath the ripped wallpaper.

But, she didn't.

At that moment her only concern was Puca as she pressed her hands against his chest and tried to force a breath back into his lungs.

Lola crawled off of him as he took a gasping breath. Grabbing his shirt to cover him up. She didn't want Callie or Erik to see him like this as he struggled to breathe. She pulled her sundress on, pressing her back against the wall as she wrapped her arms around her legs. Her chest shook as she tried to hold in her sob.

She didn't know if she'd killed Puca, but nothing she had done had helped the man she loved.

His breathing was shallow, gurgling with the water that had filled his lungs. Lola didn't know that his connection with Merrow was the only thing keeping him alive.

The door creaked open. Lola couldn't help the fear that ripped through her. She didn't want to see Erik to be reminded that this was her fault.

Looking up at the woman, she put her hand over her mouth. Trying to hold back a sob she knew wouldn't help her. The seelie queen may be a good guy, but that wasn't what Lola had witnessed so far.

"He grows weaker." Callista said, her brown eyes moving over Puca's still form. A glimmer of something flashing in her eyes so quick that Lola barely caught it.

"I didn't mean to hurt him, I just couldn't stop."

"Of course you couldn't. It's what Erik was hoping for. He couldn't make your mother love him. There is no way that he could make you." She said, moving to sit down beside the cell as she studied Lola. "Not when your heart beats for another."

"What he was hoping for?"

"Of course, he didn't think Puca would survive. I am glad he did." The queen said, looking back at Lola. Ignoring her question. "You look so much like your father."

"You knew my parents?" Lola asked, biting the inside of her cheek.

"I do, you look like both of them, but I see more of your father in you every time we meet." She rested her hands in her lap as she looked down, "I care for your parents a great deal. I made your father a promise that I would look after you and I have."

"You keep talking like they're not dead."

"They are not," Callista said as she looked up. Her eyes seemed inhuman as they changed colors to a shade that matched falling leaves from a tree. "Everything you think you know about their deaths is a lie."

"You're lying to me." Lola said, glaring up at the fae woman. She had known that the fae were tricksters. This was sinking to a whole different level, to pull her dead parents into it.

"Everything comes with a choice, my dear girl. They knew that your grandmother would take care of you. The baby that was growing in your mother's womb wouldn't have survived in this realm. Just like the one growing in you won't survive here."

"No, you're lying to me. My parents wouldn't have left me and my mother wasn't pregnant." Lola said glaring at the floor, Callie's words finally sunk in. "I'm not pregnant."

"Yes, you are. The babe that grows within you is fae. Now I'm asking you to make a choice."

Letting her legs fall to the side, Lola brought her hand to her abdomen. She didn't feel pregnant. Not that she knew what being pregnant felt like. "What choice is that?"

"I'll send Puca to the fae realm, he will heal." She said, looking at the man on the floor before pressing her eyes closed. "But you will stay here."

"He'll survive if he goes to the other realm?"

"Yes, but your baby will not survive if it's born here. Just as the babe your mother carried wouldn't have survived." Callista said.

"Then how come I survived being born here?" Lola asked as she looked over at Puca. She didn't know if she could trust the fae queen. As she watched her lover struggle to breathe, she realized she didn't have much choice.

"You're not pure fae. Your sister is."

"I don't understand." Lola said, looking away from Puca.

"Your mother cared for Erik. She wasn't as strong as you are when it came to her korrigan." Callie said with a shrug. "Puca doesn't have much time left, you should make your choice."

"Take him, please." Lola said, hoping that she could find a way out of this. If the queen was right and she was pregnant. She needed to figure out a way to save the child, she just hoped the cost wouldn't be more than she could pay.

"As you wish." Callista said as she held her hand up a bright light formed flickering against her palm as she pushed it closer to them. It moved through the air wrapping around Puca's body and Lola brought her hands to her mouth. She wanted to yell out, to tell Callie that she changed her mind. The thought of Puca dying was enough to keep her quiet as the light reached a blinding intensity and she had to look away.

Lola squeezed her eyes shut to try to keep the tears away. She didn't want to cry in front of the Seelie queen. Puca would be okay, he would survive.

"It is done." Callista whispered, leaning back into her chair.

"Thank you."

"Everything comes with a choice, the way forward is sometimes behind you." Standing, she smiled softly at Lola.

"Wait, are they-" She paused, trying to choose her words carefully. "Is my family well."

The queen nodded her head as she moved to the door, "Yes, they thrive in our realm."

Lola pulled her knees to her chest, closing her eyes. She felt more alone than she had since before she'd met the fae men. She just hoped the queen was being truthful, that Puca would survive once he was home. Lola would deal with the news that she was pregnant later. She had no idea which of the men the father was.

Or how they would react.

Placing her hands on the floor, she moved to stand, leaning on the wall as she tried to figure out what Callie had meant. With a sigh, she turned to look at the wall behind her. Taking in the peeling wallpaper, she leaned closer, picking at the shredded paper.

She could see the faint traces beneath the faded paper. Sliding her nail under it, she grimaced as a hard piece of the dried glue wedged underneath her nail. Drawing back her hand, she sucked the cut into her mouth. Her other hand reaching up to tug the strip down.

The designs were similar to the boxes throughout the room.

It was an enchantment.

Biting her lip, she pulled another strip of the paper off, letting it fall to the floor as the door creaked open.

Chapter Twenty-Five

*L*ola dropped her hands to her sides, spinning around to face Erik. Watching him as he came into the room, she hoped he couldn't tell that she had been up to something.

"I thought you might be hungry." He said, moving closer to the cell. He sat the tray on the chair that sat outside of her cage, pulling out a ring of heavy looking keys.

"You could always let me out," Lola said, crossing her arms under her breasts. "To eat, I mean." She added, not holding her breath.

"Now Lola, I don't think that's a good idea." Erik chided as he unlocked the door. Moving to pick up the tray, "What happened to Puca?"

Looking down at the floor, Lola didn't say anything as she pressed her lips together, closing her eyes.

"So you killed him?"

Lola felt her stomach drop at the smile in his voice. How could he talk about killing Puca with such an easy-going manner? Her breath caught in her throat as he moved so quickly to stand in front of her.

"It'll get easier, dealing with his death. I take it the queen took care of his body?" He asked.

Lola nodded her head, not meeting his eyes. She didn't want him to see the truth in her eyes. The hope that still dwelled in her heart, that Puca would survive.

She couldn't help but wonder if she would be able to get past him and out the door of the shop before he caught her. At Erik's chuckle, she looked up, hoping that he couldn't read her mind.

"I wouldn't do that if I were you. You'll never make it to the front door in time." Erik said. Giving her a crooked, half smile. "Your eyes are so expressive, my dear."

"Should I call you your majesty?" Lola asked. Raising an eyebrow and pressing her lips together as he moved closer to her. Hoping that he could see what her eyes were telling him now.

"I'd rather prefer my love. It's good to see that Puca's death didn't hurt you." Erik said as he tucked a strand behind her ear.

Lola flinched at his words, lowering her arms to wrap them around her abdomen as if it would somehow keep her and the baby safe. "You should eat, you'll need your strength."

Turning, he started to move to the door of the cage. Mentally making a list of all the things he'd need to take care of for Lola and himself.

"Erik?"

"Yes, Lola?" He asked, turning to look back at her.

"Does the deal still stand? My life for theirs?" Lola asked, looking up at him.

"Yes," he said with a smile as he moved closer to her and away from the cell door.

Close enough to touch, yet he didn't touch her. She was thankful for that. She didn't want to think about him touching her after the way that Puca had touched her.

Lola bit the inside of her cheek as she looked up at him, "What do you mean when you say that I have to give myself to you. Like a sacrifice…"

Chuckling as he watched her trail off Erik's smile widened. "That's what I love so much about you, Lola. The way that you see things is so unique. I could never sacrifice you. I want to marry you."

"Marry me?"

"Yes, every king needs a queen and I think that fire in you suits me well. Why don't you sit and eat and I'll be back in a moment? I've got arrangements to make. Then we can discuss your future more in depth." He said turning away, leaving her in a shocked stupor.

Lola didn't know how to respond to his words. Placing her shaking hands on her stomach, she looked down, searching for any sign of life. She couldn't help but wonder what would happen to the fetus that was growing inside of her. If what the queen had said was right and not some sort of fae trickery.

Would Erik help her with the child if she did as he asked, or was it destined never to survive?

That thought made her throat tighten. How was she supposed to carry a child to term if it might not survive?

Stepping closer to the small table. She sat down on the floor, eyeing the green beans and baked chicken. How was she supposed to trust anything that he had given her?

She picked up the silver dome and placed it back over the

food. Hunger wasn't an issue, she needed to worry about getting out of here.

Moving back to the wall, she started picking at the wallpaper again. The more that she revealed, the more she noticed that it was glowing. Not as bright at the runes that were on the box that held the fae men. Or the ones that were on the chest that her grandmother had given her. Just a faint shimmering iridescent glow.

* * *

Merrow's eyes snapped open and he gasped. Lu let out a relieved sigh as he leaned closer to study the pale merman.

"He's gone."

"Puca?" Bodach asked, crouching beside his friend.

"He's gone." Merrow repeated, shock marring his sharp features as he clenched his teeth together. The muscle in his jaw twitching as he tried to hold his emotions in check. Not wanting to accept his lover's death. He'd never known a time that he wasn't connected to Puca and the hole that was his life force felt like an open bleeding wound.

"No, there has got to be a mistake." Lu said, watching as Merrow pushed himself to sit up with a wince.

Bodach extended his hand to help Merrow stand and gave him a sad smile. "I can trace where he last was. His magic still lingers on your skin."

"You don't think it was Lola, do you?" Lu asked as he moved to stand, his shoulders drawn as he dragged a hand through his hair. He could remember how his body had felt when he had laid with Lola. Even now he felt it was worth the risk.

"I don't know what to think." Merrow said, looking back at

his lover. "If it is, she's going to need us."

"Let's go," Bodach said from the front door. He was ready to find Lola and bring her home. Then they could figure out what happened to Puca.

* * *

Hanging up the phone, Erik smiled to himself. Things were falling into place this time around more smoothly than they had in the past. He was glad that Callista hadn't interfered as she had like last time.

Her love for that mortal man, the one that was Lola's father, was sickening.

At least his love was part fae. Erik could excuse her human side for that. He already had a spell in mind that he knew would help her get rid of those complicated feelings that she felt for Bodach, Merrow, and Lu.

Snarling as he moved about the kitchen. He didn't like to think about the other men touching Lola. About what he knew had happened between them.

Shaking his head as he fixed himself a glass of water from the tap. He realized that he would get over Lola and her dalliances much better than he'd handled her mothers.

Erik supposed he was biased, Lola was special. It wasn't just that he had loved her mother. He had, with everything that he was. Or so he had thought.

Until Lola had gotten older and worked her way into his heart. He didn't think there was anything that she could do to make him stop loving her.

* * *

Bodach strode forward, his feet pounding the hot pavement. It would have gone quicker if he were alone. He didn't want to risk the others doing something rash without him, though. He didn't trust them not to. He felt the ache as much as they did for Puca.

He didn't want to believe that the other man was dead. He couldn't accept it. They'd fought together for so long that a world without Puca seemed so empty.

"Bodach, wait." Lu's hand on his forearm pulled him from his thoughts.

"For what? We're almost there."

"Can you not feel it?" Lu asked, his eyes sparkling in the sunlight.

"Lu is right, it's the magic of the queen. Same as in the forest." Merrow said, looking towards the antique shop and the surrounding lawns for any trace of her.

"What should we do?" Bodach asked. His first impulse was to rush in there and save Lola. Then they could figure out what happened to Puca. To mourn his loss.

"We know the queen wouldn't let Puca get hurt. She has always had a soft spot for him and the care that he takes with humans." Lu said, hoping that somehow Puca was still alive.

A meow caught Merrow's attention, as a cat made its way closer to the group. Rubbing itself against Lu's legs. Merrow couldn't help but smile as an idea came to mind, if there was a cat around. There were mice. "Lu, I think this might be a job for you."

"What did you have in mind?"

Lu's eyes moved to the cat and he let out a sigh. "I think I know what he's asking." Shaking his head.

Lu let out a chuckle as he moved around the outside of the

antique shop. He was glad to be of some use, most often he was forgotten during times like these. His footsteps soundless as he looked for a good spot that no one would notice him.

* * *

Shaking her arms out, Lola let out a small sigh as the door creaked open and Erik walked in. The runes stopped glowing and almost seemed to blend back into the scratched wall. She frowned, hoping that all of her work hadn't been for nothing.

"Why are you tearing up the wallpaper?" Erik asked as he stepped closer and Lola moved closer to the bars. Being careful not to touch them.

"I'm just nervous. I don't like being trapped." Lola said, looking down at her hands. "I need to use the bathroom, too."

"I'm sorry, my love. Why didn't you call out for me?" Erik smiled as he pulled his keys out. "You won't try anything, will you?"

Lola shook her head as she clasped her hands together. Trying to look as innocent as possible as he swung the door open.

"Come with me." He said, holding out his hand.

Biting her lip, Lola accepted his hand, stepping out of the cage. Letting out a breath as the overwhelming pressure of the magic let up some.

Erik pulled her closer, his hand moving up to her cheek as he traced his fingers over her cheek. "I'm sorry, I didn't think about how the magics in here would make you feel."

Swallowing the lump in her throat, Lola looked up at him through lowered lashes. Trying to push past the feeling of fear. "It's okay, I know you've got a lot on your mind."

Lola felt anxiety welling up in the pit of her stomach as a soft smile spread over his lips. His fingers wrapping around the back of her neck as he stroked the skin beneath her ear.

"I like that you're trying to please me." He leaned in closer, whispering in her ear. "You don't have to try so hard, my sweetling."

Lola shuddered at his touch and his words, glad that he couldn't see the grimace on her face. There was a time not long ago when she would have loved to have heard those words. Now all she could think about was Erik talking to her mother like that. Of the horns that had protruded from his scalp when he lost his control.

"Erik-" she said, unsure of what to say next. Just knowing that she wanted his hands off of her.

"Lola, there is plenty of time for us to get to know each other. Why don't you rest in my room?" His words were phrased as a question, but Lola knew it wasn't. She nodded her head, closing her eyes as he let her go while he took a step back.

Lola tried to think of the men that she loved, that they would be safe after this. She just had to get her emotions under control. Trample down the disgust she felt towards the handsome shop owner.

She followed him as he led her out of the room and up the stairs towards his attic apartment.

His fingers moving over the door in a quick flurry of movements. Lola wanted to sob. It reminded her of Bodach, her love.

She longed to tell him that she loved him. That what she was doing was for them, that they would be safe. That Puca would be safe with them.

Erik swung the door open and stepped back, letting her pass

in front of him. She stepped into his dark room, holding her breath.

She hated the dark, and Lola had a feeling that she would need to get used to it with him. His hand ghosted across her lower back as he stepped behind her. Other hand going to the light switch, illuminating the space.

"The bathroom is in the corner." Erik said as he walked further into the room. "Make yourself at home, I'll fix you something to drink."

Looking around the small apartment, Lola was shocked. Downstairs may have held lots of treasures, up here books lined the walls in stacks and stacks. A few casually misplaced stacked on the nightstand by his bed or haphazardly by the armchair that sat in the corner of the room.

"Erik-"

"I know, it's a lot to take in and it's a bit of a mess. I enjoy reading very much and it's hard for me to let go of my books." He said as he lifted a pitcher of water, pouring it into a glass before turning back to look at her.

Lola blushed as he looked at her. She turned towards the bathroom. Her hip bumping a table and she let out a small yelp as she watched a vase hit the floor. The thin blue and gold porcelain smashing into scattered pieces.

Raising her eyes to his, she bit her lip. Wringing her hands together.

Chapter Twenty-Six

❧

"Not a word." Lu squeaked out as he looked up at the towering forms of Bodach and Merrow.

"My coileach is bigger than you." Bodach said. His hand coming up to his mouth to hold in his laughter. Lu glared up at Merrow, waiting for the other man to say anything about his current size.

"He is a wee-thing, but hurry on. Be safe." He said, motioning the other man towards the building. "Let us in when you're in."

Rolling his eyes, Lu turned away from the others. It would have been more dramatic if he weren't so small. He was roughly about six inches tall. Already he'd walked around the building searching for an opening that he could fit through. When he'd found it, he couldn't help but let out a groan.

Knowing that he wasn't going to hear the end of Bodach's teasing anytime soon.

Crouching down, he pushed himself into the tight tunnel that he hoped would lead him into the basement of the shop.

Belly scrapping over the rough gravel and rocks as he crawled deeper. This wasn't a fun trip. He could feel the faint tingling sensation of magic moving over his skin as he reached the end of the tunnel.

Crawling out, he moved to his knees, looking around the dusty basement. Hoping that the magic didn't let the shop owner know that he was here.

Letting his own magic flow through him, Lu closed his eyes as his muscles twisted and contorted until he was back to his normal size. Rolling his shoulders, he moved to the basement doors. Grabbing a white drop-cloth of one of the chairs, he made his way to the door that he'd seen outside of the shop. He pushed it open, squinting at the bright sunlight. Merrow handed him his clothing, and he dropped the sheet.

"Not another word, Bodach." Lu said as he stepped away, pulling on his jeans.

"You were so little. I could keep you in my pocket."

"Bodach." Merrow warned as he stepped past Lu into the damp basement, his nose curling at the smell of stale air. It reminded him of his time in the box.

"I thought you were cute, but seeing you palm size-"

"I said not another word." Lu pulled on his shirt, glaring at the men before turning away. "Let's go find Lola."

* * *

"Lola, you need not look so scared of me." Erik said, pressing his lips together as he sat the glass of water down on his dresser.

"I'm sorry." Lola's words were tight and clipped. Her eyes wide as she waited for his next move.

"Sweetling, you must be more careful."

"I will be." Lola said as she clasped her hands together at her waist.

Erik's lips twitched into a smile as he moved closer to her, "You didn't need to use the bathroom, did you?"

"No," Lola said, biting her lip. Worried that he had caught on to her plans to try to escape. "I mean, yes I do."

"You wanted to come up here?" Erik smirked as he stepped close enough to Lola that she could feel the heat of his skin through her clothing. Smell the jasmine tea that he had drank earlier, it wasn't an unpleasant smell. Just one that had her on edge.

"No, I didn't."

"It's okay, Lola. You don't have to hide anything from me." Erik brought his hand up to caress the top of her cheek as he wrapped his arm around her waist. Pulling her closer so her breasts pressed against his chest.

"No, Erik. I didn't mean-"

Her words were cut off as he pressed his lips against hers. His tongue snaking into her mouth, cutting off her protests. She brought her hand up to his chest, giving him a shove. Her other hand was trying to pull his hand away from her waist.

"Oh Lola, you seek to deny me?" He chuckled as he rested his forehead against hers. "My sweet bride."

"Please." Lola said, trying to shove him away again. It was like a fly batting at a giant as he stood next to her, unmoving.

"You don't have to beg me." Erik's lips twitched into a smile as he pulled her with him towards the bed, his hands moving over her hips. She felt his hardness press against her belly and her stomach churned.

"No." Lola shouted, trying to pry his hands away as she

stumbled, falling into his chest. His fingers tightened as he dug them into her hips. Letting out a dark chuckle, horns sprouting from his forehead. His eyes seemed to glow a bright green that reminded Lola of a glow stick in the darkness.

"Lola, I have been so patient with you. All you have to do is give into me and I will give you everything you could ever want."

"Erik, I could never love you." She said. Trying to turn her head away from him, his fingers moved to her chin, holding her in place.

"Guess I'll have to force you then."

He tangled his fingers in her hair, forcing her head to the side so he could lick and nipped up her throat. "I'd hoped that we could both enjoy our first time together."

"Erik, don't do this." Lola pleaded as she hit at him again. She brought her hands up to his face, raking her nails across his skin. Grimacing at the feel of his horns.

"It's okay, I like it rough." He growled as he let her go, pushing her towards the bed. Smiling as she tried to scramble away.

He moved with viper-like speed. His hand wrapping around her ankle as he pulled her closer. His body thrummed with the need to take her, to possess her until he was the only thing that she could think about.

Just as he was cursed to be consumed by the women of her line.

"Erik, please don't." She cried out again as his hands moved further up her leg. His other hand joining him to map out the skin that haunted his every waking thought. "Erik, I'm pregnant."

With a snarl, he climbed up her body as she struggled to get away from him. Her eyes wild and desperate, she bit at him as he brought his lips to hers. Her teeth sinking into the soft flesh of his lower lip.

"We can take care of that, the only offspring you'll be carrying will be mine." He growled at her, blood dripping down his chin.

"Please." Lola sobbed as she twisted her body beneath his, trying to fight down the panic she felt as his erection pressed against her thigh.

* * *

Bodach moved through the antique shop, searching for any signs of Lola. He could hear Lu and Merrow doing the same. Their movements didn't cover up the footsteps he could hear above them. He wondered if it was Lola and what she could be doing here.

He was more in tune with his primal side when it came to her. He paused, hearing the whispers of voices as Merrow moved closer to him.

"She's here." Bodach whispered.

Merrow nodded his head, looking up. Lu came out of the kitchen, her purse clutched in his hands.

"Aye."

A loud crash pulled their attention upwards. It was quiet after that, and Bodach felt anxiety well up in the pit of his stomach. He moved towards the stairs, Lu and Merrow on his heals as they tried to keep their steps quiet.

Lola's shout made them give up the pretense of keeping silent as they rushed towards the attic.

The closer they got, the more they could hear the sound of

Lola pleading. The admission that she was with child as she begged for him not to touch her made his heart beat faster.

Bodach slammed the door open, he stormed in. Red glowing eyes moving to where Lola lay, sprawled beneath Erik. Her head turned to the side. Eyes squeezed shut as his lips moved along her neck.

Erik looked up towards them. His tongue moving over her skin before Merrow pulled him off of Lola. Throwing the man across the room into one of the bookshelves. Books fell onto him and he let out a growl, shoving them to the side as he moved to stand.

Bodach walked forward, cracking his knuckles. He could hear Merrow and Lu checking on Lola, pulling her closer to the door.

"You shouldn't have touched her."

"She is mine. She was willing to trade herself for your safe passage." Erik said, his lips twisted into a smirk. As he glared at Bodach. "I am your king."

"I bow to no one." Bodach said as he launched himself forward. A right hook clipping Erik's chin, making him turn his head to the side at the force of the punch.

"You've gotten stronger." Erik said as he rolled his shoulders, "So have I."

He reached out, shoving Bodach hard in the chest. Smiling as his teeth grew to sharp points and his horns sprang from his skin.

Moving faster than Bodach was ready for. Erik shoved him again, causing the man to backwards. He watched Erik pull his leg back. Scrambling to his side, knowing he wasn't going to be able to avoid the blow.

Bodach looked up at Erik. He felt the swirl of magic before

he saw her.

The queen was entering the battle. He just hoped she was on his side.

Erik landed another kick to Bodach's side as the other man climbed to his knees. He fell to the floor, breath having been knocked out of him as his dark hair fell into his face.

Lu rushed over, trying to help him take Erik down. They both knew there was no way that they could kill the fae king. The queen could, without as harsh of a punishment.

Bodach wouldn't risk the judgement of being sent back into the box.

He wasn't willing to let that fate happen to Lola. Pushing himself to stand, he felt a soft hand grip his shoulder.

"Bodach, I will take care of this." Her voice was soft. Like the wind whistling through the trees as her long blonde curls danced with a magical breeze. "Lola will take you to the gate."

"My queen-"

"Go, this has been a long time coming." She smiled, her eyes turning cruel as they met Erik's. The air felt thick with the power that flowed through it. "The king needs to be put back in his place."

Nodding, Bodach moved to Lola. "You know the gate she speaks of?"

"Gate, no. I've got no idea what she's talking about." Lola said, as she took his hand in hers, pulling Bodach towards the door.

"Did you see any enchantments?" Lu asked from behind them. Merrow at his side. Their steps were quick as they moved down the narrow hallway.

"There were markings in the cell."

"Show us." Bodach said.

Lola led them towards the room where she had been kept. The walls rattled around them as they heard a masculine groan of pain along with a girlish giggle.

They stepped in and Merrow's eyes went wide.

"It's a prison, so many trapped souls." His words were soft as he stepped forward. Only Lu keeping him from going towards the boxes.

"Best if we get to the gate, They are here for a reason." Bodach said, stepping closer to the gate.

"His nephew-" Lola whispered, and Bodach let out a sigh.

"He's here for a reason." Merrow said as the ceiling above them rattled as the two forces fought above them.

"We need to get out of here." Lola's voice was filled with fear as she let go of Bodach's hand. Swiftly, she moved to Merrow and touched his arm. "You will meet him one day."

"Aye, we will."

Stepping closer to the cell, Lu bounced on his toes. "I can feel it, it's already started to open."

"We shall be home soon, my friend."

Lola worried her lower lip as she pulled Merrow with her. She needed to see them off so they could be with Puca.

"Someone has already started the enchantment." Lu said as he stepped closer. He looked over his shoulders at the others. "Do you think it was Puca?"

"It was me. Is this what the queen meant? When she spoke of the gate."

"Aye." Lu said, trailing his hands over the markings. Watching as they grew brighter. "It should take us home."

Lola nodded her head as she looked down. She knew that she should say her goodbyes. Merrow's fingers tangled with her fingers, pulling her attention to him.

"Lola, we've so much to show you."

"I can't-" she muttered. Looking up at Bodach and Lu as they started working on the enchantment.

"What? Did you think we would be leaving you behind?" Lu asked as looked back at her.

Merrow smiled as he pulled her closer to the brightly sparkling runes. "We could never return without you. Lola, you are our home."

"It's time." Bodach said, stepping back as the colors seemed to swirl into a shimmering pool of light. He looked over his shoulder at her before stepping through the gate.

Lu looked back at her with a smile, "Let's go home Lola."

She glanced at Merrow and he squeezed her hand as they followed Lu.

Epilogue

F OUR YEARS LATER

Pushing her hair out of her eyes, Lola let out a huff as Lu rounded the corner. A bright green-eyed toddler clinging to his back. Her copper curls bouncing in the slight breeze as he bounced her around the yard.

"There's your mum."

"Mummy," the girl shouted, she pointed over her father's shoulder, "Auntie Queen is here."

"Lu, be careful with her." Lola chided with a small smile as Lu galloped her around the yard. She turned her head, looking over at the Queen.

"Your majesty." She said, dipping her head.

"Lola, how many times have I asked you to call me Callie?"

"It still feels strange."

"We're family. You're sister and I are ruling the courts together." Callie said with a smile.

"I know, it's just still strange to know that I have a sister and she's the Unseelie Queen." Lola said, as she went back to pulling the weeds from the garden.

"She's doing a far better job than Erik."

Lola smiled at that. She didn't like to think about her onetime friend. She was glad that he was locked away for now, she just dreaded the day that he escaped. If ever.

"I'm glad to hear it. Hopefully, it keeps her busy so she won't fuss over the baby too much." Lola said, placing a hand over her swollen middle.

"You know she won't be able to stay away, speaking of which. I'm going to go play with Mana, before she gets here and steals her away."

Lola watched the queen as she walked over to Lu and their child, her fingers tickling the girl. She let out a squeal as she launched herself from her father's back.

A shadow fell over Lola and she turned to look up at Merrow. A grin spreading across her cheeks as he smirked down at her. The sunlight streaming through his white blonde hair making him glow. Her breath was taken away by his beauty. Dusting her hands off on her apron, she frowned. Realizing that she was trapped.

Gardening was hard work for her during pregnancy, but touching the ground made her think of her grandmother and how much she would have loved her great-grandchildren.

"You got stuck down there again, didn't you?"

"I refuse to dignify that question with an answer." Lola said, pressing her lips together with a glare at her lover. She brought her hand up to rub her swollen middle. "This one doesn't let me move around as much as big sister did."

"Annwn says that's normal." Merrow held his hand out to her, rolling his eyes as she pressed her hands to the ground, trying to push herself to stand.

Bodach pushed himself away from the tree that he had been leaning against. "You need to get ready, acushla. Your mother and sister will be here soon."

"Don't remind me." Lola said crossing her arms over her chest, If it was anything like the birth of Mana. She knew they wouldn't let up with the constant mothering that would happen to her during labor and once the baby arrived. She could only hope that the court would call her sister away.

"We could always tell them to stay home." Bodach pressed his lips together as he tried to fight back a smile.

"And have you guys freaking out, I think not." Lola said finally giving in and holding her hands out to both of them.

"What? We do great with Mana." Merrow smiled as he helped Bodach pull Lola to her feet.

"You guys would let her get away with murder and then hide the body." Placing her hands on her hips, she glared up at them.

"What can I say? She's our little princess."

Bodach moved forward, wrapping his arms about her waist. The fluttering movements caught his attention. He placed his hands on her belly. "This one, he will be our little prince."

"I told you I didn't want to know what I was having." Lola said, pushing his hand away. Stomping her foot and turning towards the house.

"Ghra, it'll be any day now." Merrow called out, chasing after her. Smiling at the way she waddled into their cottage. "We've all been harassing him to know what it is."

"I still wanted it to be a surprise." Lola said as she scrubbed at her eyes. She hated this part of being pregnant. The overwhelming emotions that she felt and how easy it was to cry. It didn't matter whether she was happy or sad. The tears just flowed. "Do you think that, Puca-"

"That I what?" Puca asked as he walked down the stairs, a book in his hands

"Nothing." Lola said as she blushed, walking closer to her love.

"Lola, you know you can always tell me anything." He said, bringing his hand up to cup her cheek. His fingertips caressing her skin, making her shiver as desire shot up her spine.

"That you'll be excited to know it's a boy." Lola looked down as he pressed his hand to her belly, feeling the fluttering kicks.

"Nothing could make me happier. Maybe the next set will be twins." His lips twitched into a smirk as he watched Lola grimace.

"I don't think I could handle you guys with twins, this baby and Mana." She looked up at him through lowered lashes.

"Lola, you'll always have us. More babies would be a blessing. They'd be a part of you, of us." Puca whispered before pressing his lips against her forehead.

A knock on the door pulled her attention away and she let out a sigh, "Let's worry about this one's birth first."

Puca nodded, letting her slip away from him to let in her family.

That thought filled her with happiness. She had a family. She had a home and it was with her fae men.

THE END

Thank you

Thank you for taking the time to read Her Fae Lovers. If you enjoyed this book (or even if you hated it) feel free to leave a review where ever you purchased the book. It would mean a lot to me and would help others to find my book.

Without you guys this book wouldn't be possible, so thank you from the bottom of my heart. XOXO

About the Author

Jane Knight, author of Wild and Blood Thirsty, Wild and Untamed, Hers for the Holidays, Her Vampire Master, The Vampire's Witch and Her Dominant Dragon is a native Texan. Wife, mother, and life time storyteller. Jane specializes in high heat paranormal romance/erotica, with a dash of humor. When she isn't writing, Jane enjoys wine, knitting, and chasing her kids and pets around.

If you'd like to email Jane, feel free to at
  Janeknightwrites@gmail.com

You can connect with me on:

- https://ko-fi.com/janeknight0471
- https://twitter.com/writes_knight
- https://www.facebook.com/JaneKnightWrites
- https://www.instagram.com/janeknightwrites

Subscribe to my newsletter:

- https://anystories.page.link/yjbv

Also by Jane Knight

Wild and Blood Thirsty

Drake Collins did not want a mate, he never had, he liked what he had and didn't want anything to change his arrangement. When he meets Abby things change and he realizes that maybe having a mate isn't such a bad thing.

Owen Walker knew the second he saw her that he wanted her, he didn't just want Abby to be something that he and Drake got bored with when they were done with her. He wanted to mark her, claim her, keep her with him, not just him but with them. He knew that she was made for them. In all his time walking the earth he had never met anyone that smelled the way she did and that smell had him hooked from day one. He knew in an instant that there was nothing he wouldn't do to have her, body and blood.

After moving to the city, Abby heads into a job interview that will change her life. She meets some very sexy dominant men, will she be able to resist them or will she fall for all of them?

Wild and Untamed

"Can a devil love someone?" Annie asked as she looked up at Stolas through lowered lashes.

"Why don't you come and find out?" Stolas smirked as he wrapped an arm around her mate. Candy felt her heart beat quicker at the demons touch as Annie glanced at her nervously biting her lower lip.

Candy knew from the moment she saw Annie that she was her mate, there was just one problem. Stolas had taken an interest in her as well, but can she compete with a devil? Or will he want to join in?

Hers for The Holidays

After breaking up with her ex, Emily doesn't want to go home alone for the holidays. She chooses instead to keep pretending that she's seeing someone and enlists the help of a fellow gamer to keep up the ruse.

Vincent doesn't want to go home alone again, so when Emily asks for his help he has no problem agreeing to pretend to be her boyfriend. Will he be able to keep his shifter status a secret when the two finally meet in real life?

CJ's family is away for the holidays, so to keep the boredom at bay he heads with his room mate to visit his family where he discovers his roommate's sister is more than meets the eye. His heart will get captured quickly and so will his dragon, there's just one problem she already has a boyfriend. Sparks will fly. in this sweet yet steamy, paranormal, holiday, romance.

Will Emily choose her pretend boyfriend or her brother's roommate?

Her Dominant Dragon

When Marcus Blackwell meets his new secretary, he knows that she's the one he's been waiting for. He can feel it and so can his dragon. He'd planned to take his time seducing her, before introducing her to his darker desires. Fate has other plans for them, speeding up his seduction. Will he be able to convince her to be theirs.

Louis knew from the moment that Amelia came into his basement that she was something special, his dragon knew it too. Now he just needs to figure out, what is she to him and his lover?

Amelia is just your average modern woman, with a bit of bratty side looking for a dominant to tame her. She doesn't know what she's getting into when she takes on the dominant dragon, Marcus and his lover Louis.

A whirlwind reverse-harem romance pulls Amelia in as her lovers awaken her desires. Drawing her into a drama she didn't know existed outside of the realm of fantasy and make believe.

CPSIA information can be obtained
at www.ICGtesting.com
Printed in the USA
BVHW031426091220
595285BV00001B/53